M000214886

CRITICALLY ACCLAIMED
ACROSS THE NATION!

"COLLINS HAS THE ABILITY TO SET IN MOTION A
SEQUENCE OF EVENTS THAT MOVES WITH THE
INEVITABILITY OF A HUGE BOULDER ROLLING
DOWN A MOUNTAINSIDE...ONE OF THE BEST!"
—New York *Times Book Review*

"Plenty of action...Collins sets authentic scenes in graphic
black and white...*Chasing Eights* is a taut, suspenseful
thriller!"

—The Statesboro (GA) *Herald*

"FULLY REALIZED CHARACTERS...HUMMING
WITH TENSIONS, THIS PAGE-TURNER IS FIRST-
RATE!"

—*Publishers Weekly*

"An undeniable sense of urgency characterizes this fine
effort...well-directed action, excitement and entertainment!"
—*Library Journal*

Other *Leisure Books* by Michael Collins:

CASTRATO

CHASING EIGHTS

MICHAEL COLLINS

LEISURE BOOKS NEW YORK CITY

A LEISURE BOOK®

May 1992

Published by special arrangement with Donald I. Fine, Inc.

Dorchester Publishing Co., Inc.
276 Fifth Avenue
New York, NY 10001

For further information, contact: Donald I. Fine, Inc., 19 West 21st Street, New York, NY 10010

The name "Leisure Books" and the stylized "L" with design are trademarks of Dorchester Publishing Co., Inc.

Printed in the United States of America.

CHASING EIGHTS

MICHAEL COLLINS

To Marian and Paul Hallenbeck

PRIME TIME

"The business of America is business."
—CALVIN COOLIDGE

Chapter One

That morning, they board the United Airlines 737 in Palm Springs, stay on in Los Angeles. Both have hangovers from an impromptu going-away party the night before, doze in their seats. The jet continues to its next stop in Santa Barbara. Their names are Messick and Gretzer.

They look down at the mud and salt marshes of Goleta Slough without reaction, without speaking. The 737 comes in low over the road to the University and Isla Vista. Gretzer points toward the campus buildings. Some are tall, some low. Long and square, L-shaped and H-shaped in the January afternoon sun. He waves toward the curving beach and lagoon beyond the buildings.

"Where's the town, Messick?"

"There ain't one. Not what I call a town."

"Maybe we find action around the University over there."

"In and out. That's what the lady said, that's what we do."

A few hundred yards from where the newly landed 737 makes its slow turn at the end of the runway there was once a tiny island named Mescalatin where more than a thousand Indians lived in their round thatch houses. A Stone Age megalopolis that Gaspar de Portola and his Europeans reached overland in 1769. The island no longer exists, was bulldozed in 1943 to provide fill dirt for the airport runways. The two men who stand to deplane know nothing of this. They wouldn't be interested if they did.

"I'll call for the guy going to pick us up," Messick tells Gretzer, "you get the bags."

Messick is the boss, more or less. He lives with the lady in Palm Springs who has sent them to Santa Barbara. A heavy-set man in his early forties, five-ten with a square face and blue eyes, Messick has been many things. A high-school fullback too poor to afford college and too short to get a scholarship. A soldier, a deserter, a federal prisoner, a boxer, a security guard, a drug runner, a bodyguard, and a businessman. More businesses than he can remember, all in sales and service: used cars, office cleaning, car washes, debt collecting, charity fund-raising, single product retailing from pornography to futons. No experience or training needed. Cash investment and cheap labor.

"Fifteen minutes," he tells Gretzer when the younger man returns with the luggage.

"Time for a couple," Gretzer says.

Gretzer drinks too much. Messick is aware of this, but he doesn't think about it. He won't unless it comes up later. Messick thinks about nothing until it comes up. He doesn't think about his past or his future, not even about the lady in Palm Springs when he's not with her. He has been with her almost a year. A long time for him. And for her. He doesn't think about that either. Messick doesn't really think at all.

"What kind of import brews you got?" he asks the bartender behind the bar on the second floor of the small terminal.

"Beer," Gretzer says, "you float away before it hits."

"Heineken," the bartender says.

"Nowhere gulch," Messick says, orders the Heineken.

Gretzer has scotch—water on the side so they don't drown it. In his early thirties, six-feet-two and dark haired, he has the lean face of a greyhound, a nose broken more than once. His face reddens when he drinks, is beginning to puff from alcohol, and there is a belly under the tailored gray slacks. His blue blazer

15

is sharp, his shirt is gray striped, his tie is blue-gray, his shoes are cowboy boots to add to his height. Next to Messick's off-the-rack two-button brown worsted, white shirt, brown tie, and brown loafers, Gretzer is a fashion plate.

"Where's the night action?" he asks the bartender.

"Downtown around State. Maybe Isla Vista."

Gretzer went to college, was expelled for selling cocaine. He had hung out in the drama department because the girls were independent, uninhibited, so after he was thrown out he drifted to Southern California with some of the aspiring actresses. Since then he has moved on the edge of the drug scene, lived from woman to woman, taken minimum wage jobs when he was down to the bone, put in a lot of beach time. This last year the women seemed to get a lot older, he lived more in his car, the beach was full of kids. He was thinking about going back east when he met Messick and the Palm Springs lady.

"The action's in Palm Springs," Messick says. "Here we're in and out. I told you."

"You just got the hots for old Sandy," Gretzer says.

The lady in Palm Springs, Sandy, is a heavy cocaine dealer. Messick flew security on a shipment from Colombia. Sandy took a liking to him, put him on as private bodyguard. She needed to take out a small-timer who had ripped her off, Messick did the work when the Colombian people wouldn't oblige. Messick moved in with Sandy in the Palm Springs house.

"Hey! Messick 'n Gretzer up here?"

The *pachuco* stands in the bar. The only other drinker doesn't react, so he walks up behind Messick and Gretzer. Short, muscular, late thirties, he wears a sharp suit, *mucho dinero*. It's a blue banker's pin stripe with a pale blue shirt, blue-and-red tie, low black boots with tassles. His eyes are bold, the black hair and mustache too long. An independent *cholo*.

"Want a beer?" Messick says.

"I take you to the motel. *Muy pronto*."

Messick drinks. "Soon as we finish the drinks, Jose."

"My name is Santos."

"Whatever," Messick says, drinks his beer.

"I will be down in the car."

"You do that, Jose," Messick says.

After the Latino has gone, Gretzer goes to the front window.

"A fucking station wagon," Gretzer says.

"You want a limo?"

"What kind of rich guy drives a station wagon?"

"How about a guy sells cars, dummy?"

Sandy in Palm Springs got to know the man they are meeting when they both bought up properties around L.A. being sold to pay off delinquent taxes. A sweet deal that could make

17

profits on resale of two, three thousand percent. All legal, if you didn't look too close at the bidding and how the places got grabbed in the first place. Legitimate, the man they are meeting, but you never knew about anyone. Messick will keep his eyes open.

Chapter Two

As Jack Price reaches to sweep the chips to him, he feels the adrenaline. Mack the Bluffer said it the time he took his savings to play in The World Series of Poker in Vegas, "What else could I ever be a world champion in? Number one?" The charge when you win, the poker face as you rake in a big one. The cascade of chips into the trough: white, red, blue, yellow.

"You backed into that one, Jack," Al says.

"Keep playing like that, Price," the Genius says.

The dealer says, "Coming around. King, big ten, bet the bullet, deuce is loose, one-eyed hook . . ."

From time to time Morgan the owner checks on the draw game in another room, brings a beer or soda to anyone who wants one. The markup is less than in a bar, Morgan cuts the pot the same as Vegas, but you don't have to take the time to drive to Nevada. It's a real game, not one of those buddy-buddies where you play with the same guys every time, serve food house to house. That is washing your foot with your sock on, kissing your sister. Jack likes to take money from someone he's never met before.

"Wheeltime," Al crows.

Jack tosses in his two pair, checks to be sure Al really has the 1-2-3-4-5. Not that most of the players are strangers. But except for Max Mellecker they're not friends, and there is always new blood. Jack catches the six inside for his eight, but the Genius has hung in for the wheel and lucked out with a seven.

"Flush takes high, seventy-five's low," the dealer intones.

Jack stands on the next deal, takes a break, wonders again what Santos Torena wanted when he called the office. Jack was out on a demonstration drive so the switchboard nitwit had to take the message.

"Mr. Torena said to say he'd meet you at the game maybe around five. What game's that, Mr. Price?"

"You don't want to know, Gloria."

The dumb little broad giggled. "You wouldn't never play those kind of games."

20

He bantered with a straight face, "What kind of games?"

"Funny stuff and all. Kinky city."

"Would it shock you that much?"

"A married man with kids and all. I mean, at your age."

"You think I'm too old?"

"Oh, you know what I mean. Anyway, you're just puttin' me on. I bet it's a softball game or maybe tennis or something."

Brower had been at the real estate office nailing down the deal, Jack had no more appointments, the lot and the showroom were empty. He called Angie to say he had to meet Torena, would be later than usual even for a Friday, would eat out. The Friday night rush at the showroom wouldn't start until 7:00. He could go to the game early, come back early. He took the back way.

Jack liked to look at the green winter mountains, the mansions in Montecito, the horses and pools and tennis courts. The freeway was necessary, you had to be able to get around fast on business, and most of the time he liked the speed, enjoyed pushing his yellow XJ and seeing the other drivers stare. One of the best investments he'd made, no matter what Angie said about guys who drove Jags. Built for the man who can handle it, will the rest be kind enough to step aside and let him pass. People were impressed, and it never hurt to impress the other guy.

The sun was low behind him as he drove down the curves of Stanwood to Sycamore Canyon and made the turn into East Valley Road. After the village, East Valley stretched out, mountains clear and sharp to the left in the early evening. A flash came from high up on Camino Cielo. The windshield of a solitary car. As soon as the kids were old enough, Jack had taken them up there. He hadn't driven it for years. Kids grew up, you had to do other things—fish, camp, take the girl to dances. East Valley became Toro Canyon Road, and soon he pulled into the lane behind the old house.

"Off early this afternoon?" Max Mellecker had said.

"Where the hell were you all afternoon?" Jack said.

"You think you're the only guy with deals?"

Now Jack has a beer, looks at the time. 4:10. Digital watches still make him look twice at the display for the real time, not just some numbers. His mind works faster with analog, but digital is the technology, and Brower bought the whole staff digitals. "You want to look high-tech to everyone who walks in, on the cutting edge. The cars run by computer now, you have to look like you know how they work. Make the customer think he has to go with progress, needs a high-test vehicle."

Jack knows it's important to stand out of a hand sometimes. Never too eager. The Genius is good at that. A cool player who takes as much money from the game as anyone. Genius got the name because he knows everything about everything. An electronics expert, he worked up in Silicon Valley, has a bunch of degrees. And because he has every crazy idea in the book. You say white, Genius says black. The nuclear family is the worse thing ever happened. The best place to learn sex is on a street corner. There is less freedom in the United States than in Nazi Germany. Sometimes Jack thinks the whole damn world is going crazy.

"Deal me in." His watch reads 4:30, he sits next to Al.

The opposite of Mack the Bluffer, Al bets only locks, the sure thing. A retired union organizer, the old kraut has a hole-in-the-wall office somewhere for renters to fight owners. Brower hates Al's guts. *"He's a fucking nightmare, always telling the stupid pachucos their rights."* Al doesn't understand the basic importance of property rights, is as dumb about that as he is about playing only locks.

"You can't win, you don't stay in," Morgan the owner says.

"You're all heart, Morgan," Al says.

Jack watches the cards fly under the light, drop in front of each player. They talk and joke but their eyes never leave the cards. It has to be the deal Torena wants to talk about. That makes Jack nervous. He watches the cards as intently as the others but they don't quite register. What the other players have. It's the best deal Jack's ever had bar none. He had to fight to make Brower let him in, it's taken a lot more money than he counted on, but it's the big one, the jackpot, and nothing can go wrong. Not this time.

"Catch an eight, make a straight," the Genius says, rakes in the pot with his eight high straight that wins both ways.

There's been enough trouble with the buyer. Rearrange the condos, add that El Parador estate to the package for more land, rezone it and unload the old mansion. Extra money all the way. But this was it. Tonight or tomorrow. Brower has the new money, and what the hell does Santos Torena want to talk to him about? The cards slide and flash and turn under the lights, and Jack finally has a hand that brings him back from Santos Torena.

"Nines full beat aces up."

No one has a low. Jack reaches for the whole pot.

"Nice hand," Max Mellecker says.

5:05. Where the hell is Torena?

"Deal me out."

Jack walks through an empty room and out onto the side porch. In the dusk a slate blue twilight sky hangs above the mountains. A long flight of outside stairs leads up to the main tower of the old house with its widow's walk. Jack climbs up to the railed platform where the wives of sea captains stood to stare out at sea and hope for their husband's return. In the cold sea wind of early January he leans on the railing to look down. When he sees nothing down there, he stares out at the red and gold layers of sunset between sky and water. Twenty miles off shore the islands are clear and sharp. He can even see valleys and bays. Only in winter are the islands so clear.

As the sky over the mountains darkens to deep navy, the far-off islands give Jack a sense of disappointment. He has been out there only once. On Brower's boat, and then they didn't land. Angie doesn't like fishing, he's never taken the kids out. As if they are too far to reach, a different world where he can't go.

Chapter Three

The dark was motionless even with a sea wind that blew through the palms and old oaks. Night is not our time. We need light, what we can see and touch and not have to imagine the dangers hidden in the shadows.

I had heard the sound that wasn't wind or imagination.

The big Victorian house set back from Toro Canyon Road near Via Real had shown no life since I'd arrived. It was all gray towers and gables and turrets with a widow's walk on its main tower. Most of its windows were closed and curtained in the last light of evening. There were no cars in the driveway. A plain house with no one home. But unless Angela Price's husband was lying to her, behind the windows covered by drapes and vegetation imported to Southern California from every semitropical corner of the world, was a professional poker game.

It wasn't the game I listened for.

The alien sound on the sea wind of the early January night.

Not from the big shadowy Victorian, but from across the road where two smaller houses were darker. What could have been two muffled shots, footsteps in the brush.

I waited five minutes, circled to cross the blacktop road away from the sea and the freeway, came up on the small houses through trees and the chaparral. They were both little more than cinder-block shacks, one darkened and neat with curtains, the other a tumbledown half-ruin in overgrown weeds.

He stood behind the tumbledown house.

A wolf face in the brief headlights of a passing car. Skin grooved like leather, a graying mustache, a dark windbreaker of no color. A western hat and worn jeans. Eyes reflected straight toward me. The one sweep of light and then only a skinny shape, a shadow rigid in the night. I moved closer. When the next car passed, its lights swept emptiness.

Cars moved in a steady drone on the freeway, passed on Toro Canyon Road and Via Real. I moved on to where the Latino had been standing.

Chasing Eights

The body lay between the broken house and a rear shed.

A heavier texture in the night that made me stop before I fell over it.

In the beam of my flashlight he had no face.

Old Captain Gazzo in New York told me you never get used to it, you only withdraw into some private nightmare where it is always midnight. Death is difficult enough, violent death is, in the end, impossible. Gazzo drew the shades down on his office windows, kept them down for the next twenty years, so he wouldn't see all the bloody bodies lying shattered in the dark glass like color negatives. They become you, you become them, and you never get used to it.

A pool of dark liquid, bone and tissue where his head lay in the weeds. Without half a head he couldn't be alive, but I took his pulse, checked his heart and breathing. There was no heartbeat, no pulse, no breath. He had no eyes to look into. A short man, thick and muscular, with brown skin and black hair worn long, in a dark blue pin-striped suit, pale blue shirt, blue-and-red tie. His black half boots had tassles. Shot in the back of the head at close range. He had been on his knees, dirt on the pin-striped trousers. A heavy gun placed against the skull, red marks on his wrists where they had been held behind his back. There were rings on his fingers, a stickpin in the tie, a gold Rollex watch, but his wallet was in his hip pocket as if he wasn't used to wearing a suit yet.

The driver's license was in the name of Santos Torena.

The pistol was in his pants. A snubnosed Colt .38.

I put the wallet and pistol back, searched around him with my flashlight. The body was still warm, the weeds were trampled all around, but I found no clear footprints. I had seen enough death to know I could do nothing for Santos Torena, went back across the blacktop to the Victorian. It was still dark and silent as if nothing had happened out in the night.

I walked around the big house listening for voices.

Poker is unlike other forms of gambling. There is no edge to the house, so it cuts the pot for its share. You play only the odds, the others in the game, and yourself. If you play perfectly, the way you know you should, you will always win over the long run. But human beings do nothing perfectly, even less act always the way they know they should, and so poker is a game of tension, of frustration, of anger at yourself. A game of self, and it cannot be played in the silence of blackjack or roulette, the isolation among crowds of horse racing. It is a game of talk, of laughs and curses, of long explanations of why one did or did not, of analysis of past hands tonight and weeks ago, of what could have happened and might have been.

I heard the voices, climbed the steps of a side porch where Victorian ladies had served tea on warm afternoons. Through the white curtains on french doors the players sat in a room beyond the one next to the porch. Eight men around the green felt table with a dealer's slot. The angle gave me four faces, two backs and only the hands of the dealer as the cards went around.

A tall man with horn-rimmed glasses and a black-and-white checked shirt under a black vest sat next to the dealer. He wore his glasses on a cord, his long red hair ragged as if cut with a knife. His eyes watched the cards of the other players, and the other players themselves.

Underweight and gray faced, a balding man in his forties sat in a blue blazer that hung too loose on his bones, a red-striped button-down shirt, bow tie. He looked at his hole cards, scanned the cards of the others with pale eyes that saw little, seemed to look out through the bars of a cage.

The third, a little man in his seventies, had the precise face of an accountant, held his hole cards tight to his chest. Steel eyes that studied both his up and hole cards over and over, calculated the value of his hand rigorously. He would be a man who folded a great deal.

Between the old man and the balding one with the caged eyes the fourth player was who I had come for.

Angela Price had described her husband well. Forty-two, a whisper over six feet and two-hundred pounds. Maybe fifteen pounds

overweight. Thick dark blond hair that had
been golden. Erect, his chest out, belly in
under a proper white shirt and blue tie,
blue three-button suit with vest. The pos-
ture of an athlete, the clothes of a successful businessman. A confident expression to
the blue eyes as if aware of people watching him.

But Jack Price wasn't an athlete, and he
wasn't confident. It was there in the belt that
cut into his waist, the shirt that bunched out of
tight pants. Pale, thick fingers almost like the
fingers of a baby. The tightness of everything
because he would not admit he was overweight.
And the face. A soft face, puffy and smooth, the
nose and chin too small. Behind the confident
expression there was a flicker in the blue eyes.
He was a man who would always feel someone
was watching him.

In the room there were only two who would
take money from the game over the long run.
The thin man in the checked shirt who studied the cards of everyone, and the owner who
cut the pot. The others never really looked at
what anyone else held, played as if they were
alone with their cards. Too busy with other
problems. Too eager and too distracted at the
same time. They played at poker, the game not
the result.

I walked through the trees to my Tempo
parked up Toro Canyon Road. I looked at my
car telephone. In my work the rule is tell the

police everything, it's the law, you need them more than they need you.

There are exceptions to every rule. Santos Torena was the man my client's husband was supposed to meet tonight. I couldn't help Torena, I needed to know more of what was going on before I talked to any police. You owe a client that much.

I called Kay. The machine answered. I left a message—the job was going to take longer, eat without me.

Chapter Four

"All I know," Angela Price said, "is he told me Torena called the office, had to meet him. He'd be later than usual again."

She was at the front window of her living room with its fake cathedral ceiling, looked out as if watching for Jack Price to appear and explain everything. She put her slender hand on the windowsill to steady herself. "You're . . . sure it was Santos Torena, Mr. Fortune?"

"His identification said so. Short, dark, muscular. Suit, tie, tassled black half boots. Long hair and a gun."

Her shaken eyes and her silence covered all the questions and answers.

"Your husband has been coming home late often, Mrs. Price, right? Long periods in the day when you don't know where he is?"

She turned to look at me. She was a tall woman, as tall as Price himself. Light brown hair of the kind most women bleach these days, with a faint touch of gray. She had slender fingers, large feet, long legs under a comfortable denim skirt. A slim woman, even lean, her arms were firm in a white peasant blouse, her breasts a shade too large for her bra. The wide skirt covered narrow hips, showed firm legs. A long oval face, large brown eyes and a strong nose and chin. It was an elegant face with a mouth intended for smiling. It wasn't smiling now.

"He's often late, but almost never so late he misses dinner. An hour or so at his poker game, at a bar with others from the agency, or at a meeting with someone. No unexplained gaps in his day until he became involved in this deal with Brower. I don't think it's a woman, Mr. Fortune, if that's what you're asking."

She had hired me that afternoon. By telephone. I don't list an address for my new office in the Summerland house. My clients aren't always well-behaved, I don't want to disturb Kay working up in her tower. In Southern California it doesn't make much difference—a universe of automobiles and telephones where you go nowhere without calling first. Her husband was coming home late, leaving his office during the day. He was distracted, evasive.

Business he said, but the only business she knew about was a deal with the owner of the auto agency where he sold cars. At first he had talked about the deal the way he always did. Not the last month. He had used all their savings, maybe borrowed against the house at high interest instead of refinancing which she would almost certainly have found out about. *"When Jack won't talk about something, that's when I worry."*

"You're sure, Mrs. Price?" I said. "Not a woman?"

"I'm sure." She wasn't, or she wouldn't have hired me. A problem with a known answer doesn't end up with an investigator. "Not that he wouldn't if he had the chance, but it would have to be easy. It's not his vice. Too much effort, and he doesn't really like women all that much."

People who talk about someone who is late, or has vanished, almost always stand at a window. Like widows on their walks at the top of the house looking out to sea for their lost whaling captains. The hope that is part of our genes. There was sadness in her voice. Not for her, but for him. She'd tell me about it sooner or later.

"You're sure it's this deal with Mr. Brower."

"No, but it's all I know that it could be."

"And Santos Torena was part of it?"

"That I can't tell you. Torena works for Ed Brower too, but not at the car agency. In his real estate office. If he's . . . was part of this deal, Jack didn't tell me."

"It could be something else?"

"It could be anything that involved making money, a business success, Mr. Fortune. That's all Jack would put the effort into, the time and the money."

"What are you worried about, Mrs. Price? Your husband or the money?"

She turned at the window to look at me. There was anger in her eyes, but it wasn't directed at me. At something else, maybe herself. A power, too, that didn't let the anger show anywhere else. Control I sensed had been learned over a lot of years when she had smiled and gotten nowhere. She came to sit on the couch that faced where I sat in the matching armchair. It was the first time she'd sat down since I'd told her about Santos Torena.

"I'm worried that Jack has gone too far this time. That Ed Brower has dragged him into something over his head, and over our heads. That this time he's not risking only our money but even the house. This time I wanted to know what he was doing, what was going to happen to my life." She reached for an onyx box on the coffee table in front of the pale brown couch. She hadn't smoked when we met earlier after she called me.

"You said he usually told you about his business."

"I said he talked about his business. The glittering hopes and wonderful prospects. Not the details. Business details are man talk."

Bitterness, sadness and sarcasm all mixed together in her voice in the room with its high ceiling, exposed beams.

"Exactly what did he say when you asked him about the deal, about the money and the possible loan?"

"What he always says, does. He laughed—this was going to be the big one, the brass ring. Our money would triple, perhaps more. The loan he simply evaded, then denied, then got angry. When he doesn't want to talk about something, he gets angry. He gets angry, I back down. A perfect marriage." Her own anger took over from sadness and bitterness. "This time I was going to do something, take some action."

"I'm the action?"

"I want to know, stop him before he kills us."

The power I sensed in her was stretched on a raw edge. She was doing something she'd never done before, excited and worried, sure and unsure. Not afraid of her husband. There was nothing of that in her voice. Afraid of herself. Of doing what she had never done.

"The house is only in your husband's name?"

"Of course." She smoked, looked around the room, up at the cathedral ceiling that wasn't a real cathedral ceiling. "Do you like the house, Mr. Fortune?"

It was a typical ranch house in the kind of good tract that appears somewhere in Southern California every few seconds. On the fields and hills where there had been only brown wild

oats and dusty green old oaks the last time
you looked. Around the big and small cities
from San Diego to Santa Cruz, Palm Springs
to Bakersfield. This tract was older, had grown
into its landscaping. A solid house, maybe three
thousand square feet. But there was no pool, little land, the neighbors close on both sides. A five
hundred thousand dollar house. Small potatoes
in Santa Barbara.

"I'm still a New Yorker," I said. "Any house is
foreign territory to me."

"But do you like it?"

"I wouldn't rent it for myself," I admitted.
"Don't you like it, Mrs. Price?"

"No, I don't like it. But it was time to buy a
home this size, this was the cheapest one we
found. Our Mesa house had appreciated, a good
businessman sells and buys bigger. It's called
leverage, right? We had to buy it the way we
had to move to California." She smoked, shook
her head almost in wonder. "We were in Tulsa
at the time, he got an offer from Jens Spear at
Spear Industries, so out we came."

"Spear the Kingmaker? Mr. Conservative?
Friend and benefactor of governors, senators
and presidents?"

"Himself. Jack had bought Spear Industries
reverse osmosis units for the oil company, met
Jens Spear. The old man liked him, liked his pre-
law and rural background, knew and liked his
father's work in Minnesota Republican politics,
and offered him a job. The money was good but

not great—Jens Spear didn't become a billionaire by overpaying his staff—but Jack wanted to work for the great man. Spear offered me a job too, so we moved out."

She stopped to listen to a car drive into the cul-de-sac out front. It parked at the next house. "My job turned out to be nothing. Jens Spear always got what he wanted, had made up a job for me. Gofer for everyone, backup secretary. Then it didn't work out for Jack. It was his first real setback. No reason, the Jens Spears don't give reasons."

"Does this deal you're worried about involve Jens Spear?"

"Old Jens died years ago. But Ed Brower worked for Spear too. He was higher up than Jack. After Jack got fired, he had a series of management jobs, tried his own business. We managed to get by, moved through four cars, three houses, two kids, part-time jobs for me, but nothing ever really worked out for Jack. He joined Ed Brower at the car agency two years ago. Assistant sales manager with an option to buy into the business. He came home excited to the sky, he was on his way at last."

She laughed and shook her head. I heard a kind of pity in her voice now, even scorn. I didn't envy Jack Price. I didn't envy either of them.

"You sound like you don't believe that, Mrs. Price."

She stubbed out the cigarette in an onyx ash tray on the table. "You may as well call me

41

Angie, almost everyone does. I was Angela at home, but Jack likes Angie." She was up again, walked back to the front window. "All salesmen at the agency are assistant sales managers. They all have an option to buy into the agency. Ed Brower knows what he wants."

The scorn and the pity, even the bitterness, softened in her voice as she stood looking out at the cul-de-sac, watched for her husband's yellow Jaguar. Maybe because Jack Price believed Ed Brower so easily, or believed him at all. Angela Price didn't believe Ed Brower.

"Can you tell me anything about Brower's deal?"

"Only that it's a large condominium project to combine land and existing units, renovate, and sell the package. It excites him, but it worries him too. Like a small boy with a lot of money he knows he shouldn't spend for candy. As if he wants the deal desperately, Mr. Fortune, but is scared of it too."

"If it is Brower's deal that has him scared," I said. "If he isn't into more than losing money or even your house."

She was silent at the window. "He's the way he was when he got the job with Jens Spear. That's what worries me, as if we're back at the beginning." She suddenly shivered. "He's on a high, excited, eager, the way he was before we went on a business trip to Chicago with old Spear almost twenty years ago."

Chapter Five

Jack and Angela have been at Spear Industries a year when they go to Chicago with Jens Spear. It is not a sales trip, the old man does not bother anymore with the details of his business. The conglomerate is building a new headquarters in Santa Barbara to tie all the companies into a unit. It will be a monument to Jens himself, although the old man considers all that he's done in business and power politics as his true monument.

"You get a goddamned stone when you're dead. What a man builds, owns, changes, that's his monument."

They fly in the company jet: the old man, Controller Sid Beckman, Ed Brower, Jack and

Angela. Brower is assistant to the vice-president for corporate affairs, will be in direct charge of the project. Jack is the old man's personal gofer. Angela is along to take notes. Money and decisions are involved. These Jens Spear bothers with.

The construction companies come to the suite each day, present their designs and bids. Each night the old man, Brower, Sid Beckman and Jack discuss them. Then it is the turn of Shea Construction, which has built other projects for Jens Spear. The night before, Frank Shea himself calls to invite them all out on the town.

"He always does," Sid Beckman says.

"Shows a damn good attitude," Jens Spear says.

The old man will not join them. With a pacemaker, no gall bladder and a new hip, his days of nights on the town are over, if his cigars and twelve-hour work days are not, no matter what the doctors say. But there is a fierce surge of memory in his faded blue eyes.

"I'll tell you about nights on the town."

He launches into stories of nights that ended barely in time for a fast shower and shave before the office. Bacchanals where salesmen were lost for days. The all-male revels of The Bohemian Grove with heads of every government department and important national corporation, and the yearly rides of the Santa Barbara Rancheros Visitadores in the company of governors, senators, and ex-presidents who rode from ranch to ranch as the Californios had done for centuries. Only now they rode from motel to motel, and prostitutes waited to service them.

"If I know Shea," the old man says, "there'll be some nice friendly ladies for all you boys."

While Brower, Beckman and the old man grin, Jack can't seem to think of what to say so says nothing. He even smiles with the others. Angela has to say it.

"Jack and I are married, Mr. Spear. I guess you forgot."

Brower and Sid Beckman stop grinning. So does Jens Spear, but there is a difference. Brower and Beckman are embarrassed. The old man is angry. He has been made to look uninformed, even stupid. Jack should have had another secretary assigned to the trip.

"What the hell are you doing on this trip then? I pay Jack enough to keep his wife at home." The old man glares at Jack. "Damn women in business. It used to be when a man had to go he found a tree and pissed. Now we have to put executive johns in for women, remember our secretary's married to our assistant."

Frank Shea arrives all smiles and backslaps and hard grips.

"Jens, you can't let me down. I got four of the best ready to trot. You want to disappoint a hot lady? No offense, miss."

They have to tell him.

"Married?" Frank Shea grins.

"They are, Frank," Ed Brower says.

"Sure."

"No," Sid Beckman says. "Really."

"Really?"

"Really," Angela says.

Frank Shea recovers smoothly. "So, how many are we then? Will you and Jack be joining us, Mrs. Price?"

"It sounds like fun," Angela says. She knows it is important for Jack to go with Brower and Beckman and Frank Shea, tries to save the situation. "You don't have to change plans for me."

"Maybe one small change." Shea beckons to a young man with him. The young man hurries out. Angela is aware that somewhere a lady will be paid off and told her services will not be needed this night, sorry, we'll make it up to you, honey.

Shea turns to old Jens Spear who is still annoyed. "So we'll be five after all. I can still make it six, Jens. Say the word. It's going to be a bash."

Jens Spear finally smiles. "I forgot more damn bashes than you'll ever see. Go on, have fun, tomorrow we work."

They are driven to a restaurant in some old mansion where there are no prices on the menus. Waiting at a secluded corner table are three women. They are well-dressed, attractive, and not out of place in the rarified atmosphere of the restaurant. They are stiff at first. Angela knows that is because she is there, but Frank Shea makes a few pointed remarks, and they quickly relax.

At dinner nothing is stinted. The conversation among the men is animated. Angela makes an attempt to participate, but for the most part they ignore her. The other women move close to the men. Jack does not move close. A gulf develops in the evening. The other couples almost cuddle, and Jack and Angela watch. They go on to a nightclub where the gulf widens, end up in an ornate apartment with Jacuzzis in the bathrooms and a real old Wurlitzer jukebox against the wall near a bar. A hall leads to the bedrooms.

They split up in couples. Jack talks to Angela about the meeting tomorrow and the prospects of the bidders. He analyzes the importance of the project. The jukebox plays old live songs. Angela listens to the others. Sid Beckman's small woman, by far the youngest, is eager but shy. She is not well educated, knows it, and wants to learn.

"I'd sure like California. You got great colleges."

"There's a UC in Santa Barbara. Some profs work for us."

"Indiana's a good university, but there's better jobs here in Chicago."

Angela can see the blonde in one of the bedrooms, like a white melon on the bed as Sid Beckman undresses. Why does the woman always undress first when money is involved? She can see the blonde on the bed, Sid Beckman naked on top of her, and it is all as cold and dead as the porcelain washbowl in the corner.

Ed Brower holds his tall woman's hand, stares intently into her eyes. His voice is low and hypnotic, soft yet urgent.

"The Bahamas. I like to go there when I'm all strung out, the work's getting to me. Sun and sand and blue water and nothing to do all day except lie around on the beach. Later we eat, dance, take in the gambling."

"I'd like that."

"Nassau's good, but the smaller islands are better."

"I get two weeks in July," the tall girl says.

"Perfect."

"I'm a receptionist. Tonight's a favor for Mr. Shea."

Angela can see all three women on the beds down the hall. They have forgotten Jack and Angela, forgotten that Angela isn't another one night stand doing a job for the boss, helping get an important contract. Frank Shea picks up his woman to carry her to the bedroom. She kisses him and laughs. The small blonde pulls Sid Beckman up. Ed Brower hurls his glass against the wall. The liquor drips down the flocked wallpaper, a dark stain spreads on the thick carpeting.

"What the hell are you talking about?" Brower demands.

The tall girl stares at the floor. "Not tonight."

Frank Shea is beside Ed Brower.

"This stupid bitch says no screwing tonight!"

"What's the deal, honey?"

"I don't feel good."

"You got paid."

"You can have it back." The tall girl looks at Brower, "If you meant it, you'd wait. All that about the Bahamas, Nassau."

Angela realizes Brower has overplayed, has tried to pretend that the gaudy old jukebox is real and not a fake idol with a heart of coins. Pay your money and take your choice. The man who feeds the coins calls the tune. But every maudlin lyric is true if the listeners believe, and the tall girl has believed the songs and the lies. She can't return to the game.

"I got bad cramps."

Frank Shea looks down at the girl. Brower turns so sharply he almost falls, walks to the door and out. Sid Beckman hurries after him. Frank Shea swears and follows Brower and Beckman out. Angela touches Jack, and they join the exodus. Down on the night street, Ed Brower smokes under a street lamp. Jack and Angela stop some distance away near the cars.

Frank Shea says, "That's the last she works for us. Look, I know a real house. We can at least get the ashes hauled."

Sid Beckman says, "It's late enough."

Ed Brower says, "All right, Shea, lead me to it. I'll fuck them bowlegged."

They take one of the cars. Jack and Angela join Sid Beckman and are driven to their hotel. Up in the hotel room Angela looks out at the city where rain has begun to fall. Naked, Jack comes up and rubs against her, his penis hard and ready.

"Angie?" Sex is heavy in his voice. The night has made him sensual, something he rarely is since their wedding.

She goes into the bathroom. She feels sick, leans against the wall, sees the naked blonde, the tall girl, and Frank Shea's woman. All the motions, smells, tastes, without anything but the needs of body and ego. A scalp at the belt. The ashes hauled.

When she finally comes out, Jack has gone to bed, his face turned to the wall. She stands again at the high window and looks at the lights of Chicago at three in the morning. She feels that the rain will fall forty days and forty nights and someone will have to build an ark on top of the Sears Building that is the tallest in the world.

Next morning they are all in Jens Spear's room by nine. The sun, refracted by the bottles on a serving cart, casts a rainbow on the wall behind Jens Spear's head. Frank Shea arrives at ten. The drawings and data are spread on the table in front of Jens Spear. Brower pushes a drawing toward the old man, nods to Shea.

"These are damn fine drawings, Frank. You used a good man."

"Money talks," Shea smiles. "I like that design."

Brower nods. "It's a powerful concept, J.S."

Angela sees that Brower is selling not for Spear but to him. Frank Shea wants to build this particular building, and Brower is pushing it. For a price, of course, but that will come later. Jens Spear drinks his martini, leans back. His rugged old face is expressionless. The powerful man who rose from nothing by his own effort and is not easily fooled.

"I talked to Bill Peters over at GM. Bill, I said, make damn sure you do business with a company that has talent . . ." Sun fills the room with a sleepy warmth as Jens Spear tells his story. Listening is part of working for, and selling to, the old man. He reaches the punch line, laughs, and waits. They all laugh. A split second late, but Angela sees this doesn't bother Spear. He even likes it. They laugh whether the joke is funny or not. Because Jens Spear told it.

"You can tell a story, J.S.," Ed Brower says. "So, what do you think of that building?"

Jack has not seen what Brower is really doing, brings another drawing forward.

"Did you see this, Mr. Spear? A lot of imagination, and looks like good floor space too."

Ed Brower goes to the cart for fresh drinks.
Jens Spear looks at the new drawing, looks
at Jack.

"Imagination and more floor space, Jack?"

Brower returns with the drinks, is angry but
tries not to show it. Frank Shea is casual.

"People'd sure look at it," Jack says.

"We'll talk about it after lunch," Jens Spear
says.

Good food is as much part of the old man's
world as nights on the town. What he is entitled
to because he is Jens Spear. The power and
the glory. So the food comes on a parade of
carts pushed by silent men in white jackets
who hurry in and out as they once did for
kings and lords. They eat, the old man tells
another story—of the time he paid fifteen million dollars for a moribund company everyone
said he was crazy to buy, since then had made
a profit of $1.75 billion on the company, and it
now accounted for fifty percent of Spear Industries' profits.

"That's what you call damned good business,
but it took guts to see it," he says, waits as the
coffee and eclairs are served and the waiters
leave. "Okay, we get down to real work."

Angela has a sense of great distance, of seeing
them and the room isolated, detached. Sharply etched in black and white like a Daumier
print. Brower and Shea intent and insistent.
Sid Beckman the doubter, the critical voice.
Jack alone, uncertain. When Jack does make

some comment, no one looks at him. Until the old man holds up the drawing Jack admired earlier.

"This you want me to build, Jack?"

It is a small skyscraper, all glass and steel in the style of Mies van der Rohe.

"It'd get a lot of attention, Mr. Spear. It's beautiful."

"Beautiful?" Jens Spear looks up at Jack, speculative. "Okay, it wins some goddamn prizes. They love it at Harvard. Am I Lever, Seagram, Carbide? They want a big show in New York. But if I build this in Santa Barbara they send for the straight-jacket. I'm a western-er, not a Park Avenue queer."

It is then that Angela knows Jack will not be with Spear Industries long. Jens Spear bites the end off his forbidden cigar, says, "We got a damned good bid from McGregor in Canada."

Frank Shea dismisses McGregor. "Hell, you can't work with a foreign outfit. Too many complications, and bad P.R."

Jens Spear smokes. "What about Schiller? Sid likes them."

"They have offices in California," Beckman says. "They do good work and the price is more than competitive."

"You can't work with Schiller," Brower says. "Remember that warehouse in San Diego three years ago? Tulsa before that?"

"They were both good jobs," Sid Beckman says.

"Okay jobs," Jens Spear says, scowls at his cigar. "Old Schiller had too many foreign ideas, but he was a businessman. When the god-damned son took over, the place went to hell. The union runs the company. Wayne Schiller never contributed a dime to my fund raising, never bought a damn dinner ticket. The son-of-a-bitch is a liberal. No, I don't do business with Schiller."

Frank Shea smiles. "And that leaves us, right, J.S.?"

"Or Acme," Jens Spear says softly, almost slyly.

The silence this time is electric. Angela feels it.

"They have the lowest bid," Sid Beckman says.

Beckman says this without expression, as if he believes it should end the discussion, but knows it won't.

Frank Shea nods, "I guess they can beat our bid, if not our work, Sid. They hang right on the edge, no extras. We don't do that kind of job. With us each job is special, custom-made, and that costs. Personal service, a building tailored for you. We couldn't work like Acme even if we lose the contract."

"I don't trust Acme," Ed Brower says. "In a crisis, where are they? If we need special changes, what do they charge?"

"Look, Jens." Frank Shea sits on the long conference table, bends down. "I'll say it straight—

they've got no class. We cost more, but we've got the class. We spend, we let the world know we're building a monument to Jens Spear. We work with you. They give you a generic building, just another customer."

Jens Spear blows smoke. "I'll tell you about Acme. I make a phone call to Wyatt, he's busy. Long-distance and urgent, and he's too busy to talk to Jens Spear. Playing goddamned golf, Wyatt's busy! The son-of-a-bitch doesn't even call back. I want new plans in three days. Impossible. To *me* they say impossible. Not even Wyatt, some goddamned engineer. Do they think I buy a building over the goddamned counter?"

Angela realizes it isn't the right numbers that count, it's the right words. Frank Shea and Brower have said the right words. Acme Engineering has not.

"This calls for drinks all around," Ed Brower says.

Sunlight like thin gold in the elegant hotel room. Jens Spear as solid and gaudy as the jukebox last night. The right words at the right time. Last night and today. One woman is much the same as another, and twenty companies can do the job.

Chapter Six

Morgan the owner stands behind Jack Price. "So where is your buddy Torena tonight?"

It's hold-'em, the Genius raises before the flop. Jack calls with his pair of Queens, trips on a Queen, Ace, ten flop, two of them diamonds.

"He's not my buddy," Jack says.

The Genius bets the pot, Al and Jack call. A six of clubs helps no one. Al raises the Genius, tells the world he has the high straight. It is a big pot. The Genius calls. So does Jack, prays for a pair to fill him, make him a winner.

"He works for Brower," Morgan says. "Get Brower into the game. New blood."

The last card is the ten of hearts. Jack bets the limit on his full house. Al folds. The Genius

raises him. Shit, shit, shit! It has to be aces.
Unless it's a bluff. Jack calls.

"Aces full over Queens full," the dealer says.

Jack slams his Queens on the table, then tries
to grin as the new deal goes around.

"What's up with Torena?" Max Mellecker
asks.

"He left a message he wants to talk to me."

"About what?"

"How do I know?"

Max couldn't come up with the cash to go
in with Brower, is left out, can hardly stand
it. Disraeli: *The secret of success is for a man
to be ready when his time comes*. Jack is more
than ready. He's done okay so far, but okay
isn't the big enchilada. Angie holds him back.
She doesn't have the push, the drive, to go for
the top. Jack knows he has to do it for both
of them. His watch reads 7:13. The cards go
around in the cone of light over the green felt
table. There is something so peaceful about it,
warm and easygoing. It doesn't matter what is
going on outside, what you have to do, who
you have to keep happy. You can relax and
not worry about some stupid beaner. Christ,
the goddamn *cholos* have no damn concept of
time. *Mañana. La dolce vita. Hey, no sweat,
man*.

"You know why Sunday morning's the best
time for driving in L.A.?" Jack says.

"No," the Genius says, "but I bet we're going
to find out."

"Jews are in Palm Springs, Catholics are in church, the blacks are in jail, and the beaners can't get the car started."

Morgan the owner and a stranger laugh.

"That's not funny," Al says.

"Some black comic told it," Jack protests.

"And you loved it," the Genius says.

"For Christ sake deal," the second stranger says.

Jack looks at his watch: 7:30. Santos Torena isn't coming to the game tonight.

"Cash me in."

He has an hour before he should be back at the showroom. He drives the Jaguar back into town and the *barrio*.

He has always taken clients past Santos Torena's house in the *barrio* when he wants to prove it is bad to own the best house in a neighborhood. "Look at it," he says as he drives past the house. "Bigger than all the shacks around it. Real brick on a full acre, air-conditioned, a two-car garage. Those wrought iron fences enclosing the whole acre, a pool with a diving board, aluminum awnings, and a garden it takes two gardeners to keep up. Sure, it makes the guy who built it look important in the community, but who buys it if he wants to sell? No one sees the little dumps around it and pays what it's worth. The other houses set the price level, the place is a terrible investment."

Now there is one lighted window beyond the wrought iron fence, and the front door is open. The pool is black in the moonlight. Ghetto-blaster music over the whole *barrio*. In the seedy frame cottages all around, Jack sees the flicker of TV sets. No paint outside, but TV inside. A TV is on through the lighted window of Torena's house. The heavy wrought iron gate is unlocked. Jack picks his way along the brick paths between the flower beds and under the jacaranda and avocado trees, climbs the steps of the front porch, looks through the screen door into the room where the TV drones and flashes.

"Do you want Santos or Francesca?"

Jack peers into the darkness of the brick front porch and knows the woman. Torena's mother-in-law. She was at one of Brower's mandatory parties. Jack had gone alone because Angie had one of her damn writing classes, remembered wondering why the hell a guy would bring his mother-in-law to a business party? *"Probably wants her to keep an eye on that hot daughter of hers," he had told Max Mellecker. "Or maybe because she speaks better English than Santos does."*

"Santos, ma'am." She isn't a lot older than he is, he feels stupid calling her "ma'am," but he doesn't know her name.

"He has not come home from work yet. If it's important I can give him a message."

She lies in the dark on a sort of rope hammock striped all colors. In dark pants and a white blouse, she is light for a beaner, has brown hair where it isn't gray, talks English almost as good as he does.

"He called me in the office. Said he wanted to talk to me, would meet me at the game, er, Mrs. . . . ?"

"Inez Ortega. Game?"

"The regular poker game he plays in. I'm Jack Price. We met at a party at Ed Brower's house."

"You came alone, told everyone your wife had to stay home because your children were ill. What did Santos want to talk about, Mr. Price?"

Jack doesn't know if he ought to laugh or be insulted, so he smiles. "That's what I came here to find out."

"You work for Mr. Brower with Santos?"

"I'm at the car agency."

On the dark porch her teeth are white in the night. There is a reflection higher on her almost unseen face as if her eyes were watching him intently. "You are part of the important new business Santos has been telling us about?"

The man is there behind him before Jack hears any sound at all. He jumps when the voice says something in Spanish and then English. Low and harsh.

"Where is your daughter, mother?"

Inez Ortega's voice from the hammock is just as harsh, "Ask her husband, *cabron*."

"When we find him. Now we ask you, old lady."

"Look in the house, maybe she is there."

The man steps past Jack without a glance. A thin face sunburned almost black, the skin grooved like leather. Limp mustache, a colorless windbreaker in the light from inside the house. A tan Stetson that looks real to Jack. He bends close to Inez Ortega, eyes as light as a coyote. In the yard beyond the porch two other men stand in long white dusters, white pants, white shoes.

"Where is she, *chingada*?"

"She is a grown woman, Paz."

"She is a Latina, she tells her mother what she does."

They talk, threaten and deny, sometimes slide into Spanish, and Jack watches them and the silent pair in the garden. They don't watch him. He isn't there. He doesn't exist. Less than nothing, an Anglo with no connection to them or what they want.

"You tell her Paz wants to talk. You got it, mother?"

"Not Santos?"

"He comes, you tell him same thing."

The skinny man, Paz, walks past Jack and down across the garden with the two white shadows following him. Inez Ortega gets out of the hammock, stands looking toward where the three men have faded into the night. Jack looks too.

Chasing Eights

"Who were they, Mrs. Ortega?"

"I'll tell Santos you were here," she says.

She still stands and stares at the empty *barrio* night where the three men have vanished.

"Is Santos mixed up with them?" Jack says.

"That is not your business."

She walks inside the house.

Chapter Seven

"Jens Spear let Jack go a year later," Angela Price lay on the couch, her arm over her eyes, looked up from time to time at a grandfather clock. It was past eight. "Oh, very smoothly, of course. Spear wasn't his niche. He could develop his potential better somewhere else. That's how it's done on the executive level. Ed Brower even got him a job with a local distributor of Spear water conditioners."

"What about Brower? Was he fired too?"

"Not until old Jens died. The new CEO fired him. It didn't matter, he was on his way by then. He'd been the old man's fair-haired boy, Jens Spear liked having a disciple. His own sons had been a big disappointment. Spoiled rich kids who didn't want to work, not self-made men like himself." Her laugh on the long couch was scornful. "You know the real story of Jens Spear, self-made man? His father was a salesman who made twenty thousand a year before World War One. He sent Jens to prep school and Yale. Football star, class president. Jens married a chemical tycoon's daughter, went to work for the father. Got a nest egg by selling 'medicinal' whiskey during prohibition through drugstores—a deal he always laughed about, said was borderline but legal. After a lot of years doing well but nothing special, he bought a failing company for peanuts, hit a change in the market, and it became the biggest money-maker he ever had. He rode on that for forty years, preaching hard work and rugged individualism." Her laugh on the couch was less scornful this time, almost wondering. "It's hard to believe anyone could have that much gall or blindness, whichever it was."

I said, "Has Brower always helped Jack?"

"Off and on," she said. "Jack considers Brower a good friend."

"You don't?"

"I don't think Ed Brower has friends."

It didn't answer my question. About Jack or about her or about why Brower helped Jack Price over the years, even off and on. What had been in it for Brower? Sometimes I sense a void, what I'm not being told, like a black hole in the room.

"What did he do without Brower?"

"Everything. Personnel manager at TEM-PO. Public relations with Santa Rosa Sciences. Publications vice-president at General Electronics Research. Personnel again for a franchising chain. Other jobs I can't even remember."

"He got fired all the time?"

"No, mostly he quit." She reached for a cigarette from the onyx box on the rosewood coffee table. "The job was never good enough. The grass was greener somewhere else. He didn't get the credit he deserved. Raises weren't fast enough. The work was boring. It was a dead end. We finally saved enough money and he started his own company."

"When was this?"

"About five years ago."

"You worked with him?"

"We had the kids by then, he couldn't afford day care. I tried to write books and articles at home to help out."

"What kind of company was it?"

She put her hand behind her head, watched a pattern of light on the cathedral ceiling. "They called it Your In-House Systems. It was supposed to produce promotional, P.R. and direct-mail pieces from start to finish to save companies from having to have their own departments and overhead. It wasn't a bad idea, lasted almost two years, but really never got off the ground."

"Why didn't it get off the ground, and who were 'they'?"

"Max Mellecker and Randy Castro. They were in it with Jack. They both had jobs, so he ran the shop. It never got off the ground because he couldn't start small, work out of the garage until he had enough clients. He got full office space, leased a ton of equipment, had shiny new desks and carpet on the floor. Hired secretaries and editors and computer operators to sit without much to do. The overhead killed him before he had a chance."

I'd known too many like that back in New York. Actors who didn't want to act, just wanted to be *actors*. Writers who had the word processor, the printer, the envelopes and labels, the manuscript boxes, but never wrote. Painters who wore all the wild clothes, looked like great artists in the bars.

"How did it last two years?"

"By selling enough routine office services to limp along. They always lost money, but slowly. Then Randy Castro ran for City Council. They did his campaign stuff, and Jack borrowed against what he billed Castro." The moving light on the ceiling was reflected from somewhere outside. "Castro lost, couldn't pay up, declared bankruptcy, and our money went down the drain."

There was almost a resignation in her voice, she was used to watching their money go down the drain. But not this time.

"What did Jack have to say about it?"

"He couldn't believe such bad luck." She stubbed out the cigarette, sat for some time in silence. "He had to act like IBM when he was a mom and pop store. Castro played the U.S. Senator when he wasn't even a boy scout, had no chance from the start. Only Max Mellecker had any sense, refused to put up more money."

"And Castro left Jack holding the bag."

"They both held the bag." She listened to a car that parked three houses away. "They were using each other. Castro couldn't have run if Jack hadn't done all the flyers, ads. He counted on winning to pay it off. The perks and power and favors he'd get and hand out. Jack expected to have his private councilman, a 'friend' at City Hall."

"Is Castro in this Brower deal?"

"Randy moved to San Francisco two years ago."

"Mellecker?"

"He only lost some money, he and Jack are still friends. We'd socialize, but I can't stand the wife. She likes what she has too much, took the Your In-House Systems flop pretty badly, blamed it all on Jack."

"That why you don't like her?" I said. "Loyalty? Defending your husband?"

She looked up at me, reached into the onyx box for another cigarette. She was smoking a lot. Behind the control there was more uncertainty, tightness, than she wanted to show.

"You don't think I'm telling you the truth. You think I've got some hidden reason for sending you after Jack."

"Let's say I wonder why you're so worried about a husband you don't seem to like."

"Love," she said. "I don't love Jack. The children still love him and need him. Children need a father and a mother. I'm worried about their future, about our future. I'm worried we'll end up on the street with nothing after twenty years of marriage. I love my children, I'm scared for them. All right?"

"Nothing's all right when murder's in the picture. Murder and money."

"We're not talking about that kind of money."

"It's not the amount that counts, it's the need,"

She was silent again. "Me?"

"Where were you since we talked earlier?"

"Here."

"Alone?"

"The children are on overnights at friends' houses. With Jack out there doing God knows what, I'm glad they are. They're at that age where they're too young to understand but old enough to be hurt. You have children, Dan?"

"No."

"Junior high can be a terrible time if the house isn't a happy one. Susy knows her father is a sexist, Mark hates our fights. I feel tied down and Jack's always busy." She suddenly stood once more, walked to the front window again. "Go ahead, suspect me. Be a detective. That's what I want. Maybe you can stop Jack from ruining us all."

Her back to me, she had the tight body of a woman half her age. What we do to ourselves, good and bad, can say a lot. Grow apart, look different. The body fits the role. Jack Price was out-of-shape and overweight. The businessman too busy to keep fit no matter how much he tried to find the time to go to the health club. Angela Price looked like a cheerleader.

"I hope that's all you have to worry about, Mrs. Price."

The body of Santos Torena out there in the dark night seemed to lie on the floor of the living room between us.

I said, "Tell me everything you know about Torena."

"I don't know much. That says something about us, doesn't it? Of all Jack's friends and associates, I know the least about Torena." She shook her head. "He's . . . He was a general handyman-supervisor for Brower's real estate holdings. His wife is named Francesca, I met her once at a party and she spoke better English than I did. They have a house Jack says is too good for the *barrio*. That's all I know."

"An expensive house?"

"Jack said a good house. I don't know how expensive."

"Give me the address, and listen to me. I didn't report the body. I'm going to be going to Torena's house, snooping around. You and Jack will come up. Sooner or later the police will find Torena. If they come to you you're surprised, you understand?"

She nodded.

"What about Max Mellecker?"

She gave me his address.

"Anywhere else Jack might go this time of night?"

"Perhaps to visit my mother. She lives in a board and care on Olive Street. Jack wanted her to live with us, the patriarch taking care of his own. But he didn't want to do any of the caring. Mother decided to live at the board and care. Jack never understood. He hated his own mother. She was a judgmental type he could never please. He called her the She-Wolf." She turned from the window. "I sometimes wonder what he calls me."

Chapter Eight

The flashing lights of police cars surrounded the brick house in the *barrio*. A crowd stood in the street in front of the wrought iron fence, silent and watching the police mill around inside.

It was a bigger house than any of those around it, smaller than those of the Anglos on the Riviera above. Light from all the windows reflected in the pool and lit the garden behind the yellow crime-scene tape on the iron fences. Inside the fence, Sergeant Gus Chavalas stood in a clump of police and coroner's deputies at the foot of the brick steps up to the front porch. He nodded to the patrolman on the gate to let me in.

"Passing by?"

"Business." I told him about Angela Price's worry over her husband.

"Santos Torena wanted to talk to this Price tonight?"

"That's what she says."

"She say if they talked? Where Torena is?"

No one had found Santos Torena yet, or they hadn't told his family or the SBPD.

"He was supposed to meet Price at a poker game in Montecito. I don't know if they talked. What happened here, Sergeant?"

He took me to where the assistant coroner was crouched over a man sprawled on his back. He had been wearing all white: silk shirt, satin tie, slim pants, patent leather shoes, silk socks and a long white duster. *Barrio* chic. The clothes and the duster were red now, his chest a mass of wet blood, his empty eyes looked up at the dark sky.

"License says he's Vicario Silva, L.A. address. Shot three times with a big Magnum from maybe ten or fifteen feet. He had a ten-inch pig sticker under his right arm, a neat sheath inside the duster. The way he's lying the shooter could have been on the porch, but the mother-in-law knows nothing. The wife came home after we got here. She knows nothing. Neighbors know nothing. We can't find the gun in the house or anywhere around."

In his place I'd have come to the conclusion that Chavalas was telling me he had come to—

that Santos Torena had probably shot Vicario Silva, the family and neighborhood were covering. Standard for any ghetto. Protect your own. But I knew what Chavalas didn't.

"Any idea who he is? What he did?"

"The patrol people in the area think they've seen him with a *chicano* mafiosi named Paz Linero, but he's unknown to us."

"Who called you?"

"Anonymous. Some nervous neighbor."

"But no one's come with a story?"

"They have to live in their world, not ours."

"Torena lives in both."

"Yeh," Chavalas said.

"You going to talk to the ladies of the house again?"

"Right now. You wouldn't want to come along?"

Inside the house the two women sat in the overstuffed living room. There was everything money could buy. Two color TV sets, two VCRs, a full-sized stereo, home wet bar, brass fireplace set, paintings, heavy drapes, couches, stuffed chairs, end tables and coffee tables. Standing lamps, hanging lamps, and table lamps. Through an ornate arch the dining room was just as stuffed.

"Have you remembered anything more, *senora*?"

Chavalas works on his Spanish image. It's useful for a policeman in the *barrio*. He's a second-generation Greek. The older woman, stiff and erect on a couch, shook her head at him but looked at me and my missing arm. She would be Torena's mother-in-law, I was something unknown, and therefore, in the *barrio*, to be watched.

"Tell me what you do know again, Mrs. Ortega."

"Why don't you leave her alone, Chavalas." The younger woman sat angrily, legs crossed in pantyhose and high heels under a severe black dress decorated with nothing more than a rope of pearls. Taller than her mother, five-feet-seven-or-eight, she would be Santos Torena's wife and tall by Latino standards. Slim, small-boned and turned out, she had the eyes and curved nose of Aztec carvings, the curled brown hair and almost perfect oval of her Castilian ancestors. Her English was American without accent and only the smallest Spanish inflection. "If you want to be the important detective, ask me where I was again, what I was doing. Maybe I'll make a mistake, trip myself up. More domestic violence in the *barrio*."

"It's all right, Francesca," the older woman said. "I will tell the officer what I didn't see. All he wants is to find proof that Santos killed that animal."

I said, "How do you know he was an animal?"

In her fifties, almost as slim as her daughter, she had the same brown hair going gray, spoke the same American English with only a shade of Spanish intonation, wore slacks and a white blouse. Despite the more liberated clothes, she was less confident than her daughter, and it was the daughter, Francesca Torena, who stared at my empty sleeve and spoke.

"Affirmative action, Chavalas? One-armed cops?"

"Dan's a private investigator."

"Dan Fortune," I said. "What did Mr. Torena want to talk to Jack Price about tonight, Mrs. Torena?"

"Did he want to talk to Price?"

"That's what I've heard. Was it about the Brower deal?"

She watched me, then shrugged, "I wouldn't know. Ask Price."

Chavalas said to the mother, "How *do* you know the dead man was an animal, Mrs. Ortega?"

"I know a hundred like him. They are all animals."

Chavalas sighed. "Okay, tell me again what you know about tonight."

What she knew was that she had been inside the house waiting for her son and Francesca to return from work. Both were late. She heard voices outside, thought it was them, turned on the coffee-making machine in the kitchen, heard three shots. She waited ten minutes to look out. I heard the laconic story, but listened more to her voice. To both their voices. American-born and raised. American voices,

American clothes, American attitudes. Tied to, married to, surrounded by, a world across a border three hundred miles and another universe away. It couldn't have been, or be, an easy realization or acceptance. Isolation in the older woman, anger in the younger.

"And I worked late, Sergeant Chavalas. That's in the law offices of McDonald and Cebellos, guess which one I work for. The traffic was bad, I stopped at Brower Management to see if Santos was there. I . . ."

"Was he?" Chavalas said.

"Mr. Brower did not know where he was. Mr. Brower does not check every move of his employees. Mr. Brower is a liberal man. I stopped in some bars to look for Santos. I went to my cousin Emilio's house. Santos sometimes plays chess with Emilio. He wasn't there, so home I came to a dead man and our busy police force. Now I am trying to be pleasant while I wait for my husband who our police are sure murdered the man in my yard."

I said, "Who do you think murdered the man in your yard?"

"Mama?"

Francesca Torena stood and walked into a hallway on the far side of the gaudy living room. She returned carrying a small girl in a thick pink sleeper suit who stared at us all from half-awake eyes. Her black hair in braids, the child hid her face in her mother's shoulder. Francesca Torena soothed the child with a kind of fierce possession, a need to touch.

"One animal kills another. There is always violence in the *barrio*, ask Chavalas. It is the explosive Latin temperament." She stroked the small girl, glared at me. "How do I know who killed the man, Mr. . . . Fortune, is it? You're here, so unless you came to murder the animal in my yard yourself, you came to talk to my husband for someone. Who would that be, Mr. Fortune?"

"The man your husband wanted to talk to: Jack Price."

"He is a liar," the mother-in-law said. "The car salesman came here himself no more than an hour ago looking for Santos."

"Price was here?" Chavalas said.

I covered, "I came here looking for Price or Mr. Torena. I'm working for his wife. She's worried about Brower's deal."

Francesca Torena stroked the child's dark hair. "What is she worried about?"

"She thinks something's wrong with the deal."

Chavalas said, "Did your husband tell you anything about it, Mrs. Torena?"

The child stirred against her, made small sounds. "He said it would make us money. I've told you all I know, Sergeant, now I have my children to take care of."

She walked out of the room on her high heels and disappeared along the hallway to the bedrooms. The older woman, Mrs. Ortega, sat like a political prisoner ready for more questions. Chavalas didn't seem to have any, I couldn't ask what I wanted without revealing I knew Santos Torena was dead.

Chavalas said, "A man will stay on guard after we leave, Mrs. Ortega." And to me, "Let's have some coffee, talk about your client."

Chapter Nine

The Oasis and The Jalisco Cafe are on Milpas Street. Santos Torena has talked about both places. Jack doesn't like Latino bars where the patrons and bartenders all stare at him, so he sits out in the Jaguar for some time before he goes in.

Paz, *peace*, the mother-in-law called the guy who looked like a flea-bitten coyote. *Peace* wasn't what the bastard had looked like to Jack, and whatever Torena is doing, Jack wants no part of it. If it's something that could threaten the deal, Jack will tell Brower even if it costs Torena his job. No one is going to louse up this deal on Jack.

In the bars he has a beer before he asks

about Torena. "I'm looking for my friend, Santos Torena. He been in here tonight?" A friendly laugh. "He wanted to talk to me, but we missed."

Dark eyes and dark faces, hats and mustaches. They always have black mustaches.

"Santos and me, we work together."

He remembers an Adult Ed dinner, a big literary event with William Saroyan. Angie wanted to go, and it didn't hurt to be seen taking an interest in community affairs. Saroyan didn't believe in ethnic stuff, nationalism. A citizen of the world, when he looked in a mirror and saw his Armenian mustache he knew he should shave it off, but never could. No mustache, no man. Jack shakes his head over the crazy ideas people get.

"Thanks for the beer. If Santos does come in, tell him Jack Price was looking for him, okay?"

Jack walks quickly to his Jaguar in the dark lot, decides to try Torena's old cafe on Cota Street. Torena's not there either, but the new owner says he was in for a *fajita* around four. Jack leaves the same message. He has nowhere else to look, so he drives up to the real estate office, finds it still open. *Edward A. Brower, Real Estate Management*.

It is a big old two-story Spanish Colonial three blocks off State Street. Office and apartment in one, all for business use, of course. Out of the way, but in a prime house Brower'd sell for a bundle when he'd finished using it. *Walk-in business I don't need, Helen is my whole office staff, who do I impress with a regular office? Selling cars, booze or pastrami, you need to give people what they expect to see. Here, I can suit myself.*

As he goes in, Jack sees the banker across the old-fashioned oak desk Brower inherited from Jens Spear. The banker looks at Jack, and back at Brower, mouth and hands and head talking hard. J. Wesley Clark, County Trust. Jack knows Clark, Clark doesn't know him. When Jack buys into the car agency, Clark will know him. *A banker is a man who tries to give you money when you no longer need it.* Jack remembers that from college. Dr. Samuel Johnson, or maybe Ambrose Bierce.

"Be with you in a minute, Jack."

Jack sits in one of the soft leather Eames chairs. He always takes one of them, puts his feet up, lays his head back against the leather. The smell of good leather reminds him of his father's desk back in Minnesota where he used to sit for hours in his father's high leather reclining chair. Brower's office is the old living room of the house. There is a dining room, family room, and library all turned into conference and meeting rooms. Kitchen and bar for business parties and political fund raisers.

When Jack buys into the car agency he'll need a bigger house, or maybe a separate place like this. It would be a good investment, with the whole second floor a private apartment that could be rented out, or kept the way Ed does for when meetings run so late you're too tired to drive home. A place to put up important out-of-town clients, or his visiting relatives.

The banker stands. "Soon, Ed?"

Brower nods. "Don't worry."

"How do I do that? If you don't come up with the money soon we all sink without a trace. Don't worry, you say." J. Wesley Clark shakes his head, walks past Jack and out without a nod to Jack, without seeing him.

"Nervous bankers, right, Jack?" Brower smiles. "You're out late. Wait, it's Friday, right? Aren't you supposed to be on the floor selling cars? You can't sell me a car."

Jack gets up, walks to sit across the desk from Brower where the banker had been. "How come you're here, Ed? Is something new wrong with the deal?"

"Nothing new, don't worry until you have to. I've just a lot to do before tomorrow."

Jack tries to smile. "I'm sweating it out too, right?"

Brower laughs. "I suppose you are, but there's nothing to sweat, believe me. The short-term note for buying the El Parador estate isn't overdue until Monday midnight, I've got the approval on the new loan, the cash comes through tonight. Tomorrow at the latest."

"We're cutting it pretty damn fine."

"A cliff-hanger, but it was the best source. I

could have moved faster for more interest and less security. With none of us able to come up with more cash our books stank, I had to go for the best I could get to cover the due note." Brower shrugs. "I told you it's all legal but on the edge. Under the table, will cost us a hefty interest. But with the deal on the line we had no choice, we'll get it back in spades at closing."

"That's great," Jack says, nods, doesn't get up.

Brower studies Jack. "You have something else on your mind, Jack? Something I can help you with?"

"You know where Santos Torena is? Did you talk to him tonight?"

"Not since this afternoon. Why?"

"He called the agency, wanted to talk to me."

"About what?"

Jack shrugs, chews a fingernail. "He never said. He was going to meet me at the poker game out in Montecito, but he never did. I've been looking for him, can't find him."

"Francesca was in looking for him too." Brower shakes his head. "I hope he hasn't gone and gotten himself in some goddamn trouble. Not right now."

Jack feels the alarm, what has been worrying him ever since Torena called. "He couldn't hurt the deal, could he? I mean, we're just waiting for the money, right? Tonight or tomorrow?"

Brower swivels behind the desk. "Anything

that happens can hurt any deal. They're as deli-
cate as antique clocks. Trouble could still scare
off the buyer."

The thought of something going wrong makes
Jack's stomach feel cold. He's been this way for
months, ever since Ed told them he had to come
up with more money to pay off a short-term note
or the deal could fall through. The goddamned
loan they got when the buyer insisted they add
the El Parador white elephant to the package.

"What kind of trouble could he be in, Ed?
Why would he want to talk to me about it?"

"How do I know what kind of trouble? You
know Santos, he moves pretty fast and loose
down there in the *barrio*. He's probably looking
for someone to help bail him out of some fix."

"He'd go to you first, wouldn't he?"

"Maybe he couldn't get in touch with me."

"He knows all my cash is tied up in the deal."

Brower shrugs. "Then perhaps he wants to
talk to you about something entirely different."

Jack feels his neck redden. Brower always
does this to him. The same thing Jens Spear did.
Make him feel almost stupid. Brushed aside as
if he couldn't keep up, couldn't think. The same
way Ed always makes him feel short. Brower
is taller, but not that much. Tall and elegant,
that's how they always write. *The distinguished
Edward Brower, tall and elegant in white tie and
tails, led Academy president Mrs. Nelson Lehman
out for the first waltz at the Annual Opening Ball
last night . . . Tanned and fit, belying his fifty*

*years and prematurely gray hair, club president
Edward A. Brower held pro Roscoe Tanner even
for the first four games before losing the charity
match at The Sycamore Tennis Club, 6-2.*

"Did he put more money into the deal too?"

"We all did, Jack. Sink or swim, right? Up
the ante or lose it all, and I don't like losing
money."

"Maybe it is the deal he wants to talk about,
Ed. Something you don't know?"

Brower stands. "Look, for God's sake, what
could Santos have to talk about on the deal?
There's nothing more to do until we get the
cash, and we're getting the final paper tonight
or tomorrow. So it couldn't be the deal. Now,
how about a beer?"

Brower stands there confident and reassur-
ing, and, after all, what can Santos Torena
possibly have to tell Jack about the deal Jack
doesn't already know?

"Why not?" Jack says, laughs.

Brower goes into the kitchen, returns with
two John Courage Ales and two glasses, pours.
No bottles for Brower. Jack drinks the beautiful beer. His fourth on the night, it makes
him feel light-headed. Light-headed and worried again.

"Santos wants to talk about something, Ed."

Brower drinks his beer. "He skates too thin
sometimes. You know the way they are down
in the *barrio*. Any ripoff for a buck."

Jack makes a mental note to have no more

87

beers, or Angie'll never let it pass when he gets home. "I guess when you're poor, don't have a decent job, you do what you can."

Brower drinks. "The poor, or underprivileged as we're supposed to call them now, got that way from their own laziness and the fifty years of socialist government started by FDR. That son-of-a-bitch Roosevelt, as Jens Spear used to say. When Jens was a boy people worked like hell because there wasn't any damned welfare."

As he finishes the good John Courage, Jack decides there isn't a lot of difference between Ed Brower and Jens Spear, except Ed is smoother, doesn't swear so much. That, and old Spear had been a hell of a lot richer. He guesses that Brower is getting close, with the big house in Hope Ranch and this place and all his other holdings and deals. All Jack wants is a piece of it all for himself.

Brower drains his beer. "You aren't in some kind of side business with Santos, are you Jack? That could be pretty bad right now. If you are, you better tell me before we talk about you buying some of the agency."

Jack protests, "What would I know about those kind of deals?"

"And you didn't talk to him tonight?"

"We never found each other."

"That's good," Brower said. "He's got some rough friends and rougher enemies. You don't want to mess with them."

Brower smiles again. Jack smiles back, and hears the sounds from above. Someone is moving around in the private apartment. Light footsteps, small sounds. Brower looks at his watch.

"Don't worry about Santos," Brower says. "It was probably some little problem we haven't even thought of. If it had been important, he'd have found you."

Jack nods, but thinks about the private apartment upstairs. He doesn't think it's Ed's wife up there. Angie'd raise the roof. She can raise a goddamn mean roof. Almost as bad as his mother: The She-Wolf. *They're your kids, too, Jack, I'm not raising them alone, you hear? I want you around this house a lot more, around the kids.* Another woman for Ed Brower, and it isn't right for a family man, but Angie's always working on her damned writing, so why not a place like this . . .

"You look tired, Jack." Brower is standing behind the big desk, his beer glass empty. "You better go home, get some sleep. It's all a piece of cake now."

"Friday night, Ed." Jack stands too. "Got to go sell cars."

"That's my tiger," Brower says.

Outside Jack sits in the Jaguar. He doesn't want to sell cars tonight. He hasn't had any dinner, but he doesn't want to eat. He wants another beer.

Chapter Ten

A small Asian hunched inside a thin wind-breaker at the bus stop across Milpas Street from Winchell's Doughnut Shop. An even smaller black woman at the stop danced on roller skates, unaware of the Asian or anything but her intricate steps and rhythms.

"What does Mrs. Price think is wrong with Brower's deal?"

Chavalas had two jellies, I had a chocolate old-fashioned. The coffee was bitter, but it was hot and cut the sweetness.

"She's not sure anything's wrong, but Price is nervous, edgy, not telling her anything. Price has made bad deals before, but this time it looks like he's gone in with everything they have and more, she wants to know what's going on."

"You dug up anything on the deal so far?"

"I only got the job this afternoon."

"That sudden?"

I told him about Jack Price calling her to say he had to meet Santos Torena, would miss dinner. "I guess it was the last straw. She decided she had to find out."

"Or she has a real reason to worry she didn't tell you."

"Possible."

"Could be why Torena wants to talk to Price."

I nodded. "You know anything about Brower's business?"

"He's important in this town. Holdings, investments, real estate projects. Sits on our best boards, juggles all kinds of businesses. Sometimes you hear what he's supposed to be pushing, but you don't know."

"What do you hear now?"

"He's in a condominium buy and sell that stands to make a bundle. That sounds like the deal Price and Torena are with."

"Anything else?"

Chavalas wiped his mustache, licked his fingers. "Rumors he's in deep in a development over in Nevada. Very big."

"Could Price be part of that? It's so big he's nervous?"

"I don't know Price or what makes him nervous."

We'd both finished our doughnuts. Chavalas didn't seem to be in any hurry to leave. He got up for coffee. The place was almost full, more coming in on a Friday night. The owner looked at Chavalas and at the clock, but didn't say anything.

"Torena's ambitious, works hard, has the best house on the block." Chavalas stirred his coffee. "It's not getting out of the *barrio* for him, it's going Anglo but taking the *barrio* with him, you know what I mean?"

"Beat 'em at their own game?"

"Something like that." He looked out the window at Milpas Street in the early night. Santa Barbara isn't that different from any small American city outside the South or the old factory belt. Most of the cars that pass in the *barrio* are driven by Anglos, the people on the street are mostly Latinos, blacks and the new Southeast Asians. "He showed up here six years ago from L.A. I'm pretty sure he's Mexican born, came up when he was young but not that young. Never has talked English so good."

The small Asian still hunched inside his windbreaker at the bus stop while the black woman did her silent dance on roller skates around him.

"He bought a Mexican restaurant when he came here, did some cooking, put on a tie and moved into business pretty fast. He kept the cafe as a base until last year, went into real estate and did some building. That's when he had the house built. Got everything at cost, I guess."

"Just like a real wheeler-dealer."

The roller skate dancer had finally caught her bus. The Thai or Khmer or Vietnamese was still at the bus stop with no one to watch.

"On the edge of fraud a couple of times, then nailed on a little extortion racket." Chavalas shook his head. Maybe over what people try to get away with. Or maybe over their need. "He was pulling in thousands in illegal rent from low-income tenants in some units he owns in the *barrio* and the west side. Mostly lone women with kids on housing assistance under the Section 8 program the city operates with federal funding. Minority women, young Anglo single mothers, all working lousy jobs, struggling to make ends meet, afraid of getting evicted and having nowhere to live if they complain about it."

"His own people?"

"Some Latinos didn't give him a medal. But is was a first offense, all a misunderstanding. He paid most of the money back, so the judge only hit him with a suspended and probation. He went on to new challenges. Alone and with Brower. Brower is sort of his mentor, the guru. Torena pays off as field honcho for nuts and bolts."

"What does his wife do?"

"Works. She's American, her mother too. The family's an old one here. She's smart, been to college, holds down good jobs. Lived in L.A. a while, probably helped Torena get a start down there."

Across Milpas the small Asian in the windbreaker had finally caught his bus. It's not easy to learn your way around a strange country, or find the right direction in a different world.

"You think he's involved with Paz Linero and the dead guy?"

Chavalas shrugged. "Unless Vicario Silva got killed in his yard by accident."

"It happens."

"Especially in a *barrio*." He looked at his watch. "Paz Linero's the honcho of an illegals smuggling operation. Vicario Silva was probably one of his *mules*, brought the illegals up from the border after the *coyotes* got them across. Up here, they 'sell' them to employers, people who need maids and gardeners, the big farmers. There's good money in it."

"You think Torena helped at this end?"

He buttoned his jacket against the chill settling in outside. "Depends if he needed money, how much and how fast."

Modern America was built by, on and around the automobile, and auto dealerships carry weight. To prove it, when they widened the freeway through Santa Barbara they put in a new exit that leads straight off to auto dealers row on Calle Real.

Ed Brower's showroom was one of the largest, a blaze of cars and light inside an expanse of plate glass. Neither Jack Price nor Max Mellecher were there. With a horde of sales people, they weren't being missed, but it wasn't cars the woman who came up to me had on her mind.

"You're looking for Jack Price?"

"You know where he is?"

"No. He isn't at home, he isn't here."

"How do you know he isn't at home?"

"He had a customer return ready to buy. I called his home, no one answered. Is anything wrong, Mr.—?"

"Dan Fortune. You know Price well?"

"There is something wrong."

She was short, slim, wore her hair long on the shoulders of a soft beige wool suit with stockings and high-heeled suede pumps to match. Dark hair, aquiline features, almost a miniature of Angela Price, and her voice carried more than the concern of a colleague. A strong echo of Angela Price, without the beauty. Not that she was unattractive. Everything was right, the combination just missed. Call it aura.

"I'm just looking for him, Ms.—?"

"Claire Broberg." She saw my one arm, black beret, old duffel coat. "You're not police, or state, or insurance."

"You sell here with Price, Ms. Broberg?"

"I'm the Controller. Officer of the corporation. Ed likes titles. Actually, I'm the bookkeeper-accountant." She smiled. It helped the aura. She had small teeth and deep hazel eyes. "Process server? Credit check? Is Jack behind on some payment? No, it wouldn't be that. Unless . . ."

"You seem to know Price. Maybe we could talk?" My voice implied we'd both talk if we were alone somewhere quiet. She glanced around the crowded showroom.

"You know where The Elephant Bar is?"

"Out on Hollister?"

"Twenty minutes."

She had picked a place ten minute's drive from the showroom where her co-workers would be unlikely to go for a break. A place crowded and noisy. A chain, The Elephant Bars, one of the myriad machine-cooked, mass-supplied restaurants without quality or character that have swept the country and probably the world. This one's gimmick was fake safari, complete with plaster African trophy heads and overhead *punkahs* run by motor. Most of the patrons were young, the drinks were large.

I took a corner table on a raised platform between the long bar and the entrance, had a Beck's, and Claire Broberg arrived less than five minutes behind me. She had beer too.

"All right, what trouble is Jack in? Who are you?"

"Dan Fortune. A private investigator."

"Christ," she said. "Angie."

We both drank our beers.

I said, "What makes you think that?"

97

"Jack's a solid guy. Home and job. The kids and the house. No one else would put a private eye on him. What does she think he's doing, holding out some of his commissions?" She shook her head in disgust, drank her beer, put the glass down hard. "Don't tell me she thinks Jack's got a tootsie."

"That's not possible?"

"I guess anything's possible, but I'd put a month's salary against it." She leaned back and let her glance sweep the room and the raucous young people. "I don't think Angie would really care if he did have another woman. Not enough to hire a detective anyway."

"You've made a study of the Prices?"

"You don't have to be a weatherman to know which way the wind's blowing. It's been obvious for years Angie isn't happy. She never comes to company functions unless it's mandatory like Brower's Christmas party at the Hope Ranch house. Jack comes along, pretends to have a good time, laughs a lot, but you can tell he's not happy either. I don't know what the trouble is, but it's something. He works his ass off, she doesn't give him the time of day. What kind of marriage is that?"

"Ever talk to her about it?"

"No."

"Him?"

She finished her beer, looked for a waitress. "Sometimes."

"Recently?"

The waitress arrived instantly. It's a swingers' bar, tips depend on the speed of the drinks. The overage boys want the right mood as fast as possible. So do the girls.

"We go to The Pepper Tree, or Red Robin, or Harry's Plaza. I don't keep a record. We go every week or so. Sometimes in a gang, sometimes a three- or-foursome, sometimes the two of us. Talk a while before I go home to my kids and he goes to Angie."

"Kids?"

"A two-time loser with two trophies. Girl and boy same as Jack."

"What do you talk about? Just the two of you."

She tried to pour from her empty bottle. "When do you tell me why you're looking for Jack?"

"To ask him about a deal he's in with Ed Brower."

"The condo deal?"

"Sounds like the one."

"Why?"

"His wife's worried. He's in deeper than usual. Acting nervous, secretive, not telling her anything."

The waitress brought our beers. Not quite as fast as I'd expected. Either my duffel coat and beret didn't look like the uniform of a swinger, or she thought we were too old for it.

"How does she know? She never cares what he's doing."

"Apparently she does, and he tells her. Until now."

"Unless maybe Angie's heard something."

"Such as?"

"I don't know, Fortune. It's a standard buy low, stitch together, sell high. I've got a few dollars in it myself."

"So does Santos Torena," I said. "Did he happen to talk to you today about the deal?"

"Santos doesn't work at the agency. He's Brower's expediter in the real estate office. Goes out among the plebians."

"You didn't see him today? Maybe looking for Price?"

"No."

"Earlier you started to say Price would never be behind in payments, unless . . . What was the unless?"

She took another long drink of the beer, licked her lips. I couldn't tell if she was nervous or thirsty or just liked beer.

"Unless he needed a lot of cash."

"Any reason to think he might need cash?"

"No. But Jack's always looking for one really good deal to get him started. He has everything it takes, Fortune, he just never had a break."

"Is that what you talk about? His need for a break, a good deal? Just the two of you?"

She finished the beer, waved to the waitress who came even faster. Maybe we were swingers after all.

"So I like Jack. Angie's all wrong for him, and I know about that. My first husband died last week. He was a boy in my high school who liked surfing more than going to class. He grew into a great-looking guy who never found any work that gave him the thrill of admiring women on the beach and horses at the track. He never held a job longer than six months the whole time we were married, never sent a support payment on time since we divorced. But he was dead, my girl had lost her father, so we went to the funeral. The good news is Matt never did remarry, Sharon inherits his estate. The bad news is there isn't any estate. Matt never lost his love for the horses and the things money can buy. All Sharon gets is a Porsche we don't need and a condo mortgaged to the scalp. My second husband wasn't much better. I know about bad marriages."

The waitress brought her fresh beer. "You think Jack might have a tootsie, and maybe it's even me?"

"Is it?"

"Not yet." She looked down at her fresh beer. "If you're looking for hanky-panky, maybe you should look at Angie instead of Jack. There was this party they gave right after Jack joined the agency . . ."

She held her beer in both hands as she talked.

Chapter Eleven

Claire arrives at the party with her date, a recently divorced assistant public defender. They are late because the defender has his sons for the weekend, had to wait for the reliable older sitter he needs so he can stay the night with Claire. She finds the assumption annoying, decides the defender won't need the sitter, but knows that time, events and need can change her mind.

There is a good crowd, mostly business people Claire knows, but more strangers than she has expected. At most parties she goes to everyone knows everyone else. Claire does not see Angie, but Jack is across the room with Ed Brower and Max Mellecker. He sees her, waves once, goes back to his conversation. He holds a drink, leans with one arm against his mantel-piece in a formal blue suit, seems to be making a speech to Brower who is smiling.

No one comes to the door to greet Claire and the assistant public defender. Jack's wave told her that Angie is handling arrivals while he does his job of making drinks and mixing with the men. But Angie is not in sight, and eventually it is the daughter, Susy, who comes to greet them shyly, direct them to the food and the bar. The boy is out in the yard playing a violent game with two neighbor boys, ignoring the adult party.

They get white wine at the bar Jack has set up out on the patio, Claire introduces the defender to some people from the agency, makes a point of going up to Carolyn Brower who is being talked to by Maggie Mellecker outside the glass doors into the living room. Maggie is dressed up as usual, wears every jewel she owns, is making a point of talking to the boss's wife. Mrs. Brower is smiling but not listening. She is watching her husband.

"Brower hasn't lived with her out in Hope Ranch for years," Claire tells her defender. "He has an apartment over his office, goes to the house on weekends for the kids. If he isn't busy."

Claire and the defender finally find Angie in a corner of the family room with seven of the people Claire doesn't know. Angie is not the

center of the group, that is a smaller woman with an ex-model's face, a lively manner,
and a way of leaning forward when she talks
as if she is near-sighted. Claire now vaguely
recognizes her as a mystery author who has
been written up in the *News-Press*. Another is
a heavy, black-bearded man obviously waiting
for the mystery writer to stop talking. All the
rest, including Angie, listen eagerly, except an
older man beside Angie whose attention is else-
where.

"He's got his eye on Angie," Claire says,
smiles. "Did you see his hand? On her shoulder?"

"So he's an old friend," the defender says.

"Christ, you're no fun," Claire says.

She knows Angie has ambitions to write
books, so maybe the defender is right, and
when Jack comes to greet them in the living
room he doesn't seem to have any troubles, is
jovial.

"Hey, you look fabulous, Claire. I don't believe
I know your friend." Jack beams at the assistant
defender.

Claire introduces them, the defender compli-
ments the house.

"It was the right time to move from the Mesa,"
Jack says. "I needed more house to go with the
better jobs, my own company. Probably have to
move up again soon, more entertaining and all."

"What business are you in?" the defender
asks.

"Jack's at the agency with me," Claire says.

"A real opportunity," Jack says. "I've known Ed a long time. I did have an office service company, but the town turned out to be too small, you know? Can't win 'em all, right?"

Angie finally appears to replenish the hors d'oeuvres and get dinner ready. The older man is not with her, and she does not smile as she goes through her hostess tasks while Jack continues to hold forth among the guests. She moves almost furiously in the main rooms and on the patio, then disappears into the kitchen.

Dinner is going to be late, Claire and the defender have a third glass of wine, join Jack, Max Mellecker and Ed Brower who are talking about the state of the nation.

"It's these illegals," Jack is saying. "We let them into the country, they live ten in a room, take our jobs, crowd the schools, and never even learn English much less what democracy and this country mean. They're going to suck us dry, take the opportunity away from real Americans."

"All they want is a chance, Jack," Mellecker says. "What's so important about English. We should learn their languages."

Ed Brower laughs. "Better they don't learn English. They're the only way we can get strawberries, gardeners and housemaids. They learn English, they hear about welfare and don't have to work."

"Welfare'll kill us all," Jack agrees.

"Welfare and Washington," Ed Brower says. "It wouldn't be so bad if we made them at least work for the money, stopped them from breeding so fucking much. Christ, they have more kids—"

Angie walks past them with a tray of cocktail franks she has forgotten to put out. "Women on welfare have forty percent fewer children than women in general. That's statistics, Ed, not hot air. In L.A. County, welfare people have fewer than two children per family. Only one percent of welfare recipients cheat, less than half the families get aid for more than two years, and what welfare pays wouldn't support your dog."

"I'd like to see those statistics," Brower smiles.

"So would I," Jack says. "I never—"

"I'll put them in the mail," Angie tells Brower, tells Jack, "Dinner will be fifteen minutes. Give them all another drink."

A buffet dinner, Claire and the defender eat out on the wall near the hot tub under the floodlights Jack has rented with propane heaters for Santa Barbara's cool summer nights. Jack goes around making sure all the guests have enough heat and light. It is the first time he reminds Claire of her father who always directed everything when he and her mother had a party.

Angie's writer friends have joined the main party to eat, and after dessert, when Angie has left the kitchen and coffee is being served by her daughter and two girlfriends, a general conversation begins. After a time, for some reason Claire misses, someone brings up the name of the great medieval French writer, philosopher, theologian and lover, Pierre Abelard.

"Ouch," Jack grimaces, sticks out his tongue, laughs.

"It hurts just to hear that poor guy's name," another man groans.

"What you get for messing with a nun."

"And probably deserved it," a woman says.

The heavy, black-bearded writer says, "She wasn't exactly a nun. The times were a lot different, it was common for priests like Abelard to be sexually active. The castration was more the result of an angry father, an aristocratic family feud."

"Abelard was actually glad it happened." This is Angie's older writing friend who is sitting near her in the living room. "He was pleased as hell when they cut his balls off—it freed him to think and write without the temptations of the flesh to get in the way. He could do what he wanted, and with no moral guilt of tampering with God's will. Since Heloise's father had it done, Abelard could even say it was the way God wanted it."

The bearded man says, "Heloise was the furious one, it hurt her a lot more."

"Tell us about it," a woman laughs.

After the laughter stops, it is Angie who says, "We probably have more Abelards around than we know."

Jack, who has drunk more than usual, says, "What the hell does that mean?"

Angie has not drunk much. "It means I expect there are a lot of men in this room who wish they didn't have a woman around so they could get on with what they want to do."

"It means," the older writer says, "what our average male today fears most is freedom, real freedom for everyone."

"Bullshit," some man says, angry.

Jack laughs. "Someone's nuts, and it sure ain't me."

"I don't know," Ed Brower says. "Angie and the gentleman may have a point. A lot of us are afraid of real freedom."

This sets off a heated discussion until most of the guests become bored and drift away into other rooms, the shadows of the yard. Some, angered by the discussion, leave. Claire and the assistant defender take a lively part in the talk, Claire on Jack's side, the defender somewhere between Ed Brower and the older writer. By the time they get out on the patio for some air it is late, the defender wants to leave.

This is when Claire spots Angie going into the hot tub. Jack is still in the living room talking, but Angie isn't alone. Claire moves closer with her drink, sits on the rear wall. The man

with Angie is the older writer. They are both
naked, which is the custom in hot tubs at parties, and they are not alone in the tub, but they
are close together with only their heads above
the water.

Claire feels a wave of sympathy for Jack.
She finds him through the window, still in his
three-piece blue suit and tie, drink in hand,
talking earnestly to three men from the agency.
They are all nodding as if what they are talking
about is very important to them. Ed Brower is
not one of them. Carolyn Brower is alone on a
couch, Max and Maggie Mellecker are having
a low but angry argument. Claire on the patio
suddenly wants to leave.

She and the assistant defender stop for a
nightcap at The Elephant Bar, are at her door
before she discovers she has left her purse at
the party. They drive all the way back from
Camino Corto. The party is over, the house
dark, but Claire is certain her purse is out on
the patio where she watched Angie and the
writer in the hot tub, so carefully opens the
side gate and walks quietly around the house.

At the back of the house there is light from
a single room where the drapes are open on
sliding glass doors out into the patio. Claire
finds her purse on the brick wall, then hears
voices. Outside the circle of light she looks into
the room. It is the master bedroom, and Angie
stands in the room with a drink in her hand.
Jack is propped up in bed naked, the covers up

to his waist, a book in his hand.

"What are you reading?" Angie's voice comes clear through the open doors. She is wearing a white terrycloth robe.

"How to operate a selling business."

"You're not running the agency."

Jack says nothing, returns to his reading.

"I'm sorry about tonight, the party."

Jack puts the book down. "I don't know what you want, Ange. I do my job, why won't you do yours? Is it so hard to be a wife, the hostess? To be nice to the guys I work with, the people who can help me? You're the whole damned night with those deadbeat writer friends of yours. How does that look to Brower, all the agency people, the other businessmen?"

"I know, Jack." She puts down her drink, lets the robe drop to the floor, stands naked. "I want it to be better between us. Let's make it good tonight."

Jack stares at her. "Christ, is that all you think about?"

For a long moment, perhaps a full minute, they stare at each other. Then Angie picks up the white robe, puts it on, picks up her drink, and walks from the bedroom.

Jack sits in the bed. He starts to read his book again, then throws it at the wall. Claire watches him lie down in the bed, lie rigid. His hands are under the covers. She sees the bedcovers begin to rise and fall as he turns out the light. In the night Claire hears the unmistakable rhythmic creaking of the bed springs, the steady rustle of the covers.

She returns to the car and the defender. When they reach her house again, she shakes her head at the door.

"It's awful late now, I'm tired, okay? Call me tomorrow."

The defender is angry, but he leaves. Claire doesn't know if he will call again. She doesn't care. She is thinking of Jack and her father.

Chapter Twelve

Beyond the sweep of light through the show-room glass, Jack Price searches the distant interior for Max or Claire. Other salesmen bend close to customers who touch the shine of painted metal, but he sees no Max or Claire. The rear stairs from the night parking lot echo narrow as he climbs. Cluttered, cramped, its single window overlooking the showroom floor, Claire's office is empty.

"Mr. Price?"

At the top of the back stairs the woman stands with a big handbag hanging from her shoulder. Small and slender in dirty jeans tight on her belly and ass. God, what kids wear today. Mexican for sure. The hooked

Indian nose and brown skin, but her hair is brown and curly and she doesn't sound like a *pachuca*. Pretty, and not as young as Jack thought at first. Some kind of red shirt and a bright striped wool poncho. The handbag as big as she is. One hand is inside the bag. Not a kid, a woman, and Jack knows her.

"Mrs. Torena? Hey, I've been looking for Santos. He wanted to talk. I went to your house, he wasn't there. I—"

"I'm here, Mr. Price. I have to—"

"I ought to go down on the floor."

"A few minutes. Please."

She keeps her right hand inside the big handbag that hangs in front of the colorful poncho. *Please*, she says, but Jack hears no "please" in her voice. He isn't sure what he hears, but he backs into the office and sits down with his back to the window and the showroom below. She closes the door, her hand is still inside the handbag.

"Why did you want to talk to Santos?"

Jack spreads his hands, smiles. "You've got it wrong, Mrs. Torena. He wanted to talk to me."

"About what?"

"How do I know? I never found him." He leans toward her, smiling, the way he leans toward a customer when he finally gets one to his desk. "Look, he called me here about 3:00, 3:30, said he wanted to talk, it was important.

He'd meet me at the game, but he never showed up. So—"

"The poker game at Morgan's in Montecito?"

"Right. I waited, and—"

"You were there from when?"

"Me? About four, I guess. So when—"

"But you didn't talk to Santos? You never saw him?"

"That's right. So I—"

"You can prove that, Mr. Price?"

"Prove?" Jack still smiles and leans toward her, but the smile grows thinner each time she interrupts him with another question like some police interrogator in the movies. "There were a lot of players. I took a walk outside once, but—"

"Were you involved with Santos and Paz Linero?"

"Who?"

"Paz Linero. Vicario Silva. Nacio Cruz. The *mules* and *coyotes*."

Jack is confused. "I never heard of guys like that. Me and Torena we're both—"

"But he said he had to talk to you today, it was urgent."

"That's what our girl said. I mean, I didn't talk to him myself. He was going to meet me—"

"You know St. George. Were you working with him too? Is he what Santos wanted to talk about?"

"St. George? The only St. George I know stuck a spear in a dragon, and—"

115

"He plays in your poker game too, Mr. Price."

"There's no St. George in—"

"A tall man with horn-rimmed glasses he wears on a cord. Long red hair, very ragged. He talks a lot."

"The Genius? He doesn't even know Torena."

"He knows Santos, Mr. Price. He was at the game tonight? Did he leave at any time?"

"He was there, I didn't notice if he . . ."Jack stops his own sentence this time. He stares at the big, expensive handbag with her right hand still inside it. "Why do you care if the Genius left the game, Mrs. Torena? Why do I have to prove I didn't talk to Santos? Has something happened to him?"

"When you took your walk, you saw no one? Paz Linero? St. George, or, as you call him, the Genius?"

Jack shakes his head. "What's happened to Torena?"

"He was worried this morning. He wanted to talk to you this afternoon."

"Something's happened to him, hasn't it?"

She stands against the closed door in the tight jeans and the multi-colored poncho, her hand still hidden inside the big brown leather handbag, and Jack knows why Santos Torena didn't come to the poker game.

"Santos is dead, Mr. Price. He was shot to death across the road from your poker game in Montecito. He went there to talk to you, and he was shot to death. I found him out there, Mr.

Price. I'll find who murdered him."

"Jesus," Jack says. "God."

Francesca Torena says nothing, only stands in the small office above the showroom floor with her hand inside her bag.

Jack's mouth is dry. "Have the police—?"

"The police don't know. Or perhaps they do by now. It doesn't matter. Santos had a lot of projects, but it was you he wanted to talk to. What would it have been about?"

"I told you, Mrs. Torena, I don't know. I mean, we both work for Brower, but not together. There's only the condo deal. We're . . . we were . . . both in the deal. That's all."

He knows what's in the handbag. Once he had wanted to have a collection of guns. He would make his own hardwood cases with velvet linings and hang them on the walls of his den when he had a real den. Over the big desk he was going to have with the high-backed executive chair.

"I'm going to find out, Mr. Price," Francesca Torena says before she walks out of the office.

Jack waits for some time after her footsteps have echoed down the narrow back stairs to the parking lot. She has brought death too close. Violent death. It can't have anything to do with him, but he has been looking for a man who was dead, and that scares him. Claire hasn't shown up, Max Mellecker still isn't down on the floor through the window. He should go home, tell Angie about Torena, but he doesn't want to

117

talk to Angie, not yet. The kids are on over-nights, and he doesn't want to talk to Angie. He wants to go back to the poker game.

As he drives the dark roads of Montecito, Jack wonders about Torena and the Genius. The Genius never talked about doing anything with Torena or anyone else. All the Genius talks about is the whole world and what's wrong with everything. When he isn't raking in a pot or telling everyone else how to play the game. Torena only played once in a while, Jack has never seen him even talk to the Genius.

Jack parks on the lane behind the old Victorian, stumbles through the dark to the rear door.

"Seats're open, Jack. Both games."

Max Mellecker is gone, but the Genius sits in the same seat, the usual long rows of chips in his tray slots. Jack sits down, the cards fall in front of him. He can hear voices in the draw game in the next room. It is warm, calm, even soothing. The constant rhythm of light, easygoing talk that never stops yet never interferes with the flow of the cards, the clatter of the chips, the smooth pulse of the game.

The Genius smiles. "Glad you came back, Price. Can't win if you don't play."

"Can I to talk to you a minute, Genius?"

The Genius studies his cards. "After the game."

"It's about Santos Torena."

The Genius watched a diamond six turn in the middle, tosses in his cards. "Deal us out a hand."

They walk into the room inside the door of the side porch.

"I didn't know you knew Torena," Jack says.

"I know him. Why?"

"He's dead. His wife said she found him dead right near here. Shot. She heard he wanted to talk to me, so she was looking for me. She's looking for you too, and some guy named Paz Linero. A *mule* or *coyote*. St. George, she called you. She said he had work he did with you."

The Genius looked toward the curtained windows. "We heard sirens, noise across the road. The deputies didn't come here. Probably won't make connections until tomorrow. Did you tell her where I was?"

"She knows you play out here. What did you do with Torena, Genius?"

The Genius rubs his lean jaw, watches something past Jack. "Santos wanted to talk to you. Is that what you said?"

"Called my office, said he'd meet me here."

"He never came here?"

"No."

"You know Paz Linero?"

"No."

The Genius nods. "The police will look for Linero and his *mules*. Don't worry about it, Price."

"But it was me he wanted to talk to."

119

"There is that." The Genius reaches into his shirt pocket, takes out a business card. "If you want to talk, or need a quiet place, call or come round. Anytime."

The tall, lean redhead smiles at Jack, walks back into the card room. He scoops up his chips, cashes them in with Morgan the owner, and is gone. The deal goes around the green felt under the cone of light. Benny is still there, and old Al, but everyone else Jack knows has gone home. All strangers.

Jack sits, looks at his down cards. He has an ace-king of clubs, a great hand. He forgets the Genius, Santos Torena, death and what he should be doing. He bets and watches the flop out on the table as the dealer turns the three cards. Queen, ten of clubs, four of hearts. The bet is checked to Jack, he bets the limit. Benny and two other players stay. A three of spades. Jack bets half the limit. No one raises. The final card is a nine of clubs. Jack has a lock, the sure winner, and there is no low. He bets the limit, only Benny calls with a pair of aces.

Jack hangs his jacket on the back of his chair. The cards drop lightly before the players. Jack listens to the soft click of the chips, the drone of the dealer, the easy voices of the players. He stacks the chips from his big win in the troughs. Morgan the owner brings him a beer, he makes a small joke about how much a free beer costs you at Morgan's, the players beside him laugh. There is no weight and no time.

No outside world. Only the circle of green felt beyond time or space. The cards, the chips, the banter, as ritualized as a church service.

In half an hour Jack has lost back all he won with his big locked flush, looks at the business card the Genius gave him: *Stanley St. George, Ph.D., Electronics Consultant, 29 Padre Lane.* Santos Torena is dead. Francesca Torena is carrying a gun and talking about *coyotes* and *mules*. The Genius left the game early, gave Jack his card in case Jack needed a quiet place. Jack knows he has to find Ed Brower, talk to him.

"Cash me in."

Outside in the night, Jack stands and breathes. He has to ask Ed Brower where he is getting the money they need to make the deal long after the whole world has closed for business on a Friday night. Or has the whole world closed? Maybe that was it. A bank in Hong Kong. Tokyo. Singapore. It was, economically, one big world now. He had told Susy that when she asked what Wall Street was—that the Tokyo Exchange was almost as important as New York now, that Wall Street could no longer tell the rest of the world what to do, that half of America was owned by the Japanese and the Arabs, that all businesses were becoming global, that . . . *"God, Dad, I'm sorry I asked."* . . .

Something moves in the night behind the old Victorian.

Jack's eyes aren't accustomed to seeing outdoors at night anymore. There was a time when he could see a rabbit run, when he, Angie and the kids camped in the high Sierras, but now it is all a blur of shadows, of movement that could be bush or tree, animal or man. Until the Victorian's door opens again to let out another player on his way home, and Jack sees the man in the long shaft of brief light.

A man alone under the trees watching the house.

The razor thin brown face, sunburned almost black. Hard skin grooved like leather. Mustache. Hat. The skinny man from Torena's house who looked like a flea-bitten coyote. Paz Linero. Cold black eyes that seemed to glow yellow in the flash of light and look directly at Jack Price.

Then the door closes and there is only the night.

Jack hurries to his Jaguar. Almost in panic, he backs and turns in the narrow lane, watches the night for the face to leap into the hood, stare in at him through the windshield.

Chapter Thirteen

Sergeant Chavalas's unmarked car stood behind a black-and-white inside the gate of Edward Brower's beachfront mansion in Hope Ranch. I parked in the shadows under a stand of eucalyptus.

Chavalas wouldn't call on Brower himself just to look for Santos Torena or Jack Price. The sheriff's deputies must have found Torena's body, informed SBPD, and Chavalas was here to talk to Torena's boss in what was now a murder case. Torena had died in the county, but Vicario Silva had been shot down in the city. It was a joint case.

After fifteen minutes, the iron gate swung open as soundless as a ghost in the night.

Chavalas came first, then the patrol car. After ten minutes, no one else came out. There was a call box beside the gate.

"What?" A man's harsh voice, not friendly.

"Dan Fortune to see Mr. Brower."

"Call my office in—"

"It's about Santos Torena and Jack Price."

There was a silence. When the voice returned it was smooth, neutral. "They work for me, Mr. . . . You said you were?"

"Dan Fortune. A private detective, Mr. Brower. You don't know me, but it won't take long."

Another silence. "All right. The gate opens on its own when you drive up."

Through the gate and up the drive, I parked facing the white-walled house built to look like an adobe hacienda. It wasn't old enough to be real adobe, was so overgrown with trumpet vine, bougainvillea and wisteria that its size was impossible to tell. The front door, in adobe style, was small. A heavy door framed by decorated wood beams under a brown wood balcony on the second floor. The door opened before I could ring.

"Mr. Fortune? Please come in."

She had a motherly face and figure, smiled under carefully waved gray hair. Her dark eyes had pain in them. An expensive black cocktail dress with bare shoulders bulged in all the wrong places. A triple strand of pearls didn't help her eyes. She saw my empty sleeve, looked like a mother hen, but said nothing.

"He's in the TV room."

It was an enormous house, there had to be servants. As we went along a two-story entry hall I heard voices across a formal dining room with a table long enough to seat at least twenty. She had answered the door before I rang, sent to open it so the servants wouldn't know I was there. The living room was three steps down and deserted as we passed. She left me at the open door of a smaller room with a TV set, wet bar, and windows over a wide lawn. The lawn was lit by floodlights on the tall palm trees between the house and the edge of the cliff above the beach and the sea.

"Sit down. Fortune? Is that it?"

"Dan Fortune."

The only place to sit was a low chair facing him, its back to the row of windows, the lawn, and the sea. He looked at my missing arm more like a prospective employer than a mother hen.

"Which war?"

"My own."

I would have said he'd already made up his mind he didn't like me, except that he wasn't a man who liked or disliked. He judged. What you could do for him. How you could be useful. If he could see no value for him in you, you didn't exist.

"You know Torena and Jack Price well, Mr. Fortune?"

"Never met either of them."

Seated in a leather wing chair, he was in his late forties, six-feet plus, trim but not thin. Toned by health clubs and well-draped by expensive clothes. California distinguished, not Cape Cod. A dark gray cashmere jacket, soft blue shirt, blue striped tie, gray slacks, gray socks, black loafers. Smooth gray hair, a lean face not at all rugged. Dark brown eyes and a tan. A man who would fit in anywhere, and probably had.

"You came to talk to me about two men you never met?"

"I didn't have time to meet Torena. Why do you think he was killed, Mr. Brower?"

He studied me. "The police only told me fifteen or twenty minutes ago. When did you know?"

"Earlier. You have any ideas why someone would shoot him? At least two men?"

He continued to study me. "The police said nothing about two men. You seem to know more than they do."

"They probably forgot."

He looked past me at his floodlit lawn outside the windows. "Why would I know anything about someone shooting Santos Torena?"

"He worked for you."

"He worked for himself." He looked back at me. "The police say another man was killed too, a *mule* in an illegal alien ring."

"Vicario Silva from L.A. Did you know him too?"

126

When he stood he was taller, six-two at least. His control of his anger was remarkable. At the bar he opened two bottles of beer from the refrigerator. John Courage Ale, they looked like. Only the best. He poured them into twelve-ounce steins, handed me a stein, sat in his leather chair again. The anger still burned back in his eyes, but he had it in hand.

"Who are you working for?"

"That's confidential."

He studied me again. He would study everyone, look for what he could use, how best to handle the person. "Lenders wouldn't send one man. A team of accountants is more their speed. The Nevada Real Estate Board?"

"What did Torena want to talk to Jack Price about?"

"The buyer? Checking up on me? No, wait, probably from someone I owe money. Of course, right? But which one?"

His answer to his own question seemed to satisfy him. He must have had a lot of creditors. It was either an act to lull me because he'd made up his mind to handle me some other way, or a decision to back off and see what I would reveal if he kept me talking.

"Are there that many?"

"Business runs on credit. You know that."

"What did Torena want to talk to Price about, Mr. Brower?"

"Ask Jack."

"You know where he is?"

"At home, I suppose."

He was good. If I said I knew Price wasn't at home, he'd know it was Price I was looking for. Price I was interested in, not Torena. I could play the game too.

"When did you last see Santos Torena?" I asked.

"I'm not sure, who pays that much attention, right? I think about 3:00 P.M. We talked over repairs to some rental units."

"When did Francesca Torena come looking for him?"

"You get around, don't you? If I ever need a detective, I know where to look. Are you local?"

"In the phone book. Francesca Torena?"

"Around seven or seven-thirty, I don't watch the time."

"Does Torena's death affect the deal you and Price and he are involved in?"

"Of course not."

"Who gets Torena's share now?"

"His wife, I assume. It would be part of his estate."

"Can you tell me about the deal?"

He shook his head in disbelief. "You're something, Fortune, you know? All right, if it gets you off the wild goose chase. In the simplest terms, we bought a large complex of new condos from a corporation that had to unload before they sold a unit, built more units on adjacent land, swung a deal for a big estate right next to them nobody had lived in for years, got it rezoned for multiple, and have a buyer interested in the package who will pay almost twice what we put in. Quick buy-sell, sweet profit."

"What's the catch? What did you have the original owner and someone else didn't?"

"There isn't any catch, as you put it. Simply business. A matter of the right place at the right time, information other people don't have, clout to swing the zoning, and the credit to get cash quickly. The original people couldn't put the package together."

I said, "You mean they didn't have the local influence to get zoning changes, the local power to squeeze owners, and the inside knowledge of a buyer ready to pay high for the package."

Brower shrugged. "That's about it. Good, solid business. Of course, there are conditions. We have agreed to redesign the condos, turn over the estate land ready to build on, but those are only details."

"Details you needed more investment to handle?"

"You have to spend money to make money."

"In Nevada too?"

He drank, wiped his mouth. "I've been very cooperative when I don't really know who you are, Fortune. Santos getting shot has nothing to do with me. He dealt in questionable businesses on his own, some pretty rough associates like that Vicario Silva. If you want to know who shot Santos, I'd say look there."

"You don't deal in questionable businesses, Mr. Brower?"

He looked sorry for me. "You mix so much with criminals, Fortune, you see chicanery under every rug."

"No chicanery under your rug? Not even a little?"

"One man's chicanery is another man's good business. I never went out to find a business that would render a service to mankind. You think Edison went into business to help mankind, light up the world? Hell no, and without Edison, we'd still be burning whale oil. If I keep a lot of people employed, make and spend money, I'm doing my service to mankind. Greed is part of everything we do. I don't find anything wrong with that."

"Somehow, that doesn't surprise me."

"I worked damned hard for everything I have, I see no reason why everyone shouldn't do the same."

"No subsidies, no tax breaks, no government contracts?"

"Those things simply build and protect incentive." He drained his stein. "Now I do have business. I hope I've been some help, whatever it is you're investigating."

I looked out through the wall of glass that faced the wide floodlit lawn and the cliff and sea beyond. Far out I saw the lights of oil platforms between the mainland and the dark shadows of the Channel Islands.

"Your incentive seems to have been well protected. Too bad those oil rigs spoil the view."

"They can put a hundred more rigs out there, it would be fine with me. The country needs oil, and if my country doesn't come before my view I don't think much of my country."

"What about your environment? You might not have a country or a world."

"Bullshit. It's the environmentalists who will ruin the world with their elitism. Okay, preserve a hundred acres of the redwoods up north, show them to the kids, but let the lumbermen make a living out of the rest. There's too much selfishness in the world. The country needs timber, oil, and jobs. How many people will end up going up to that Alaskan wilderness in the next hundred years to suck their thumbs and write poetry?"

"What's the difference between your good greed and their bad selfishness, Brower?"

"Greed is productive, helps everyone. Selfishness doesn't."

He stood up. Somehow he'd signaled the woman in the black dress to show me out. He didn't introduce us. She walked ahead of me in silence until we reached the front door. As she opened it, she smiled the most humorless smile I'd seen in a long time.

"Will my husband be going out now, Mr. Fortune?"

"He didn't say, Mrs. Brower."

"Yes, of course." Her smile remained fixed.

"You have to push the button on the release box inside the gate to open it."

She stood in the doorway as I drove toward the gate, her arms hugging herself as if she were freezing. She didn't see all that much of her husband. This had been one of his nights at home, her night, and because of me it might be ruined.

I pushed the button, drove out but not away. In the shadows of the grove of eucalyptus I parked and waited.

He'd told me the rough details of the deal he was in with Price and Torena when he didn't have to. When the rich or the powerful tell me what they don't have to, I start to look under the rug.

Chapter Fourteen

Jack Price parks behind the darkened office of Ed Brower. The only car in the lot is a Dodge station wagon. Jack sits in the car. He feels stupid. Santos Torena was smuggling illegals, was shot by those *mules* and *coyotes*. They'd cut their mother's throat for a dime and give a nickel change. Anyone who gets into that kind of thing is a damn fool.

Jack is still in the Jaguar when the Rolls-Royce comes into the lot, and Ed Brower hurries through the dark to his office. Jack hesitates, lets Brower walk all the way across the lot and into his office. He swears at himself. "Shit." Always worried about doing it wrong. Afraid to look bad. He gets out, slams the Jag door, follows Brower.

In the office, Brower comes from the kitchen carrying two beers. He sees Jack, holds out one of the beers.

"You've heard about Santos?"

Jack shakes his head to the beer. "His wife told me. She found him, knew he wanted to talk to me tonight. She's looking for a *coyote* named Paz Linero too, and one of the guys in the poker game. I've seen that Linero a couple of times. Hanging around, watching, asking after Francesca Torena. He was shot. Santos. Right near the poker game."

Jack moves farther into the office as he talks, until he had reached the desk. Brower walks on with the beers, gives a bottle to a big man lounging on one of the couches, his legs stretched far out, feet in cowboy boots. The big man sucks on the bottle, stares at Jack. The second stranger in the room is older, sits in an armchair reading a thick paperback book. Brower returns to his desk, sits down.

"That game out in Montecito?"

Jack stands at the desk. "What happened? I mean, who? Why?"

Brower says, "The police didn't tell me Francesca found him. You're sure that's what she said?"

"I think so. I mean, yes, I guess so."

Brower looks up at him. "You all right? Sure you don't want a beer?"

"No. I mean, yes. Okay, I'll have a beer."

Brower goes into the kitchen. Jack looks at the strangers. The younger one still stares at him. Maybe thirty-five, way over six-feet, dark hair, still sucking on the beer bottle as he stares. He has the kind of red face you see on guys who drink a lot, and his belly hangs over his gray slacks. A blue jacket, nice gray striped shirt and a blue-gray tie are sharp, but his cowboy boots stretched out where he lounges on the couch look all wrong. Brower hands Jack a John Courage and a stein.

Jack looks at the two men, says, "How come you're here so late."

"Business. Did Francesca say anything else about Torena's shooting?"

"Just that she found him."

"Did she say when?"

"Early, I guess." Jack sees his hands shake, takes a long drink of beer. "All the time I was looking for him he was dead." He drinks again, glances at the strangers, back at Brower. "How come you're not home? Something else's wrong, isn't it?"

The big stranger laughs. "You think something's wrong, Jack? You worried, Jack? Hey, everybody worries, right, Jack?"

Jack sees the other stranger's face for the first time when he lowers the paperback. An older guy, he looks at the younger with cold blue eyes. "You drink too much, Gretzer."

In his forties, Jack guesses, the older man has a square face, is light-haired and heavy at five-ten and over two hundred pounds. His cheap two-button brown worsted is wrinkled, he wears a brown tie and loafers.

"Fuck you," the younger one, Gretzer, says.

Ed Brower says, "You didn't tell a man named Fortune I was at the Hope Ranch house on Fridays, did you, Jack?"

"I don't know any Fortune."

"Dan Fortune. A private investigator."

"Investigator?"

"He came to the house to talk about Torena and you. Seemed to know a lot about you. Even that Torena wanted to talk to you before he got shot. How did he know that?"

"I guess someone told him. Francesca Torena or maybe that Mrs. Ortega, the mother-in-law. Who's he working for?"

"That's what we wonder." Brower finishes his beer. "You're sure he never talked to you? He seemed to know all about you and Torena being in a deal with me. He wanted the details of the deal, some other deals I'm involved in."

"Not from me!"

"He's out there nosing around, Jack. Someone sent him. Maybe it's the other things Torena was doing, maybe not, but we have to make sure he doesn't get in our way. If he talks to you, you know nothing, tell him nothing. Understood?"

The older stranger has lowered his book again. This time to look at Jack. The younger, Gretzer, walks past the desk into the kitchen, comes out with another beer, leans on the door frame. Jack looks at both of them, then at Brower behind his desk. His own voice is hoarse in his ears.

"You're not getting the money from a bank. Not on a Friday night or Saturday morning. You're getting the money somewhere else. That's what Torena wanted to talk to me about."

In the office that seems to echo with the silence, Jack hears the late traffic distant on State Street, a few passing cars closer on Santa Barbara Street, finds himself listening for the movement upstairs. A familiar sound. Reassurance. All the women Ed has up in that apartment while Carolyn sits out in Hope Ranch waiting for him to come on Friday night, maybe stay until Saturday night. Jack knows he could never do that, a family man.

"What would you do if you're right, Jack?" Brower says. "If I tell you no one will get hurt, and nothing can go wrong. Does it bother you? Worry you?"

Jack's mouth is bone dry. "Worries me, I guess. I mean, is it . . . dangerous?"

"Everybody worries, Jack," Gretzer says.

The older stranger has closed his book, put it into the pocket of his brown suit coat. He sits with no expression on his square face. Totally blank behind his blue eyes.

"I need a partner, Jack," Brower says. "I want to get out of the agency. I'll sell it all to you if you want. Now that's an opportunity. You don't want to spend your whole life working for other people. You do all the work, and someone else takes home the money, the position, the prestige. You want to be the one who gets rich, puts his family in the big house."

Brower goes into the kitchen, brings out more John Courages. Gretzer takes a bottle, shows his teeth to the older man who still sits doing nothing but watch Jack and Brower. Brower pours the two beers, hands one to Jack, sits again.

"It's what built this country," Brower says. "Working to get rich. The rich build the middle class, and the middle class are the strength of the country. Everyone trying to get rich, that's the name of the game. Not everyone makes it all the way, in a democracy inequality is inevitable. A lot of people stay down there working all their lives for other guys. You have to work to make sure you're going to be up there at the top. You have to take some risks."

"Hey, Jack," Gretzer said. "Don't think about it, right? Just go home and hide, tomorrow it's all cool."

Brower drinks. "Messick and Gretzer are experts. They were sent by a friend down in Palm Springs, you don't have anything to be concerned about, no one does. It's all going as planned. Go home, get some sleep."

Gretzer says, "No sweat, Jack. A piece of cake."

The older one, Messick, says, "He going to blow it, Brower?"

"Of course not," Brower says. "He'll do fine, right, Jack?"

"Maybe old Jack wants to come with us," Gretzer says.

Messick still looks at him. "He got anything on his mind, Brower? Him and that Fortune?"

"Jack don't know any Fortune, right, Jack?" Gretzer says.

Brower says, "Just go home, relax, watch some TV, go to bed, and by morning we'll all have what we need. If anyone comes to talk to you, you never heard anything. Okay?"

Jack wipes a dribble of beer from his chin. "Okay, Ed."

"That's our Jack," Gretzer grins.

"Drive home carefully," Brower says. "Don't even think about it."

Messick and Gretzer both watch Jack as he leaves.

Chapter Fifteen

It was after 10:30 in the shadows of the eucalyptus trees. Half an hour, and no car had come
through the automatic gate.

Either I was wrong about Ed Brower, or there
was another way out. I drove along both sides of
the wall, circled on the cross road. The service
entrance was on the next street behind the big
house, and it was open. I could see the garage
behind the house. It was also open, only one
car in a three car garage.

I took the back way out of Hope Ranch past
Hendry's Beach—the local name for Arroyo
Burro County Park. Everyone likes to be in
the know. It looked like Brower had guessed
I'd wait and watch, had slipped out the back

way. Which meant he had something to hide. Angela Price could be right.

In the city, Brower's office in the house three blocks from State Street showed light in only the upstairs windows. No cars were parked in the lot.

It was time I talked to Jack Price, or Angela Price again if she still didn't want him to know who I was. If Jack Price were home I would play the role of an anxious writer acquaintance of Angela Price who had a novel idea he wanted to discuss until I knew what she wanted me to tell him.

I drove the freeway north to the house off Turnpike Road in Goleta. Cars were parked in all the driveways, but there was no yellow Jaguar. Angela Price answered my ring. She was surprised to see me. Surprised, concerned, nervous, and eager, all at once.

"Did you find him? Talk to him?"

"He's not home?"

Tall in the doorway, she wore slim gray slacks and a blue turtleneck under a navy blazer. Silver earrings with blue New Zealand Paua shell hung from her ears, her brown hair was combed back soft on her shoulders. It wasn't a going-to-bed outfit.

"No," she said. "The police were here."

"Sergeant Chavalas or the sheriff's people?"

"Chavalas. I think that was his name."

"When?"

"Perhaps half an hour ago."

142

Right after they left Brower.

"What did they ask?"

She turned back into the house, I closed the door. She bent for a cigarette from the box on the coffee table, walked the room as she talked. The silver sandals on her feet caught the light from the single table lamp.

"They wanted to talk to Jack, asked where he was. I told them I didn't know, I was worried, that was why I hired you. The dark one who did the talking knew about that. Was he Chavalas?"

"Yeh. We talked earlier at Torena's house."

She waved the cigarette. "He wanted to know how close Jack had been to Santos Torena. Had he had trouble with Torena? What was Torena involved in? Who were Torena's other enemies? I said other than who? Jack wasn't an enemy of Torena, was connected to Torena as far as I knew only as an employee of Ed Brower and in this new condominium deal. Then he wanted to know what I thought was wrong with the deal. I said I didn't know anything was, but I didn't like how Jack was acting. Did I know Francesca Torena? Did Jack? Had he ever mentioned a Paz Linero or Vicario Silva? She shook her head, earrings flashing. "Do they always hammer at you like that? Question, question, and hardly wait for answers? Skip around until your head swims?"

"It's one technique. Looking for a slip, some automatic response that tells them something."

"What could I tell them? I hired you because I don't know what Jack is doing. What do they think I can tell them?"

"They don't necessarily believe you, Mrs. Price. They have to consider you might have hired me because you know something, want to know more. To get something for yourself. To put on pressure."

"That would mean I was lying to you too."

"Yes."

She stopped in front of the fireplace. She held to the brick mantel with her free hand, looked down into the fireplace. "Do you think I'm lying?"

"I'll find out."

Three unburned logs were neatly arranged in the fireplace with kindling ready to light. "You have a difficult trade. You have to investigate your clients as well as what they have hired you to investigate."

"It's about the same as any relationship. Marriage, work. You trust, but keep your eyes open, and don't really expect perfection."

She laughed aloud. "I would have thought your work was a little worse than most marriages or jobs."

"I don't get people at their most trusting. Was that all they asked?"

"When Jack gets home, have him call Chavalas." Her cigarette was almost burning her fingers. She dropped it into the fireplace. "I had the impression he was more than a little

144

interested that Jack wasn't home, would probably look for him."

"Your husband is an unknown piece in two murders. They'll keep their eyes open, but as far as I can tell the house isn't staked out, and that means Chavalas still thinks some of his rougher playmates probably killed Torena. When Jack does come home, I want to talk to him first. You're sure he hasn't been home and gone out again?"

"I don't think so. I had to go out for a while, but he would have left a note."

"Where'd you go?"

"Some school business. Mother's work, according to Jack. You never found him at all?"

The sleek clothes that showed her hips and full breasts didn't look like school-business clothes any more than go-to-bed clothes. Then, what did I know about the modern PTA?

"I didn't find him or talk to him, but I talked to a lot of people."

I told her about Francesca Torena and Inez Ortega and the second dead man, Vicario Silva. What Chavalas had said about Ed Brower, and what Brower had said. That Brower had left his Hope Ranch house, but his office was empty except for light upstairs. "It looks like the murders were probably done by Torena's *coyote* friends, but Brower has something he doesn't want known. I made him nervous pumping him about the deal, and he went out the back way. He and your husband could be together somewhere."

"He's never been this late, Dan."

The room in the empty house, and the street and cul-de-sac outside, were heavy with the silence as we both thought about it.

"He'll probably be home soon. Maybe he was closer to Torena than you knew. Maybe something is happening none of us know, but I can't do much more until I talk to him. When he comes home, don't push him. Hold him here, and call me."

She nodded.

In my Tempo I drove home to Summerland. She hadn't tried to keep me there, make me wait with her in the empty house.

The Spanish hacienda-style house we rent in the beach enclave of Summerland had light in the kitchen and dining room windows. Kay watched TV in the darkened living room.

"You'll ruin your eyes."

"Dinner's in the oven."

"You shouldn't have waited up."

"Why not?"

I couldn't think of a really logical answer. She smiled, stood up. She's as tall and slim as Angela Price, about the same age, but her hair is darker and more auburn, and her face is less perfect. More angular, with wider-set eyes that look at you with a steadiness that has become calmer since I decided to move

out from New York and try my luck in the
West. We rent the house together, her office
is in the tower, mine in the extra bedroom. So
far it's working.

"You want to argue or eat or go straight to
bed?"

"How do you know I didn't eat?"

"Motherly instinct. What odds do you want
me to give you?"

"Put it on the table."

She refuses to eat in the kitchen. The dining
room table was set with place mats, silverware,
real glass, bone china and flowers. While I ate
her pork chops with onions and new carrots,
she shared my Assam tea with me, and I told
her about the job.

"You think Mrs. Price should have asked you
to stay?"

"What would you have done? Alone in the
house, worried, your husband very late, and
two murders hanging over you?"

"Maybe she still didn't want him to know
she'd hired you."

"She didn't have to tell him who I really was,
leave it to me to get what I could without letting
him know."

"Not all women are afraid of being alone,
Dan." She drank the good tea. "You think she
could be going out again? Or was expecting
someone else to come to the house?"

"Or knew her husband wasn't coming home
at all. For one reason or another."

The dishes were mine. Dishwashers are a godsend for a one-armed man, turn two-steps a dish into the one step of real two-armed people. Upstairs she waited in bed. I sat at the foot, on the thick king-sized black-and-red Japanese comforter.

"Is he a fool or a victim?" I said. "Has he flipped out, gone bad?"

"Perhaps all three," she said.

I took off one boot. "Our founding fathers were believers in John Locke's social theories: Life, Liberty and Property. But most people in the colonies didn't own property, so when they framed the Declaration of Independence they realized that an appeal to property wouldn't make their fellow colonists eager to fight the King for them. That was when someone, probably Jefferson, came up with the brilliant idea of substituting 'the pursuit of happiness' for 'property,' and the poor went marching off to beat King George."

"You think Price is being duped? Is in trouble?"

I held the second boot. "People who gun down the famous have usually brooded themselves into a kind of insanity that sees the killing as giving them what the victim had. Like drinking the blood of a strong enemy in primitive worlds. When you want something everyone is supposed to be able to get, but you can't seem to get it, your thinking can get pretty twisted."

"Call, see if he's home."

She handed me the bedside telephone. I dialed, held for a long time. No one answered at the Price house. I sat while Kay watched me from the bed. She looks good in a blue nightgown.

"She's gone out," I said.

"Go and find both of them," she said.

We smiled at each other. I put my boots back on.

"It could be all night."

"I'll be here when you get home."

Maybe that was something Jack Price had never really understood. Or maybe he'd never been sure where or what home was.

When I had my duffel coat back on, I kissed her, went down to my office to get my old cannon.

NIGHTTOWN

"I hope I break even tonight,
I need the money so bad."
—NELSON ALGREN

Chapter Sixteen

Somewhere a clock chimes midnight over the howls of drunken youths in the parking lot.

All but one State Street movie house has let out, the crowds of teenagers, students, single adults and couples from twenty to forty wander up and down State between the music clubs, fast-food joints, restaurants open to the street, bars, and coffee houses. On the street itself there are fewer cars. The contacts and agreements have been made, the offers accepted and rejected, the Friday playing and partying gone indoors or out to Isla Vista.

At the bar next to the parking lot where the youths sing and scream in the night, Jack Price drinks his beer. It is the third bar since he left

Ed Brower's office, one beer in each, restless among the night crowds. Sensible, he has had some fettucini in The Chase Grill, a dessert of frozen yogurt at TCBY, sits now with another beer at the bar of The China Castle.

Nothing can go wrong. Brower said it. Brower and Messick and Gretzer. The experts.

He wants to know and he doesn't want to know.

He wants to go home and he doesn't want to go home.

He is afraid to tell Angie, and afraid not to tell her. He has nothing to tell. And too much. If he goes home Angie will get it out of him sooner or later. Scream at him. The kids awake in their rooms listening to her rage and his anger at her rage. If he goes home he will tell her about Brower and Messick and Gretzer. The deal will never happen. The deal has to happen. This time. No matter what Brower is going to do.

He wants to know and doesn't want to know.

He has another beer, remembers that the kids aren't home tonight. Just him and Angie.

He has another beer.

Inside the tiny office on De la Vina, Al who only plays locks at the poker game works at a desk piled so high with papers Jack can't see any wood. Al reads some papers, makes notes on a pad, drinks coffee. Jack figured Al would work late, go back to his office after the game. Bet only locks, play the sure thing, and work when everyone else plays or sleeps.

Jack closes the storefront door. "You always work so late?"

The little man shows no surprise on his wrinkled face. "At my age I don't sleep so good, and the game's closed down." Al examines Jack from head to toe. "You come to help us poor folks fight the landlords, Price? Your boss ain't gonna kiss you."

Jack looked around the tiny, cramped office with its rows of filing cabinets. Papers and folders are piled on every surface.

"How'd you get into this? You're not Latino."

"You fight against the bosses all your life, you don't stop, buy a condo, go play golf in Florida when you retire. Who wants to stay home, do nothin'? Poor guys need help, Latinos are the biggest group around here gets shit on."

"Some of them do pretty damned good. Like Santos Torena."

"Torena got help, decided to be a boss, exploits his own people. A slumlord and worse. Torena's high on our watch list."

"What can you do for the beaners anyhow?"

"I can teach them their rights."

"Owners have rights too, Al. You ever work for them?"

"Owners got plenty of people, plenty of clout, plenty of laws and plenty of money working for them. Latinos got lousy living conditions, plenty of rats and cockroaches, laws that work mostly against them, and jobs below a minimum wage that's already below the poverty line."

"Nobody has to be poor in this country. Not if they work."

"Nobody has to be poor anywhere, Price, but it don't have a lot to do with working or not working. It got to do with how much of the value of what they make they get, and how much they pay for what they got to have. All my life I worked to get one bigger an' the other smaller."

"I don't like unions."

"Why not?"

Jack picks a pile off the only other chair in the cubicle office, sits down. "A man who owns a business has a right to run it his own way, hire and fire who he wants, decide what he can pay. If you don't like what he pays, you find a job you do like. Unions make workers lazy, inefficient, and unproductive."

"Where'd you learn all that?"

"Everyone knows it."

"You mean someone told you, you believed, never asked any questions. I asked questions, an' I heard different answers."

"Then you listened to the wrong damn people. You sound like those Marxists who want to blow up the world. Castro, and that Pol Pot, and all the rest. So maybe some things are wrong, but you have to have law and order."

The little man rummages around his desk, finds a small notebook, reads from it. *"When the weak or oppressed assert the rights that have been long denied them, those in power inevitably resist on the basis of the necessity for tranquillity."*

"Marx, Lenin, Castro or Mao?"

"Earl Warren, our good Californian U.S. Chief Justice."

"Ed Brower would say it's the same thing."

"I know what Brower would say, what do you say?"

Jack doesn't know what he would say. Not really. You had to have law and order to protect democracy, but a U.S. Chief Justice wasn't some crazy Marxist or radical.

Al sighs. "So what'd you come here for, Price?"

Jack looks back out at the windy street through the window. "You know the Genius outside the game?"

"A little. I helped out some friends of his."

"You know his real name's St. George? Stanley St. George?"

"I guess so. I mean, yeh."

Jack chewed on a fingernail. "You know what he was doing with Santos Torena?"

"Are they doing something?"

"They were into some deal or maybe project together. I didn't even know they knew each other outside the game."

"Something wrong with that?"

"I guess not." Jack looks out the window again. "Torena was killed tonight."

"Killed?"

Jack looks at Al. "Shot, Al. Right outside the game."

Al has to let it sink in. "Jesus. Who done it, Price?"

"The police don't know. That's why I'm wondering about what he was doing with the Genius."

"Christ, I don't know. I seen them together a couple of times. The Genius got a lot of crazy buddies, but I never heard they was doin' anything special. Hell, I don't even know what the Genius does. Don't have a job far as I can see, spends most of his time in that big house o' his. I never been inside."

"How'd you help his friends?"

"He sent two Latino guys was gettin' evicted for havin' too many people livin' with 'em. I got the landlord to back off, told the guys to keep the parade down. No big deal."

The cluttered little office is beginning to depress Jack. "You never heard anything illegal about the Genius?"

"Never heard nothing except he was a big electronics whiz once up north."

Jack gets up. "Chief Justice Warren really said that?"

"Sure did."

"I never knew that."

"A lot you don't know, Price."

Chasing Eights

*   *   *

They stand near his car.

The skinny Latino *coyote* again, Paz Linero, with one of the others in the long white dusters. They look into the Jaguar, talk in the almost deserted parking lot.

Jack stands across Chapala Street. The two Latinos finally separate, the skinny one going right toward Anapamu, the heavier one left to Victoria. Jack gives them five minutes.

Then he hurries to the Jaguar, watching every movement in the night, and drives out of the lot.

Chapter Seventeen

Max Mellecker's house hung on a slope below a rustic side street above Foothill Road. Weathered redwood in the night, it had been added onto many times, rambled on levels hidden by overhanging oaks and pepper trees. Among the sleeping houses all around, it showed light. A Dodge Aires and a Honda Civic were in a carport that leaned under the weight of a massive purple bougainvillea. On my third ring the door opened on the chain.

"Yes?"

Jack Price's one-time partner in the P.R. business, and fellow car salesman, still wore the red-striped button-down shirt, but the bow tie and blue blazer were gone. A canvas vest and paint-stained chinos were in their place on his scrawny frame.

"My name's Dan Fortune, Mr. Mellecker. I'm trying to find Jack Price."

"Why? Who are you?"

"I'm a private detective." I showed him my license. "His wife hired me."

"Angie? He isn't at home?"

"Not yet."

He stared at my empty sleeve. "Come in then."

The rooms were small and furnished with elegant and well-polished Victorian antiques. Formal and overstuffed, but not cluttered. A woman in a purple and gold robe watched TV in an enclosed porch that faced a broad deck and a distant view between ridges of a wedge of city lights and one glowing oil platform out at sea. At the far end of the house Mellecker led me into a large studio-like room with a wall of glass that faced the same view of city and sea between the ridges.

I sat in a canvas chair he pointed to.

"You have any ideas where Price might be?"

He sat facing me. "The game's over, the showroom's closed. Maybe he went to talk to Ed Brower about their condo deal. He was looking for Santos Torena. I suppose he could be with him."

"He isn't with Torena."

I told him what had happened to Torena, and what I'd done so far. He didn't say anything,

looked past me at the walls of the large room.
I realized he was looking at what was on the
walls. Every inch that wasn't a window or a
door was covered with paintings. Watercolors
and oils. Seascapes. Even I could see that the
color was bold and daring, the work strong.
They were almost all the same scene in fifty
different guises, times, conditions—the views
through the glass wall of the room.

"I didn't know Torena well," he said at last.

"Did Price?"

"I don't think so."

"Only through Brower and the condominium
deal?"

"Through Brower anyway."

"You think Brower was what Torena wanted
to talk about?"

Mellecker shrugged, studied his walls.

"What would Price and Brower have to talk
about on the deal this late?"

He gave a shiver as if physically breaking
away from the walls. "Any kind of last-minute
hitch they'd have to work on."

"Without calling home?"

"Jack can forget, get carried away by business."

"How about Claire Broberg?"

"I guess it's possible, but he'd have made
some excuse to Angie, some cover story."

"Unless he forgot to call."

He stood and walked to the wide row of windows, looked out at the wedge of city lights in

the distance below, the sky glow of the city beyond the ridges.

"Where would he go if he was in trouble? Worried about the deal? If something was wrong?"

"Is Jack in real trouble, Fortune?"

"It's past midnight, he's not home."

He continued to look at his night view.

"You think Torena wanted to talk about the deal," I said.

"What else could it be?"

"Would Price kill over the deal, Mr. Mellecker?"

"Of course not. No!" Across the city outside the windows lights were growing fewer after midnight. "No. Of course not." He sat down. "This deal means a lot to Jack. I can feel it. But he wouldn't kill anyone. I don't think he could, except maybe in self-defense, by accident. I don't think most people could." He shook his head. "No, Jack wouldn't kill anyone."

I heard the *but* in his voice. "What would he do?"

"We're a lot alike, Jack and I. Two midwestern middle-class boys who did what they were supposed to do. The only difference was I had a chance to be something else. I was going to be a painter, went to art school a couple of years. I wasn't good, the other students weren't what I was used to, and everyone kept telling me a man had to make his mark, get somewhere, have a position, be on top. So I went into business. Jobs I didn't like or couldn't do, bad investments, abortive schemes."

He pointed to his seascapes. "All the time I never stopped painting. I got better. A Sunday painter like Henri Rousseau, but not a primitive. The view from this room. My Mont St. Victoire. I'm not Cezanne, but I'm better than I was. My father ran a feed store back in Iowa. I worked in it summers. I liked working in the feed store, painting when there weren't any customers. I'm a lousy businessman, might have been a good storekeeper, but I was supposed to be ambitious. Me and Jack. Except I don't think Jack ever thought of being anything except his father bigger and better. His idea of rebellion was to leave Minnesota. I think he sees this deal as his last chance. He couldn't kill, but I think he could do almost anything else."

The woman who came in disagreed, "Jack Price can't do anything at all, and you know it."

She was a small woman with dark black hair and a pinched, discontented face. The long purple-and-gold robe covered what looked like a decent figure, and her small feet were in purple slippers.

Mellecker stood up, "Maggie, this is Mr. Fortune, he's looking for Jack. Mr. Fortune, my wife."

She carried a cup of coffee, sat between us. "I can go a long time without Jack Price, or that wife of his for that matter. Stupid and incompetent with our money, perhaps worse.

Max never would let me see their books. The children are grown, thank God, but look at this house. And he lets Jack Price pour our money into one of his rathole schemes."

"It was a good idea, Maggie," Mellecker said. "We just didn't have enough capital to ride out the start."

"You're gullible, Max, if not plain dumb about business." She took a cigarette from the pocket of the robe, lit it, waved the smoking match at Mellecker. "At least Jack Price has ambition, drives a Jaguar, knows what he wants to get for himself and his family. If he wasn't so stupid, had a different wife, he might be someone now."

"You perhaps?" Mellecker said.

"It might have worked out better all around."

I talked between them. "Why is Angela Price a bad wife?"

Maggie Mellecker waved away cigarette smoke. "She has about as much ambition as our Max here. With a drag like her, it's no wonder Price gets half-baked ideas. Her and her delusions and oppositions."

"What delusions and oppositions?"

Mellecker said, "Angie wants to write, doesn't think Jack belongs in business. She could—"

"She thinks she's an 'artist'! Too good to help her husband establish himself. Well, she'd better watch out for that Claire Broberg. That one's after Jack for sure. Not that Angie'd probably give a damn."

"Why not?"

"We've heard things. She's out jogging as soon as Jack's at work and the kids are in school. She keeps in shape, and it isn't for Jack Price."

"Angie has her own life," Mellecker said. "Maybe we all should."

"What do you think that means?"

"Just that it's good to know what you want to do."

"I know what I want to do." She stood up. "I want to have the life we've worked for. I want us to enjoy what we have before we're too old. I did my job in this marriage."

They stared at each other. I sensed it was an old pattern with them. She turned away. "Don't stay up all night. It's not good for you."

After she had gone, Mellecker watched the closed door of the studio room. "She did her job. Kept the pressure on. I haven't been a very good subject."

"Angela Price doesn't do the same with Price?"

"Angie lives her own life."

"Not his?"

"Not what he lives now."

"What would Angela do to save the deal if it was going bad?"

"I don't know, Fortune. She's a strong woman. She wasn't when I met Jack, but she is now."

"You know what changed her?"

"I think she saw Jack for real, saw herself for real."

A woman who didn't love her husband anymore, but needed him, needed her children, needed him not to fail again. What would she do if she saw him about to blow what could be his big chance to succeed?

Mellecker said, "You haven't asked the important question, Mr. Fortune."

"What's that?"

"What would Ed Brower do if this deal began to go sour, if something threatened to go wrong."

"You think Brower would kill?"

"I read a lot. Mostly at night when I can't sleep and a painting isn't going well. There's a short story by Somerset Maugham. It's about this man in Monte Carlo who makes his living winning at the roulette table. He always bets only red and black, doesn't make a fortune, but enough to live on. Everyone knows him, and they all want to know his system. Finally, he's about to retire, and he tells this young man how he does it. He stands around the casino until he spots someone who's desperate, has to win, a matter of life or death. A young couple broke and with no jobs, an old man whose son needs an operation, a husband whose wife is about to leave him for a rich lover who he knows will ruin her. He spots them—and he bets *against* them."

"That's Ed Brower?"

"Maugham wrote as if it were cosmic fate, an evil universe. But it's only the psychology of using people who are desperate. They all betray their desperation by everything they do, by how they play roulette, so they can be used, conned, manipulated. It works in everything—art, money, love. The person who *needs* always gets used, taken advantage of. And there's always an Ed Brower to do the using."

"Most people would do the same if they could," I said.

"The Browers do more. You play poker, Fortune?"

"If I don't have to deal."

He glanced at my empty sleeve. "Sorry."

"*De nada*. Tell me about Brower."

"Brower does business the way Mack the Bluffer plays poker. Mack plays in the Montecito game. He seems to always want you in the game, tells you how good you are, what bad luck you had when you lose. He calls me and Jack and anyone except the Genius to persuade us to go to the game that night. He's our 'friend,' but he does anything he can to lure or fool us for one more dollar. Never pass up a pigeon even if he's your best friend."

He looked at his paintings. The same view again and again. In a hundred different lights, times of day, angles, media, as if he wanted to get one small point of his universe right.

169

"Pigeons sometimes become hawks," I said. "What if Santos Torena was a pigeon who became a hawk?"

"I guess it would depend on who wanted what, on what else might have happened." He thought about it for a moment. "Ed Brower likes to talk about Thomas Edison all the time. Edison is the true American, a free man. Did you ever hear the story of Edison and George Westinghouse?"

Chapter Eighteen

The year is 1890.

Thomas Alva Edison has been having a series of good years. He's invented a carbon transmitter that is an advance for Bell's telephone, will help to make it practical. He's given the world the phonograph, such an original idea the U.S. Patent Office couldn't find a record of anything like it in its files. Ten years later he improved it with a motor drive and cylindrical records that will make it truly commercial, and the eminent Doctor Johannes Brahms has called Doctor Edison all the way from Germany on Bell's invention, aided by Edison's work, to praise the wonderful gift to music, the great step for mankind.

It is eleven years since he first demonstrated a successful electric bulb, certainly the crowning achievement of his career, although he will go on to do much more work, and will amass 1,003 patents before his death in West Orange, New Jersey, in 1931. That is some 603 more than his arch rival, George Westinghouse.

Westinghouse himself is to figure prominently in the events of 1890, together with Edison's years of perfecting the electric bulb, and the invention and exploitation of practical methods for the generation and distribution of the electricity needed to make his bulb glow in every home and office and shop in the country and maybe the world.

This is a lot of homes, offices, and shops, and there is a great deal of money to be made by the man and company that gets the contract to put in the system.

Edison and his company had developed the first electric power system in 1882 by the use of low-tension direct current. George Westinghouse and *his* company, in 1884, had brought out an alternating-current system that uses light, easily installed wires compared to the expensive installation of heavy-wired direct current.

Edison has a problem.

George Westinghouse's system is clearly superior. He has the facts and the figures to prove it.

Thomas Alva Edison has imagination and

know-how. It is time to see what can be done with those, to be inventive—as much in business as he is in science. In a time-honored tradition that goes back as far as the itinerant peddlers of the Middle Ages, and probably a great deal farther, and is as recent as the famed village-to-village Yankee peddler and snake-oil pitchman, Doctor Edison decides his best chance lies in making his rival's product look bad, discrediting it in the public eye.

George Westinghouse's alternating current has one big defect that plays right into Edison's hands—it can kill people.

Alternating current, used improperly, is lethal. Edison, who knows a good P.R. ploy when he sees it, decides that this will be his ace. He will demonstrate to the country and the world that the Westinghouse system is far too dangerous for mere ordinary people to risk taking it into their homes and offices.

He recruits a young engineer named Harold P. Brown, sends him around the country to demonstrate the fatal potential of George Westinghouse's alternating-current system. Brown does this by traveling from place to place across the land staging public shows in which he electrocutes unlucky and unsuspecting stray cats and dogs and even horses.

The scene shifts to New York State.

In progressive and civilized New York, the good people have become disillusioned with hanging as a method of removing their worst criminals. During the 1880s, they had established a state legislative commission to decide if hanging should be abolished. As 1890 approached, after carefully observing a goodly number of hangings, witnessing the usual mess, stench, macabre mishaps, and slow strangulations, the commission has decided that hanging must be replaced. The question is, with what?

Enter Harold P. Brown and Thomas Edison's traveling show to discredit the superior commercial system of George Westinghouse. The carnival arrives in Albany, state capital of New York. The commissioners on the committee to investigate hanging see the efficient demise of the various vagrant cats and dogs, instantly grasp the potential. But a cat or a dog isn't a person. They are considerably smaller, for one thing. Something much closer to actual people is needed to help decide on the prospective application.

Can young Mr. Brown, using George Westinghouse's terribly dangerous alternating current, dispatch, say, an orangutan?

Mr. Brown can and does. The ill-starred ape even catches fire, is quite a sight with its fine red hair merrily burning.

This doesn't dampen the enthusiasm of the commissioners for their brilliant idea—an electric chair to rid them of *their* vagrant villains with less mess, and less chance of mishaps. After all, Thomas Edison himself has demonstrated the absolute lethality of George

Westinghouse's alternating current, and human beings are far less likely to catch fire than orangutans.

Edison instantly sees the devastating public relations coup in this concept. The entire nation will be watching the electric chair kill a human being who could, of course, be any of them if Westinghouse's system is allowed to enter homes and offices.

George Westinghouse isn't slow either. Men dying in chairs powered by his system to light the bulbs of the world is not going to do much to drum up business. He swings into action to block the new application of his system.

The pawn becomes one William Kemmler, an illiterate axe-murderer from Buffalo. Convicted and sentenced, he sits on Death Row at Auburn Prison while Edison, Westinghouse, the State of New York, and, eventually, the Supreme Court, fight it out.

Westinghouse battles long and expensively to save William Kemmler. He hires the best lawyers, even the leading lawyer in the nation, spends over one hundred thousand dollars which, in 1890, is an enormous fortune, carries the battle all the way to the Supreme Court. But in the end Westinghouse loses. Edison wins, William Kemmler is executed by alternating current.

Unfortunately for everyone, efficiency is not a mark of this epoch-making event. Kemmler fails to die from the first massive jolt. Doctors are horrified, executioners panic. The second electrical jolt is held so high for so long that William Kemmler is literally cooked.

The public is revolted. Newspapers opine there will be no more executions by electric chair. Tom Edison has made the good fight for his system. But, alas, alternating current, despite William Kemmler, eventually defeats direct current in the homes and offices of the world. Cheap installation beats public safety every time.

Chapter Nineteen

The yellow Jaguar was almost invisible up the rural street of trees and thick bushes, had not been there when I went into Mellecker's house. It was dark, but I sensed someone in the driver's seat.

I walked close to the trees, my lone hand on the old cannon in my duffel coat pocket. There are no sidewalks on the hill and canyon streets of Santa Barbara outside the downtown area, and the Jaguar was parked as close to the trees as it could get as if for warmth or safety. I had to tap on the window before he rolled it down. He looked at my empty sleeve with uneasiness behind the mask of confidence, an edge of panic around the smile painted on his face.

"You must be Fortune." His voice was too loud for the dark street. "You're really a detective? Did you follow me up here? I didn't see you. What's going on?"

"You wife hired me, Price. You must have talked to Brower after I did. You tell me what's going on."

"Angie?"

"She's worried there's something wrong with the Brower deal. Too high a risk, maybe even illegal."

"She hired you to check on me! Follow me!"

The Jaguar door swung open so abruptly it almost knocked me over. In the thin light from Max Mellecker's house Jack Price seemed shorter, more overweight. He had forgotten to stick out his chest, pull in his belly. The dark blond hair was disordered, his white shirt open, the collar stained with sweat even in the cold January night. His blue tie hung loose and crooked. The three-piece blue suit was still properly buttoned, but the crease was almost gone from the wrinkled trousers.

"Look, Fortune, I don't know what the hell Angie has on her mind, but there's nothing wrong, believe me."

He grinned man to man. Who could understand women?

"You know Santos Torena and another man are dead? Shot? Murdered?"

"His wife told me. About Torena. I don't know anything about any other guy."

I heard the fear in his voice, but defiance too, dismissal. It had nothing to do with him.

"Francesca Torena told you? When? Where?"

"She came to the agency. Around nine-thirty, ten. I think she's got a gun. I told her I didn't know anything about Torena, or about *coyotes*. She wanted to know where the Genius was too. I didn't even know the Genius knew Torena."

"The Genius?"

"Stan St. George. A guy in our poker game. I never even knew his real name."

"Have you told all that to the police?"

"The police?"

"They want to talk to you. You better go in and tell them what you know."

"I don't have anything to tell!" His rage exploded in the night. "Angie's crazy! Another one of her stupid ideas. Always going off on some dumb thing of her own. Well, this time she's wrong all the way. Hiring a detective! I'm going to make a bundle this time. I'm going to buy into the agency, maybe take it over. Brower's got better to do, he's going to sell the whole dealership to me."

"Is that what Brower offered to get you into the deal?"

"Brower didn't offer me anything. I heard about the deal, made him cut me in. I did it, Fortune. On my own. You tell Angie I know damn well what I'm doing, it's all under control."

"Why don't you tell her?"

179

Michael Collins

"Because I'm not ready to go home yet!"

I hadn't watched him long in the poker game, but he was the kind of player who would always give back what he won. A man who needed to be liked, admired, and the moment he was a winner he would become expansive, friendly. Relaxed, outgoing, talkative. He would lose his concentration, his attention to the game, and his money. And he would never know why.

"Go to the police, Price. Tell them—"

This time I heard the car before it parked behind the Jaguar. A sleek old Cadillac. I eased my hand around the old cannon in my coat pocket as they got out, one on each side of the car, walked toward us far enough apart so one shot couldn't get both. Price saw me look past his shoulder, turned. Every muscle in his face and body tensed to run. The skinny one saw.

"Hey, man, don' be nervous. Ever'body friends, right? You do like the one-arm guy."

The same thin face, a mustache, dark windbreaker I had seen near the body of Santos Torena in the brief light of a passing car. The same worn western hat, eyes that seemed to have no color at all. Not alone now, the heavier man a step behind and five steps to his right like a ghost in the night in his white pants, shirt, shoes and long duster. A white ghost with a dark face and mustache, a dark hand with a gun in it.

"Hey, I see you guys before, right? Like 'round Santos? You maybe know where is Francesca?"

180

In greasy jeans and rundown running shoes, he didn't look like the head of any kind of operation, but he had to be Paz Linero, the *coyote* boss Chavalas had talked about. Jack Price's white face told me he knew who Linero was.

"Where'd you see Mr. Price," I asked. "With Torena?"

Price protested, "I never even talked to Torena."

"The fat guy we see talk with Santos's old lady's momma." Linero grinned again. "You don' wanna know where I see you, Mr. One Arm?"

"I know where you saw me," I said. "I saw you."

The heavy one behind Linero growled.

"Maybe you saw Francesca Torena there too," I said.

Linero spoke some Spanish to the heavy *mule*. It was too fast for my Puerto Rican based Spanglish, but the *mule* stepped closer, his gun up.

"Maybe you kill Santos, Mr. One Arm?" Linero said to me. "Maybe you *La Migra*, some kinda cop. Sneaky, hey? One arm'n all. Maybe you got your own business, right? Free enterprise. The *gringo* way."

"You were standing over Torena, I was still at the road."

The *mule* growled louder. Paz Linero motioned him down.

"He's dead when I find him, *cabron*. Who guns down Vicario, hey, one arm? You'n Santos's old lady got somethin' goin'?" He took a step closer to me and to Price, looked at Price. "Maybe fat boy got it goin' on *madre* Ortega. Old cunt, nice'n greased, in like Flynn, hey?"

Jack Price's hands shook as he licked his lips and tried to think of what he should say. I wondered if Paz Linero wanted to know who and what had happened to Santos Torena, or to know how much we knew about who and what had happened to Santos Torena. Looking for answers or stopping questions?

"Paz!"

The *mule* was an all-white flash on his way down, his gun up and already turned toward the far side of the dark road. Paz Linero had produced a gun from somewhere, was bent-kneed going flat. I heard and saw at the same instant the *mule* did. A bright light, heavy feet in the brush of the yard next to Max Mellecker's house, a glint of metal. Price neither saw nor heard. Oblivious to everything but his own needs, he went on talking to Linero as if he saw nothing at all going on in front of him.

"I never found Torena. I never even saw him after—"

A tableau.

The *mule* down. Paz Linero down. I, me, Dan Fortune, down. Max Mellecker in his side doorway under his side light staring at the dark of the next yard where the metal glistened and the feet ran. Price oblivious, still talking.

Then motion.

Two shots from the bushes. The light gone. Mellecker gone. The white ghost of the *mule* shooting. Paz Linero mouth open and shooting. Dan Fortune, me, on my knees and reaching up to pull Price down.

"Down, for Christ sake! Down!"

Pain.

I lay on my face behind a tree next to the rural street. My old pistol was in my hand. My side was wet. On the street there was bright light, movement, and angry, pompous, nervous voices.

The wet was blood. A burning in my left side. I moved my arm. Up, down, around. On the street bright with the light from inside all the houses, the yellow Jaguar was still parked. And my Tempo. There were no other cars.

People stood out in the street in their robes, talked, gestured, debated, swore, complained, pontificated.

I sat up against the tree, put my cannon in my pocket, probed the blood on my side with my fingers. There was a wet throbbing groove in the skin, nothing more. My fingers and arm moved. No one was lying on the rural road. The Cadillac and *coyotes* were gone. Whoever had been in the bushes was gone.

The police cars turned into both ends of the street. The police climbed out, quick and alert.

A sergeant gave sharp orders. They spread out to search. The outraged citizens in their robes and pajamas got in their way everywhere. I stood, stepped out with my hand up.

Guns out, the uniformed patrolmen came toward me as spread out as the two *coyotes* earlier. They watched my lone arm as if it were some kind of trick to lull them. I would put them off guard, then whip out a rejuvenated arm and blow them away.

"Lean!"

I leaned.

"Spread 'em!"

I spread my legs. The patrolman found my old cannon but no second arm. The sergeant found my license and examined my side.

"Okay, Fortune, you'll live. What happened here?"

I told him about talking to Mellecker and Jack Price and the two *coyotes*. "Mellecker came out of his house over there, turned on the side light. Someone was in the bushes next to the house. The *mule* saw them, he and Linero went down. The bushwhackers fired first, I got hit. I guess I took cover, blacked out, and it was over."

"What about this Price? You say that's his Jag?"

A patrolman reported, "No one else here now, Sergeant."

"Where does this Mellecker live?" the sergeant said.

I took him to Mellecker's door. The wife came out scared and annoyed at the same time.

"Jack Price was afraid to go back to his car. Max drove him somewhere. I never did like those Prices."

"You know where they went, ma'am?"

"No. And I wish he'd keep his stupid problems away from us. My God, detectives and guns and shooting." She saw the blood on my side. "What stupidity has he gotten into now? I told Max—"

"Yes, ma'am, thank you." The sergeant half saluted, pulled me away with him. "We'll take you to the hospital, then get your story on paper."

"Call Gus Chavalas," I said. "It's his case."

They didn't handcuff me, but they put me into the back seat behind the wire cage with no door handles on the inside.

Chapter Twenty

"For God's sake, Jack, what are you and Brower doing?"

Max Mellecker drives in the stream of cars around the loop of Embarcadero del Mar and Embarcadero del Norte. Jack Price watches the Isla Vista students, tourists, street people and wildly dressed adults who should have better things to do this late on a Friday night. Aimless and loud, they cruise the sidewalks and half the street, block traffic.

"It's not the deal. Those guys were *coyotes*. Some private stuff of Torena's."

"Were the ones in the bushes *coyotes* too?"

"How do I know who they were? I never saw them. They were shooting at Linero."

"They shot at that Fortune, too."

"He's a detective, they were crooks like those *coyotes*."

"Fortune was looking for you, not the *coyotes*."

"That's just another dumb idea of Angie's. She's crazy."

The wandering students and street people weave in and out of the food stores and bars, the ice cream shops and tea and coffee houses. They crowd into La Jicora, the Mexican restaurant Jack likes on Embarcadero del Mar. Jack still takes the family to La Jicora. It's really authentic, someone told him.

"Angie has no reason to be worried, Jack?"

"No damn reason at all."

"Then I'll drive you home. It's late, I need—"

Jack looks out at two members of the Isla Vista Foot Patrol who walk among the crowd. "It's an old idea from way back in England. They dug it up to control the crazy kids and street drifters, the wild parties out here. It works, too. Cops on foot keep real order around a community, make the kids and druggies and bums think twice before they bother decent people."

"Let me take you to the cops, Jack," Max Mellecker says.

Jack laughs. "You're as crazy as Angie, Max."

"Is it that important?"

Up a side street Jack can see the steam from the hot tubs of Shibumi Gardens. He wants to jump out of the car, leave Max and the crowd behind. He has always liked hot tubs. Ever since they first came to California. Up on the Mesa then, working for old Jens Spear. A good dinner, some drinks and into the tub. Taking them to the tub they liked—far rear to the left under the big eucalyptus that dropped its acorns right smack on their heads—the attendants always stared at Angie. Envied him, the man who had Angie. They imagined Angie naked and hurrying into the tub where she would open and spread in the heat waiting for him. The attendants wanted to be in that tub with Angie. Wanted to be him with his woman and his house and his high salary at Spear.

"I'll be fifty, I'll be nothing. What did that football guy say? Lombardi? Green Bay Packers? Winning isn't everything, it's the only thing."

Almost once a week to Shibumi until old Jens told him to go out on his own, develop his potential. The old man was right, but it took time, and they couldn't afford to hot tub, and the kids were born and they had to move to the bigger house that had its own hot tub. A tub in your own backyard, dinner at home and no TV, wasn't the same thing. Angie expected him to paw her, make love under the water, talk, and most of the time he was too tired. After a while she stopped going in too, and now Jack misses it, can feel the aches leave his rigid muscles as he floats deep with only his face above the hot surface.

Jack says, "Torena's wife came to the agency. Asked me about the *coyotes*, about the Genius. I never heard the Genius even knew Torena outside the game."

"Torena's wife thinks the Genius could have had something to do with Torena's shooting?"

"What else? I mean, she was looking for him for a reason. I'm pretty sure she had a gun in her bag."

At the top of the loop Max turns into El Embarcadero itself, drives down to Del Playa Drive and the ocean. He parks facing out toward the lights of the oil rigs in the Channel. Max lights a cigarette. Jack takes Max's cigarette. Max lights another. Jack looks at the oil platforms out on the dark sea.

"You knew Torena and the Genius were doing something?"

"For maybe a year," Max says. "You don't listen much."

"You know what they were doing?"

"Helping street people."

"Street people?"

"Food, a place to sleep, clothes. The Genius runs it all, Torena got him stuff. At least, that's the way I heard it."

Jack sits with the cigarette, reaches into his pocket. The business card is a blur in the night. He turns on the overhead light, reads the card: 29 *Padre Lane*.

"You know where Padre Lane is, Max?"

"It's almost 1:00 A.M."

"He said if I wanted to talk, needed a quiet place. I want to talk. It's Friday."

A late moon casts long shadows in the street as Max Mellecker drives down the steep slope from the edge of the Riviera to the upper east. Jack points:

"There."

Padre Lane is tucked into the foot of the slope. Short and narrow, thick bushes, trees and hedges hide two old Victorian mansions at either end separated by the high white adobe wall of No. 29 that fills most of the lane. There is a massive wooden gate in the old wall built for the entry of horses and the rural carriages of Colonial Spain. A smaller door is set in the gate for human entry.

Max parks, Jack pulls the old-fashioned bell-pull.

"Yeh?"

Eyes look through a Judas hole in the smaller door.

"The Genius told me to come around."

"You got a name?"

"Jack Price. And Max Mellecker. We play poker with the Genius."

"Lucky you."

The Judas hole closes, Jack and Mellecker stand in the silver moonlight of the narrow lane with the dark and silent city around them. Only the faint drone of sparse late night traffic distant on the freeway.

The eyes return, search the night around them. "You alone?"

"Just the two of us," Jack says. "He knows us."

"Lucky him."

The door in the gate closes and locks behind them. A two-story white Monterey house with a dark wood second floor gallery is across a courtyard where ancient cobblestones show through cement. Light comes from inside the big old house through gaps in drawn curtains. A ragged group stands close to thick bushes and trees on the right.

"Mr. Rick died," the guardian of the gate tells them. A burly, bearded man with long straggling hair held off his sunburned face by a red band. "It was cold three nights ago, Mr. Rick died out there where he was sleeping."

A four-car carriagehouse-turned-garage with an apartment on top is attached to the old house on the left, and on the right beyond the small crowd two outbuildings stand among the trees and heavy undergrowth. The brush and bushes are as thick around the house behind the wall as on the slopes of the mountains. Exotic imports mix with native chapparral. A lot of trees Jack knows—silk oaks, silk floss with their trunks full of thorns, red and yellow eucalyptus, blue gum eucalyptus, bottle brush, pepper, avocado—and some he doesn't.

"The town killed him," the gate guardian says. "The good people. Afraid of a man who refused to want what they wanted, wouldn't be the same as they were, didn't need a house to sleep in, a TV to hide in, a job to die in."

Behind the front wall the house and its acre of overgrown land are totally hidden from the other houses and the streets. As if it didn't exist, an empty space among the streets and houses of the upper east.

"He had a sister. She says give him a military funeral. He was a Korean War vet. He used to laugh like hell about that."

Jack and Mellecker see a tall man in the center of the group digging a hole among the trees at the edge of the concrete. He wears a T-shirt and old army pants, a Los Angeles Dodgers baseball cap on his long hair. He works by the moonlight and flashlights held by the silent watchers. A seedling evergreen in a can stands on the ground beside him. He digs and talks aloud.

"An honest man, Richard Roth. A man of laughter for life and love, a man of tears for a sick world and raped country. We celebrate his life not his death. This tree will be his fitting memorial. A tree of life: clean, free, doing good for people and the planet, for the universe. A tree like Rick. Living off no one, a slave to no one. He used to quote Abe Lincoln: 'As I would not be a slave, so I would not be a master.' He said old Abe should wake up and see what had happened to his country."

Someone shouts, "Everybody drink. Rick and me used to drink together every damn day."

"He said he wanted to die on the street," another says, "and he did. I'll drink to that."

"What are we doing here? You want to do Rick a favor? Get drunk! Celebrate! No funerals. He's still in the morgue. Get drunk. Yell. That's what he'd want."

The digger sets aside his shovel. The mourners with flashlights shine them on the seedling. The gate guardian cuts the can on each side with large wirecutters. Free of the metal, the tree is picked up, carried to the freshly dug hole. The digger and the gateman set it gently into the hole. The group moves forward to throw in their own handfuls of earth.

The Genius stands behind Jack and Max Mellecker.

"The poor and forgotten, the deniers and refusers, they die under the stars, in empty rooms, on the streets where no one knows their names."

Tall, almost emaciated, he peers at Mellecker and Jack, his eyes intense behind the horn-rimmed glasses. The black vest and checked shirt have been replaced by camouflage fatigues and paratrooper boots, a khaki military beret.

"Survival of the fittest," Jack laughs. "You live here with all those street people, Genius?"

"And the civil rights marchers, zero population and peace advocates, nuclear disarmers and sanctuary workers, feminists and refugees.

Greens and reds and browns and blacks. Anyone who needs and wants help to afflict the comfortable."

Jack looks at the group planting the evergreen memorial to a dead man named Rick, at the men and women going in and out of the old house and garage and two outbuildings. Young and old, ragged and neat, brisk and busy at past one in the morning.

"Christ, who foots the bill?"

"I own the house," the Genius says.

Jack nods to Mellecker. "Max said he heard you helped out street people, Torena got you stuff for them."

The Genius looks at Mellecker. "What *stuff*?"

"I don't know. Max says maybe food, like that, but I got to thinking you and Torena could be doing business down in Mexico and that's why he was killed. Maybe you know why he was killed, you can tell the cops it had nothing to do with my deal."

"Your deal, Price? No, I can't tell the police that, but I can show you what Torena helped us with."

The Genius leads them to the carriagehouse-garage. Inside, four men sit on packing boxes working on what looks like a large desktop computer all torn apart. They are all ages, all dressed differently, from one in jeans and a soiled cowboy hat to another in a worn business suit with tie still neatly knotted. There are other crates and boxes that do not contain

195

computers or parts. Jack and Mellecker both know Ak-47 rifles when they see them, boxes of curved ammunition clips.

"Torena got us whatever we needed," the Genius says.

Chapter Twenty-One

Cleaned, stitched, bandaged and shot for teta-
nus, I sat with Chavalas in Cottage Hospital
emergency waiting room while they finished
the paperwork on my health insurance.

"You never saw them? They were shooting at
Linero?"

"They were shooting at everyone."

The Sergeant had rescued me from a trip
down to Figueroa Street, waited while they
patched and strapped me up. Now he leaned
back on the plastic couch, let the steam from
his coffee rise warm into his nose. He looked
tired, had probably been off duty for hours,
worked on his own time.

"The record shows Brower's condo deal is

going down under the name of El Bosque Homes, Inc. President is John R. Price, vice-president S.A. Torena. Brower Management Corp. is the major stockholder, holds loans to El Bosque."

"Brower has no position in El Bosque? Is he a crook?"

There were only the two of us in the waiting room, the faint sound of water heating on the coffee machine. The dark TV, the creaking chair of the solitary nurse at the emergency desk. Each second moved on the clock with a slow, stiff click of the sweep hand. The theory of relativity. Time really slows at night.

"What are you asking? Has he been arrested, charged, convicted, served time? Has he broken laws, regulations? Has he cheated, tried to cheat, skated thin?" Chavalas inhaled the coffee instead of drinking. "He's never been charged with a felony, no. He's been arrested on code violations and contempt of court, yes. He's never been convicted of anything or served any time, no. He's cheated, paid fines, skated thin when it was necessary to turn a profit, yes. Is that being a crook or just a sharp operator?"

"How has he cheated, skated thin?"

"His car agency's had its license suspended. He's in court now for raising rent a hundred percent in his Isla Vista apartments for college students. Two years ago he was involved in a big mess in L.A."

"License suspended for what?"

"Selling used cars as new, misrepresenting year and model on cars, overcharging for license and transfer fees, selling cars that didn't meet state safety standards, failing to return downpayments when a deal fell through."

"What was the mess in L.A.?"

"A conspiracy to buy up houses being sold to pay delinquent tax assessments. It's supposed to be done at open public auction so the owners get at least a fair shake, but L.A. found more than fifty houses had been sold on the same day to the same names and all for less than three hundred bucks. The sharks got together, agreed not to bid against each other, literally stole the houses. Most of them from old people."

"Sweet."

"I talked to Brower after we got word on Torena. He doesn't have a clue, he says, why Torena was shot. All his business is in great shape. We're checking on the Nevada deal and the condos here. What he owes, where, what he stands to lose, insurance, everything. From what we hear El Bosque has a short-term note due on the condos deal and Brower's so tapped out in Nevada he's got to borrow more at real high interest to pay off. Should have more by morning."

The small hours of the night are like a stage set. Artificial, fixed, a sense of unreality. I checked on the progress of my paperwork.

There was only one nurse who had to fit the paperwork between checking on earlier emergencies. She finally handed me my copies. Chavalas stood to walk out ahead of me. I had a question.

"When did you find out about Torena's murder?"

"About nine-thirty. Sheriff's people called us."

"Who told the family? The wife?"

"We told the mother-in-law. The wife wasn't home."

Outside we walked to our cars. In the late night it was like moving under water. The corners of my eyes fluttered with fatigue held just inside consciousness.

Not even a dog moved on the side street of Ed Brower's office. Close to 2:00 A.M., the upstairs was dark now, but there was light again below. Brower's Rolls and an old Chevy wagon were parked in the lot. The door opened before I could ring.

"Come in, Dan."

Angela Price, in a red terrycloth robe two sizes too big for her, walked ahead of me to a leather Eames chair with a book open face down on the seat. The single light was a lamp behind the Eames. She had been reading, had gotten up in a hurry. An old-fashioned oak desk and filing cabinets were the only office items in what was a living room. Stairs behind the desk led up to the second floor. She sat in the Eames. I sat, looked at her robe, bare feet, loose hair.

"Jack upstairs?"

Her eyes were steady. The same controlled face without a smile. Somehow not as tall in the robe and bare feet, yet in a way larger, more imposing. Or maybe more intimidating. The large breasts loose, the slim body naked under the robe. The color of passion on the long, oval face, and in her large eyes.

I said, "Forget to tell me about this?"

"No."

"Didn't think I ought to know I was being hired to discover what you already knew but couldn't tell your husband?"

"No."

"Hired me to prove Brower was pulling some kind of con on your husband because you couldn't call down on your boyfriend."

"Brower isn't my boyfriend."

"What is he?"

"Something I wanted tonight. Someone who picked the right moment to call. A diversion I needed. A challenge. Curiosity. A postponement of tomorrow. The end of something." I was going to get the story. Not justification. The strength I had sensed in her from the start was too hard won for that. What had occurred, nothing more. "He's hit on me for years, even when we all worked for old Jens Spear. Tonight he called looking for Jack, He told me about you: some detective asking questions about Jack. You worried him. He doesn't know I hired you."

"What time?"

"Ten or so. I was on my way here when you came back to the house earlier."

"Jack wasn't there when he called, so he made you an offer."

"He was never a man to let an opportunity pass." She pulled the robe closer around her where she sat, her long legs up on the foot rest. "The first time he tried was on the way back from that trip to Chicago where Jack lost what chance he'd had with Jens Spear. I'd intrigued him that night on the town. My cool sexuality, the way I handled the whores as he put it. I was better, smarter and tougher than Jack, I understood more."

She looked for a cigarette in the voluminous pockets of the oversize robe, found none. "Back then, married only a few years, I was angry, insulted. Jack was my husband, his life was my life. He was much smarter than I was. I refused to listen to Brower then or any of the times after that. He always laughed, said I'd find out, he could wait. Over the years he changed his tactics, made it more into a kind of sexual game between us, but part of it's always been what does a sharp broad like me see in a loser like Jack when I could have him."

She looked toward the dark stairs.

"He's a compulsive womanizer. I've never run

into a man with power in our society who isn't.
Our public standards say they're not supposed
to, but the private rules almost expect it. For
men, of course, not for women. It's a reflex
with men like Brower. It's easy enough for a
woman to say no to."

"You said no. Until tonight."

She started to look for a cigarette again.
"He's had the apartment upstairs for twenty
years, probably can't even remember when
he didn't cheat on Carolyn. After a time you
wonder what's behind it. All that effort, all that
chasing, all that work and energy to get into a
woman. I suddenly wanted to know what all
that need and confidence had going for it."

"What does it have going for it?"

She managed a smile. "I haven't made up my
mind yet."

It was a different smile. Ironic, honest on
the face intended for smiling. As if tonight was
stripping everything from her except herself.
The learned needs and the acquired concerns,
the expected and the unnecessary, the proper
and the false.

"Why tonight, Angie?"

She thought about it for some time. "I began
to doubt my life with Jack years ago. For a long
time I was sure something had to be wrong
with me. I was miserable, suicidal. Even after
the kids came. Jack said they'd help, I thought
they would, but they didn't. I had to know what
was wrong. Went to classes to find something

I'd really like to do, took counseling, tried to
write the way I'd wanted to back in high school
even before college. None of it seemed to help,
and Jack hated it. He was doing his job, why
couldn't I stay home and do mine? I felt guilty.
We got to zero sexually. A year ago I started
going to other men. One night stands, two and
three day flings."

"But not Brower."

"He would have been too serious."

"The other men weren't serious?"

"Just fucking. A kind of therapy."

"Brower's not serious now? A therapeutic
fuck?"

When she smiled everything about her came
alive, from her eyes to the bare toes curled on
the foot rest under the edge of the oversized
robe. "A female who fucks around, talks about
it so casually, still shocks. Even you, Dan.
Female virtue, sweet chastity. Man's greatest
invention. A male stroke of genius to keep us
in our place, where and how he wants us. It
really never existed for women anymore than
for men, but that didn't suit what men wanted,
so they invented the jewel of female virtue. A
matter of property, exclusivity, disease, and
convenience."

"So Brower's a tranquillizer? To take your
mind off Jack? A coincidence he could be the
trouble?"

She stood, went into the kitchen, opened
drawers, found a carton of cigarettes. She lit

one, came back to the Eames. "He hadn't really moved on me for some time, tonight he did. Perhaps there was something in my voice. After all the men, I'd decided to try again with Jack. For the kids. For peace. Then this deal, what I sense is happening, hit me hard. He's somewhere risking all of us and everything we have, refusing to face it, lying to himself." The cigarette carved figures in the silence of the office. "I feel a change, a shift inside and outside. It's coming apart, or coming together. Tomorrow is too near or too far. I'm not ready, or it's already over. Maybe that's what Brower heard, why I suddenly wanted to know all about him."

We both heard the light switch at the top of the stairs, saw the stair light go on. Angela Price swivelled in the Eames chair to look at the stairs. I was already facing them. His footsteps came down, stopped. Ed Brower wore a twin of the robe Angela was swathed in. On him it fitted. He looked at each of us one at a time, then only at Angela.

"So you hired him," he said. "Does Jack know?"

Chapter Twenty-Two

"Someone should know what's going on," Angela Price said. Ed Brower looked at me. "That why you came here, Fortune? To know what was going on?" He laughed. There wasn't much humor in it. "Now you know, now you go. Unless you'd like to watch?"

"I've seen the movie. It's more the boardroom than the bedroom I came to talk about."

He opened a box on the lamp table. Cigarettes had been there all along. Angela Price wasn't that familiar with the layout of the place. Brower lit his cigarette, waved the match, didn't offer one to either of us. "The condo deal again? Angie must have put quite a bee in your bonnet." He looked at Angela. "The question is, where did she get such a stupid idea?"

From the moment Brower had appeared, Angela Price had pulled in her legs, curled them under her on the Eames chair, seemed to become smaller. Maybe it has to happen to every woman who's just had the man on her, in her, holding her. But the strength of her long face hadn't grown smaller.

"From watching you work over a lot of years," she said. "From watching and listening to Jack the last two months."

"Then you watched and listened wrong."

Ed Brower didn't like being crossed, wasn't used to being crossed. He sat on the couch, smoked, his other hand in the deep pocket of his robe, one bare foot tapping the hardwood floor, as if waiting like old Jens Spear himself for someone to remove the annoyance, set his smooth path back on track.

"The police tell me you have a much bigger deal going in Nevada," I said.

"Why do the police care what deals I have where?"

"The police care about two killings."

"Which has nothing to do with me."

"Santos Torena worked for you, was part of the condo deal."

"Torena was part of a hundred deals on his own. The bigshot of the *barrio*. You and the police both know that. If you don't, my lawyers will remind you tomorrow."

Chasing Eights

I knew an old New York cop who claimed he'd never needed a lie detector. All he did was look a suspect in the eyes when he asked questions, could always tell when the man was lying. He couldn't do that today on the higher levels. Some Englishman once said that an ambassador was an honest man sent abroad to lie for his country. Politicians, cabinet members and businessmen have now joined the diplomats, learned to lie so well and often almost no one can tell what is the truth and what is a lie.

"Is the Nevada deal through a front, too?"

"What the hell does that mean?"

"It means the condo deal is."

"The Nevada deal is complicated, the condo deal here is relatively simple. I can't handle everything on my own. That's bad business. You have to know how to delegate."

"To men who have fulltime jobs working for you?"

"I said it was a simple deal."

"Especially if they don't actually do anything."

Angela Price said, "What men are we talking about, Dan?"

"Jack and Santos Torena. Jack is president of the official corporation making the condo deal, Torena was vice-president. Brower doesn't actually appear in the corporation at all."

"You mean he doesn't make any money?"

Brower's laugh had humor this time.

"He kept the real ownership, Angie."

"But made Jack president? That would have done it, made Jack put everything we had in it and more."

"We all put money into the deal, Angie. That's how business works. That's how you get rich. You'd like to be rich, right?"

"They do the work, and you make the money."

"The name of the game," I said.

Brower said, "It's a game that makes us all rich. I risk the most, I get the most."

"Except that your share of the *get* is more than your share of the *risk*, you keep getting long after the risking is over, and it's a long way from making us all rich."

"No one said life was fair. Some win, some lose."

"And Ed Brower makes sure he's one of the winners," Angela Price said. "Nothing personal, he'd do it to anyone, an equal opportunity shark. All legitimate, right, Ed? Get yours, to hell with anyone else, especially the poor and weak."

"What else should I do?" Brower said. "I'm not in business to lose, and if the poor want to live like us, the men better start working harder, and the women better start using corks."

"Now why didn't we all think of that before?" Angela Price said. "You're a man of such sensitivity, Ed."

"You want sensitivity, go back to Jack."

"He doesn't have that much either."

Brower said, "I've never found a woman yet who really wants sensitivity in a man when her backside hits the bed. Or when she's out to get a man to put her backside in the bed. Or when she's after a man to take care of her and bring home the bucks so she'll put her backside in the bed."

"Maybe that's why you never found a woman to stay with."

Brower spread his arms as if nailed to a cross. "I'm afraid I wasn't intended to be the good husband and all that. Now Jack, he's the backbone of the nation. Hardworking, faithful, a family man. Community leader, backyard barbecues, paint the house and mow the lawn. Sometimes I envy him, I really do. I simply never was able to be that. A weakness in me, I suppose.

"What horseshit. You're exactly what you want to be, proud as a peacock of every deal, dollar, and dame."

He brought his arms down from the cross. "Am I?"

"Women or a deal, it's all the same to you, Ed. Something to have, own, win. From Adam to Ghengis Khan to Ed Brower."

"Then I'm in good company, and maybe it's just the way life is. Have you thought of that?"

"If I thought that, I'd take sleeping pills."

"Because human beings aren't what you want them to be? Or think you want them to be. You came here tonight, maybe you like what I am more than you admit."

For the moment they had forgotten I was there. In a silence inside and outside the muted elegance of the office that was more like the fine Spanish colonial home it had once been, they faced each other across more than the space from Eames chair to couch.

"You never wanted me, Ed, you wanted Jack's wife. That's why I hired Dan. Fucking a woman and winning in business are the same thing. Fuck her and him. That's what worries me about your condo deal. Business or sex, you'll use anyone you can to get what you want."

He didn't laugh, but he did smile. Humorless again. He leaned to put out the stub of his cigarette in an ashtray on the lamp table, folded his hands on the lap of the robe. The sex might have changed their relationship for him, but it had not changed anything for her.

"No, I only fucked you. I like Jack. He's a good man, I'm going to make him rich. You'll like that part. When this deal goes through I'm going to sell Jack the agency. You'll be a *grande dame* in this town, the elite. All Jack needed was an opportunity and some help. I'll do what you never did for him."

"By cucolding him?"

Now he did laugh. "That's an old-fashioned word for a fine liberated lady like you. I don't think that would worry Jack too much, and I have the feeling this is a one-night thing for both of us." He stood. "Now I'm going back to bed. Come up if you feel like it, we can finish it in style, eh? You're wrong about me and Jack, and tomorrow we can all get back to normal."

He nodded to me, bent to give Angie a light kiss in passing, and walked up the stairs. The light on the stairs went out. The whole house became as silent as the city in the late night. We both looked at the darkened stairs for a time. The sound of movement upstairs quickly faded into silence. Brower wasn't acting as if he had worries on his mind, or anything important to do the rest of the night.

"You want me to go on looking?"

She had swivelled in the Eames chair to face the darkened stairs, sat with her back to me, her head tilted in speculation as if imagining herself up there. Her long connection with Brower had not changed, in bed or out, but something inside her had changed, was still changing.

"Why did you really come here tonight, Angie?"

She spoke to the stairs, "I didn't want to wait for Jack. I didn't want him to come home, and I didn't want him not to come home. I wanted to know what was happening, and I didn't want to know what was happening. I hired you to find out what Jack was doing, but it wouldn't really change anything. I hired you so I could pretend that what happened to Jack would make a difference, but I don't think it will anymore." She swivelled in the Eames and faced me. "If Jack

213

didn't matter, why not try a man who wanted me and could be interesting."

"Was it interesting?"

"Not very. Most of them weren't very interesting after the need wore off. Brower doesn't care if he's interesting to women, only that they fill his needs. He's a man of property. It's all power and acquisition. The baronial viewpoint."

"What was your viewpoint?"

"Pretty much the same, I suppose. The female version. The baroness asserting herself, bestowing a favor."

In the soft leather of the Eames she leaned back, stretched her long legs out on the foot rest. As she did, she hesitated, pulled the robe over her bare legs. It was an unconscious but nice gesture. For that brief moment I was a person, a man, even if it passed and she put her head back with her eyes closed and the weight of the small hours heavy on both of us.

"We married in college back in Minnesota. Small town kids in the big time. A seat of learning, the Big Ten itself. Jack loved it. The frat parties, the beer busts, the pep rallies, the bull sessions. His father was a lawyer, had a position in the state. Mine was a foreman at International Harvester. I was a tall, unconfident girl with vague ambitions to be a writer, a creator of literature. I'd worked on the high school newspaper, so I studied journalism and worked on the university daily. I never felt secure at the university, got poor grades, had few friends.

Jack had position on campus. He was pre-law, all his friends knew exactly what they wanted. They knew they were going to be big in law and business, had the wildest parties and still got the best grades. I was so happy when he pinned me our junior year. I knew I wanted him and what we were going to become.

"We married the day after graduation. Jack decided to skip law school, a married man had real responsibilities. He applied for jobs in management all over the country. He got one in Tulsa working for a big oil company who wanted a trainee with a pre-law background. I got a job on the local newspaper. We were there a year. I loved it. I was writing, I had my own work, my own ambitions. I was feature editor when Jack got the offer from Spear and we moved here."

Her eyes were open, but she was in a late-night trance, saw and heard nothing outside herself. "I cried a lot in those days, I was nothing at Spear, less after Jack was let go and I couldn't get any writing job. So I stayed home, kept house, entertained new friends who could help Jack's career, took clerical and secretarial work when we needed money. It was all I could get in this town. Jack quit jobs, seemed to get nowhere. Our sex life went to once a month, then once every two months, but at parties he still talked about sex all the time."

She listened to a stray car out in the small hours. It passed into the silence. "After a while he said maybe it was me working, him not getting recognition that was turning him off. Maybe some kids would help. We'd always said we wanted kids. He said kids would bring the excitement back. So we had the children. All it did was make it worse. I was tired all the time, the kids drove him crazy, he worked late to stay away from the house. I was nearly out of my mind, really came close to suicide. That was when I had my first revelation. Jack didn't care about kids, they were part of the package. *Kinder, kir, kuchen.* He'd never like me to work unless we really needed money. He never liked me going to classes. He hated my writing. He hated me to be anything outside the family. Standard male chauvinism."

In the empty silence of the office and the city, the hours heavy and thin at the same time, her voice had mesmerized me like great music that draws you into its world beyond.

"He'd taken my identity, my ambition, my potential. It was all clear, and it broke me loose. I took classes *I* wanted: writing, psychology, sociology. I went to writers conferences, wrote a novel. It wasn't good enough, but at least I'd done it, and the one I'm working on now will be better, and the one after that. I started to look at other men and they looked at me. I jogged, exercised, lost weight. I dressed better, and soon I had no trouble at all seducing any man I wanted. I learned my power, my potential, my identity."

Upstairs Brower coughed. She came out of the trance, looked at the stairs.

"He may use Jack, but not me. Maybe that's why I came here tonight, to show him I'm not Jack." She looked at me. "I want you to go on. I'm even more sure he's up to something with Jack, conning him, and I won't go down with him."

I stood.

"You'll go home?"

"I don't know yet."

"Brower doesn't act like a man with a problem."

"That worries me even more," she said.

Chapter Twenty-Three

The four men on the boxes around the disassembled computer watch Jack Price and Mellecker. The Genius sits, leans toward them almost like a question mark. "Santos got what we needed. Guns, food, ammunition, parts. His own money. He believed with us."

Jack Price says, "What are you, for Christ sake? Bank robbers? Hit men?"

"Believed with you?" Max Mellecker says.

"No-sayers," the Genius sweeps his long arm to encompass the garage and the four men working on the computer. "*Refuseniks*, dissidents, the other side of the coin."

The man in the worn business suit and tie worked on a disk drive. "They have somethin' to do with Santos getting killed, Stan?"

"What do you say, Price?" the Genius says. "You have anything to do with Santos being murdered?"

The four men seated on the boxes in the harsh garage light are like the judges of a grim tribunal, a kangaroo court in some prison camp movie, the inquisitors of an underground army, a Mafia council.

Jack protests. "I don't know anything about what happened to Torena. I got shot at myself. Ask Max. This private eye Fortune came . . ." And he told them about the *coyotes* and the ambush in front of Max Mellecker's house.

"A private detective?" This is the burly one in the hat who scowls at Jack and Mellecker.

"Working for who?" the youngest one says. He wears a beret and camouflage uniform too. Except that his are stained and faded, with lighter spots where unit patches and rank have been.

"How do I know?" Jack says. "Maybe he's after you. I mean, those guns and all, the street people—"

"We got fucking work to do," the fourth man says. Fat and young, he hasn't looked at Jack or Mellecker since they came into the garage, and his head twitches as he scowls at the Genius. The Genius motions abruptly, turns to the door. Jack and Mellecker follow him out.

Jack says, "What do you do with guns?"

"What did you come here for?" the Genius says. "Talk or somewhere quiet?"

"I don't know," Jack says. "Both, I guess.

The Genius starts a brisk circle around the courtyard, points behind them at the dark second floor apartment of the garage. "Couples get to sleep up there. Families on the street with no place to go. Most of them have skills and trades we can use and we get them jobs too. The single guys and women stay in the outbuildings or under the trees. At least its safe in here."

Max Mellecker says, "Torena could have been killed because of the work he did for you."

"It's possible," the Genius nods. "If you're outside, those inside don't want you around. Especially those in power."

As they circle the dark courtyard, Jack stares at the shapes sprawled on the ground under the trees and against the two outbuildings. At those who sit drinking. At those who read by the light of flashlights. At those who talk aloud in the night.

"What happens to them? I mean, how do they get like this? No homes, no families, nothing to do."

"Who says they have nothing to do, Price? Who says they don't have families? They're each others' families."

Mellecker says, "Do the police know about those guns?"

"The police don't worry about retired electronic geniuses who own their own home and play poker every day. Trouble on the rich upper east? Bite your tongue."

"Smuggling automatic weapons interests most police."

"Probably," the Genius agrees.

"Undercover police. Border patrol."

"That could always be, I suppose."

The Genius has walked them all around the courtyard back to the house. The only light now comes from the garage and first floor. Inside, beyond the entry hall is a large living room where people sleep, write, read, smoke and fill the house with the pungency of marijuana. They walk through two smaller rooms where more people read, sleep and work. Jack walks like a man on a guided tour of Hell. Confused and unbelieving.

"You can flop here. The kitchen's through that door if you're hungry or thirsty. Me, I need a beer."

It is a library at the rear of the house. There are armchairs, two couches, a coffee table, a TV set turned on to a late night movie, stacks of a small newspaper.

"You have an extra beer?" Mellecker says.

Jack picks up one of the newspapers, turns the small pages that look like a miniature *National Enquirer*.

THE NATIONAL ACCUSER
Voice Of The Other Side In America

Chasing Eights

ADM. RICKOVER: WORLD WILL
DESTROY ITSELF, SEES
CORPORATE THREAT

In his final testimony before Congress, the late Adm. Hyman Rickover, pioneer of the modern nuclear navy, said that the power of corporations is excessive, the world will probably destroy itself in a nuclear war.

He said both nuclear weapons and nuclear power should be outlawed, because history shows that nations use whatever weapons are available to them. "I think we'll probably destroy ourselves. I'm not proud of the part I played."

In saying that large corporations are a potential threat to American society, he added, "Through control of vast resources, large corporations have become, in effect, another branch of government, but without the checks and balances inherent in our democratic system. Defense contractor lobbyists, for example, have generally learned how to get around laws and regulations.

"Political and economic power is increasingly concentrated among a few large corporations and their officers—power they can apply against society, government and individuals."

HOMO SAPIENS AMERICANUS

Letter in TV Guide: If we get involved in a nuclear war, would electromagnetic pulses from exploding bombs damage my videotapes?

HEROIC HASHISH

Hashish carrying the insignia of Afghan freedom fighters, and stamped "Smoke Russia Away," has started to show up in the San Francisco Bay area.

Jack holds the small newspaper in disbelief. "What the hell is this thing?"

"A voice in the wilderness," the Genius says. "Call it a try for sanity."

Jack stares at the paper. "What do you do with it? Who reads it?"

"It's an underground newspaper," Max Mellecker says. "They hand it out at civil rights rallies, peace marches, nuclear protests."

Jack reads the thin newspaper as if numb. "But where do they get this crap?"

"No problem," the Genius says. "We clip it all from your own newspapers, magazines, flyers, newsletters. It's there, but no one really looks. So we put it together for everyone to see."

"For Christ sake why?"

"Because we live in a fundamentally sick, irrational system that controls everything we do and corrupts human potentiality. Because we want to change that."

"With guns?" Max Mellecker says.

"If that's what it takes, yes."

"Guns?" Jack says. "Then maybe Torena *was* killed by—"

224

"Someone's got to do something." the Genius says, drains his beer. "You want to know what we're doing? Besides running a haven for those who refuse to accept this system and printing a satiric newspaper? Okay, come and see."

The Genius walks out through the kitchen to the back door. Mellecker finishes his beer, follows. Jack takes his beer with him as they go out into the rear yard hidden from all sides by thick growth and trees.

In the pale light of the low moon, the Genius stands in the center of the yard beside what look like six or seven canvas covered statues. The Genius pulls the canvas down on one. Jack and Max Mellecker see a long tube set on a tripod stand with a smaller tube and eye-piece on top of it, all angled up into the night sky above the yard.

"What the hell is it?" Jack says.

Mellecker hits the long tube with his knuckle. It rings metallic. "It's some kind of launcher. For rockets, shells. Like a big bazooka, a recoilless cannon."

"A missile launcher, to be exact." the Genius nods. "A lot like a Stinger missile, about the same size, but my own design."

"Missiles?" Jack wonders.

The Genius's eyes shine in the night. "It so happens that this house is located directly under the flight pattern of the President's helicopter on its way from Port Hueneme to his ranch. With seven launchers, we can hit every chopper in his party, make sure we get him."

Jack and Max Mellecker stand there and look at the silent tubes that point up into the dark night sky.

"The President?" Mellecker says, "You mean Ronnie Reagan? He's out of office. He won't be flying to the ranch."

The Genius smiles. "They're shoulder-fired like the Stinger. We can take them anywhere."

Chapter Twenty-Four

Friday night must come to an end even in Isla Vista. Students must sleep, street people roll in their blankets under the bushes. Near 3:00 A.M. I drove the deserted streets. The retail stores and bookstores were closed, the movie houses dark, the bars locked. Only the last revellers, the solitary homeless, still walked in slow groups and pairs. The drinkers and the wanderers, the lost and restless. The people of the night.

Claire Broberg lived in a small house on Camino Corto on the western edge of Isla Vista. It was my last grasp at a straw to find Jack Price directly, or a good reason for him to be away from home. At least a reason his wife and I would understand. Maybe one the police would. There was light in the house.

"He's not here, Fortune. I'm watching a movie. Friday gets lonely sometimes."

"Has he been?"

"No." She held her white robe tight over her breasts in the open doorway, did not invite me in. "You never found him?"

"Found him and lost him." I told her— the *coyotes* and the attack outside Mellecker's house, the abandoned Jaguar.

"They're together? Jack and Max? What about Brower?"

"As far as I know he's cosy in his bed. If Jack shows up, tell him to go to the police."

Her head nodded as she closed the door, agreed. Her eyes didn't. If Jack Price showed up, it was the last thing she was going to tell him to do.

They waited near my car.

Two of them.

I ran.

One moment the dark street of parked cars, low fences, lawns and small houses was empty and motionless in the night. The next they were there. A tall one. A broader one in a suit. Without haste or urgency, as certain as tigers in a jungle.

The only sound their heavy feet. Their hard breathing.

My feet on the cement.

My breathing, the gulps of air.

Chasing Eights

Salt air.

The beach.

A black sea with the moon gone.

Heavy behind me, their running was out of rhythm. The tall one in the lead breathed ragged, sucked air. The broad one ran slower and steadier farther back.

Running violence.

Hard, breathless, determined, and silent.

They played no games, the silent chase was no contest. There would be no handshake for the loser.

I saw the dark grounds of a school ahead. Trees, bushes, underbrush.

Among the trees the running behind became ragged, gulped air, fell back.

I ran through the trees until the only close sound in the night was surf on the deserted beach somewhere to the left.

I listened. Somewhere there was labored breathing. The violent curse of a gasping voice. A lower voice. Fast walking and slow running. Aimless. South and west.

I walked north. Listened every fifty feet.

The breathing more distant, then nothing.

I walked faster through rear yards, across Camino Majorca. To Camino Lindo. Camino Corto. Listened in the dark corner of a yard and looked to where my Tempo stood like a staked goat outside the low fence.

If I waited, the tigers would return sooner or later. Every second brought them closer. I stepped out of the dark and walked fast to the fence and over to the car. My stomach knotted, my neck crawled, my lone hand sweated in the chill of the late night sea wind. But I went, climbed, stood at my car.

Got in, started, drove away.

My back felt as it had those long years ago on all the old buckets I sailed through the submarine zones. El Colegio Road and Storke Road were both empty. Two cars waited at the light on Hollister. The taillights of a single trailer truck led me on the hypnotic freeway back into the night city. I pulled off at Anacapa, drove to East Beach, and parked in the shadow of the palms on broad, deserted Cabrillo Boulevard.

I lit a cigarette from my emergency pack in the glove compartment, sat behind the wheel and looked at the dark ocean. I breathed slowly, let the fear shiver out like a held breath. I wondered what I was doing out in the night. I wondered who the two men were. They had wanted to kill me, that much I knew, but I didn't know why or for whom. If they really knew who I was or thought I was something I wasn't. Were they for Jack Price or against him? For Ed Brower, the Genius, Santos Torena?

The shivering stopped. The cigarette ended. I started the car, drove to the *barrio*.

Milpas Street looked like any desert town in New Mexico. Long rows of street lights and traffic lights and not a soul in sight. The side streets of the *barrio* twice as dark and just as empty. But the brick house behind the wrought iron fence also showed light. No one was sleeping tonight.

The light was in the living room and kitchen, but the voice came from the far end of the dark porch. The mother-in-law, Inez Ortega, watched me from a brightly striped hammock of the kind Indian villagers made in Central American countries. In the same dark pants and light blouse she'd worn earlier.

"You have not found your Price, mister private detective?"

She wasn't alone. So motionless I almost missed seeing him at all, an old man sat in a painted wooden chair against the brick balustrade of the porch. Hawk-nosed, his white mustache drooped long on his dark face. White hair and a wide-brimmed sombrero, its woven cord under his bony chin, he wore a loose white overshirt, white cotton pants tucked into high black boots.

"Francesca found him," I said. "Is she here?"

"No one is at home but me. I felt the need of light."

"You're up late. Waiting for someone?"

"Old Indian women don't sleep much."

"You're not that old, and not that Indian, Mrs. Ortega. Not you or Francesca or Torena."

The old man's eyes reflected the light from inside the house as they moved without his head turning. "What do you know of Indians, *ladino*?"

"I know they aren't born in Anglo cities," I said. "What do you know, *señor*?"

His whole head turned toward me. "Indians are born in the forest and in the mountains, in the earth and in the tall grass. The river is their brother. The river watches, the forest hears, the thunder speaks. The tree bleeds when it is burned. The Indian does not turn his brother into a *burro*. He does not live without a tree in a forest of stone."

"He's an old man," Inez Ortega said. "He's drunk."

The bottle was at the old man's feet.

"Santos Torena was no Indian?" I asked him.

"He is *ladino*. A burner of trees. He lives on the blood of his brothers, as the soldiers and *bandidos* in my country."

Inez Ortega said, "What does an old Mexican know?"

I saw the bottle beside the hammock, too. Both bottles were almost empty, an exotic bird on the labels, tequila or Mezcal.

"He's not Mexican. Guatemalan, the way he uses *ladino* to mean a Europeanized Indian."

"How do you know how a Guatemalan uses *ladino*?"

"If you travel and listen you sometimes learn."

She nodded as if surprised I had said something intelligent, "His granddaughter is married to a *chicano*. He's been here thirty years. An educated village chief in Guatemala, he's never left his jungle behind."

"The forest is home," the old man said. "Here is prison."

They were in that stage when they had passed through drunk and come out numb. Coherent and lucid, but not quite aware of where they were or what they were doing. Inez Ortega had lost a son-in-law, her grandchildren's father, her daughter's man, and was waiting for something. She couldn't sleep and had not wanted to wait alone. The old man was a good neighbor, even if he had never learned to live where trees did not feel or rivers see.

"They come here and lose the earth," the old man said. "They come to escape the walls in our poor countries, find the invisible walls here. They want to be what they cannot."

Inez Ortega shook her head. "My father, my husband, Santos. It's a hunger in them. They want to live on the other side of the wall."

"Torena wanted to live on the other side of the wall?"

The old man made a noise.

"He was as good as any *gringo*, better than most," Inez Ortega said. "All the time he said that."

"A *ladino*," the old man said.

I described the two men who had chased me. "You know them?"

"No."

"I described the *coyote*.

"Paz Linero," she said.

"Is Francesca out looking for Linero?"

"A woman is the fire," the old man said. "A woman waits."

Most of us believe what we are born to, accept what we find. There had been times when the women of the Indians were as fierce and violent as the men. Times when women ruled and men waited. But in the old man's time a woman waited, so all women must at all times, past and present and future, wait.

Inez Ortega said, "My daughter is a new woman. My daughter doesn't look at the floor, fold her hands. She will find them."

"Linero?"

"Whoever."

"Is there someone else?"

The old man said, "Santos is afraid. I see it in his eyes. He makes big noise at his children, at his woman. He has listened to the voices of the thunder."

I said to Inez Ortega, "Torena was upset, scared? When?"

"Today."

"You mean yesterday? Before he called Jack Price?"

I heard the step inside the house. Francesca Torena stood in the living room, slim in dirty jeans. A red man's shirt, a striped wool poncho against the night chill, and a gun.

Chapter Twenty-Five

"It took us too long to get the launchers ready." The Genius shakes his head, leans back in his chair. "I got the idea when I saw the helicopters while we were on a protest march up to his million-dollar ranch."

"You're crazy," Jack Price says.

The Genius stares up at the ceiling. "Why do we want out leaders to be rich? Because from the beginning we had to think the chief of the tribe was better. The chief had to have more shells, or feathers, or skins. Had to be a better killer of animals and enemies. The only way we know we have the right man up top is if he's got more feathers."

"You're kidding, right?" Jack says. "About

shooting down the President?"

"I knew I could build the launcher and the missile. The only problem was to find out which helicopter the bastard was in. Then it hit me—shoot them all down."

Jack laughs. "You know you are crazy, Genius."

"Someone has to start." He leans forward over his beer. "For forty years the corporate capitalist war hawks have propped up their irrational system with the cold war. The Soviets were never a real threat, had more to fear from us than we from them. Truman and Churchill created the whole fear syndrome hoax so that massive military spending would support the profit system."

Jack says, "Everyone knows the Soviets want to bury us. They even said it, for God's sake."

"Government subsidies as big as mountains, the lifeblood of private enterprise. Without trillions of tax dollars and World War Two the profit system would have died. We've sacrificed our people for the benefit of the few. We gave up housing, social services, schools, medical and mental health care, parks, and real human freedom. What we got is a nation run by the rich where the gap between rich and poor widens every day."

Mellecker says, "You think killing a president's going to change all that?"

"No, but it might get their attention."

"It'd get you the gas chamber," Jack says.

"Shit, Price. Some things are more important than a brief life of sucking your thumb and sticking it up your ass." He is up, paces like a violent scarecrow in the back room of the big house. "Look at the world you live in. They find that aspirin could maybe, just maybe, make a kid with flu or chicken pox more susceptible to Reyes Syndrome. That could kill a kid, so they want to put on a warning label. What do the aspirin tycoons do? Do they say one possible dead kid is one too many, sure we'll put on the label? Hell no. They fight all the way—the studies are inconclusive! A label might cut sales, lower profits, and we can't have that, can we?"

"A lot of money and jobs in aspirin," Mellecker says.

The Genius waves his skinny arms. "Each year more families drop below the poverty line, and what do our businessmen think up? Drive-up windows at funeral parlors so the affluent can pay their respects without getting out of the car, get home in time to watch their favorite TV show and think about nothing."

Jack Price is tired and a shade drunk from all the beers, and he doesn't know what the Genius and Mellecker are talking about. He doesn't believe all the stuff about shooting down Ronald Reagan, but he can tell that the Genius is a bleeding-heart liberal and Max seems to be agreeing with him.

"Someone has to do something," the Genius

raves. "Control over how and what we think increases every year. The whole world is being turned into morons. We don't run for office, we buy office like English lords in the eighteenth century. Candidates don't have advisers on the issues, they have marketing experts and media consultants. They don't have personalities, they have TV images. Their real views are hidden. They talk about subjects irrelevant to any issues. We don't have a government, we have a sitcom, a circus, a TV talk show. They don't educate the people, they entertain them."

"Shoot down Reagan, that's all you'd be doing too," Max Mellecker says. "The news is just another sitcom."

Jack says, "If you guys are going to talk about all this heavy stuff, I need another beer."

And he laughs. Jack has always laughed whenever anyone says something he doesn't understand or care about. Politics is not something he cares about. He is too busy on his own business to worry about what they do in Washington. When he returns from the kitchen with his beer, he sees they have been talking about him.

"You're sure you don't know why Santos was shot, Price?" the Genius says.

"I told you I don't know anything about what Torena did outside his job for Brower."

"Brower is what we're talking about."

"Something's wrong with the condo deal," Mellecker says.

"The only thing wrong is you didn't get in on it!"

The Genius sits down again, shakes his head. "You don't want to know, do you, Price? You don't want to know what I'm telling you about the world you live in. You don't want to hear the deck is stacked against you; very few win happiness in a race. You don't want to know why you lose at poker."

"I win more than I lose," Jack says.

"No you don't. You just think you do."

The hours and the tension have gotten to Jack. He feels strung out and bone weary and knows he isn't thinking straight. What is Max doing agreeing with the Genius and his crackpot ideas. If it looks like a crackpot, acts like a crackpot, talks like a crackpot, it damn well must be a crackpot. Okay, the Genius is a better poker player, but not that much better, and Jack can beat Max and the others every time.

"Somebody's getting conned around here, and it isn't me," Jack says, looks at Mellecker. "This nut says he wants to shoot down the President, and he's got you sounding like him."

In the chair the Genius considers Jack. "Sometimes, Price, a man has to act to change events, to have a say in what happens to him and his world. That doesn't make him either crazy or villainous except to those who want it all to stay the same."

"Shit," Jack says, gulps his beer. "If it's not crazy to go around talking about blowing up the

239

President, it sure as hell is when the President's not even President anymore! You're so nutty you couldn't get your act together until your whole plan went down the tubes, for Christ sake! And you talk about me not knowing what's going on."

The Genius smiles. "Presidents come and go. Perhaps Reagan will come back to the ranch alone, make it easier for us, or we could go up to Maine and have a shot at Bush. It doesn't matter. It's not the result that counts, it's doing something, making an alternate society. Our own sane world, not the insane one we were born in. It's taking charge of fate, living our own lives."

"Who would care?" Mellecker says. "Who'd even know?"

"We'd know," the Genius says.

"You blow up the President, people are going to know and they'll sure as hell care," Jack says. "Jesus, you really are off to the nut farm, both of you."

The Genius suddenly stands up, arches his beer can like a basketball shot into a waste-basket, and laughs. "But no gas chamber, Price. The booby hatch. After maybe ten years I'm out. Meanwhile I make a bundle. A contract for my memoirs. A movie. The Genius on the Johnny Carson Show. Contracts for the rights to the T-shirts, the car dolls, the posters, my picture on a poker deck. There's always a hundred angles, right?"

The bearded gate guardian appears in the kitchen doorway.

"Two guys outside. They got guns."

"You sure?"

The gate man nods. "They could be cops, or even Feds."

"All right," the Genius says. "Keep an eye on them, and you two better go out the back way in case it's you they want."

"They don't want me," Jack says.

The Genius doesn't bother to answer, motions for them to follow him.

Chapter Twenty-Six

The .357 Magnum was too big for both of Francesca Torena's small hands, but she held it steady on my belly. She looked past me to her mother in the hammock.

"What did you tell him?"

"Nothing," Inez Ortega said.

The old man said, "I told him a woman waits. A woman does not go hunting in the jungle with a gun."

"It's a different jungle, Don Umberto. And it's time for an old man to be in bed."

The old man, Don Umberto, stood with as much dignity as he could with almost a bottle of Mezcal inside him. It was better than I

could have done. He even bowed to Francesca
Torena.

"I have told him your husband was a man
afraid who heard the voices in the night. Your
mother she tells him you will find who has
killed your husband." He walked to the steps
down from the porch. Very straight, very dig-
nified, only a shade shaky and holding to the
brick balustrade. "Your husband was a *ladino*, a man who burns trees, pisses in his own
river."

He faded slowly away into the night of the
barrio that had movement and voices even at
3:00 A.M. Francesca Torena watched him go,
shook her head to her mother.

"You couldn't go to bed, stay off the bottle
tonight?"

"We told the detective nothing he didn't
know."

"That's what they make you think. He's not
even a real cop, he doesn't even have to pretend to be fair or honest or hide what lies he
tells us."

I said, "You sound like you don't have a very
high opinion of our police, Mrs. Torena."

She still held the .357 firm and steady if no
longer right at my belly. "Police, courts, judges,
lawyers, social workers, politicians and private
detectives."

"What do you know about private detectives?"

She sat in the chair of the old man. "You

have a name, mister private detective. Remind me, I forget."

"Dan Fortune."

"Fortune. Good fortune, or bad fortune? No, you're white and Anglo, that is always good fortune in this country. A WASP."

"Fortunowski," I said. "Not WASP."

She shrugged. "You could change it and pass. What do Santos and I change it to? Ravelli? Papagopolous? Say we are Spanish, pure Castilian? Pass for Puerto Rican? Cuban?"

"Any of those could be American," I said.

"None of them are really American. I know, I'm fifth generation on my mother's side. A lot more American than you, but it doesn't count. Not unless we're rich, educated, with power, and even then we can never be really sure."

"You've had some bad experiences with the wrong people."

"When you are poor, uneducated, speak the wrong language and have the wrong color you have bad experiences with all people. Today I have had a very bad experience."

"Is that why you're looking for Santos's murderer yourself? Or maybe there's another reason."

She rested the .357 on her lap, reached her hand out to her mother. Inez Ortega gave her a cigarette, lit it. Francesca Torena sat back in the chair on the dark porch, only the kitchen light still on through the windows. "Twenty years ago Inez and my father had the same dream Santos had. They were going to own a house, two cars, life insurance, send me to college. Like Anglos, real Americans. It would all happen because of a land deal they'd invested their savings in. Sound familiar?"

"Ever since the snake oil pitchman."

"Only this time there's a twist. It turned out to be the largest land fraud scheme in California history, people went to jail, the judge in the civil suit filed a notice of intended judgment that would have given the sixty-four people swindled two and a half million dollars in actual and punitive damages. My parents were the smallest investors, but it would have tripled what they invested—almost as much as the company had promised."

Somewhere near a TV talked to a *barrio* dweller who couldn't sleep.

"The case had taken ten years, the company would appeal. It meant five more years at least. Other delays were possible, the judge's award could be reduced, the other investors were old, my parents needed their savings, so they all settled for far less than the judge had said. No house, no cars, no college. It happens all the time, the rule not the exception. The whole system is set up to protect business, favor the rich, and that means Anglos. You wonder why I don't love our legal system?"

"People went to jail. Why no faith in the cops?"

"The police work for those who pay them."

"They sent those rich businessmen to jail."

"Small ones. And the Federal government put them in jail. One dead Latino isn't important to the Federal government."

"How about two dead Latinos? Or isn't the second important to you?" I said. "You shot him. Vicario Silva. You were in the house when Linero and his men came. They threatened you or your mother. You got one of your husband's guns, shot the first one to reach the steps. Linero and the other one ran."

In the tight jeans, red shirt, the bright-colored poncho against the cold, she looked like a teenager. Her face as smooth and untouched as a teen. The wrinkles and scars were in her eyes.

"You went out the way you just came in. The back way. You worked out your timetable. You went to your cousin, cooked up the cover story with him, then drove back here after you knew the police were here. News of the police moves fast in the *barrio*."

Inez Ortega said, "She got home after the police. We don't know who shot that animal."

"Never mind, mother. Why would Paz Linero and his *mules* want to threaten me, Mr. Fortune?"

She knew I was trying to get her talking, make her say what would help me, confirm my guesses. She was doing the same thing, telling me nothing, listening for what might help her.

"Maybe for the same reason they killed your husband."

247

Her hand rested on the .357. "Why would they kill Santos?"

"He worked with them. Maybe he double-crossed them. Maybe he tried to deal on his own. You'd know more than I would."

"I don't know anything about Paz Linero's business. Perhaps you have more than 'maybe' to make you think he killed Santos?"

"Maybe the same reason you have."

"I haven't said that Linero killed Santos."

"You're looking for him. Or you were. With that cannon in your purse."

She smiled. She was a beautiful woman. A woman, not a girl no matter how young she looked. "You found your client. Does he know who killed my husband?"

"Jack Price isn't my client, but I found him. Then I lost him." I gave her a brief sketch of the meeting with Jack Price, Paz Linero and his *mule*, and the unknown bushwhackers.

"Did they want to shoot Linero or your Mr. Price?"

"Hard to say. Maybe just me, maybe all of us."

She thought about that. It was the first thing I'd said that seemed to really interest her. It interested me too. Had they been attacking Jack Price, or protecting him?

"But you never saw them?"

"I never did. But I saw two other men." I described the two hard-breathing pursuers out in Isla Vista. "Know them?"

"No." She almost stroked the big .357.

"Did Linero see you find your husband dead, Mrs. Torena? Out there at the poker game? The way he saw me?"

In the hammock, the mother looked afraid for the first time. Francesca Torena didn't.

"You were there, Mr. Fortune?"

"Around five or so. Just after dark. That's when I saw Paz Linero, and so did you. And he saw you. That's why he came here after you. If he killed Santos or not, you could place him at a murder. He wouldn't like that, would want to at least persuade you not to talk about it. I might have shot first too."

The big pistol lay quiet on her legs. "You dreamed one of Don Umberto's fantasies, Mr. Fortune. I was in my office, or out on business, all day until you saw me come home."

"No, you knew your husband was dead when we first talked to you. The way you acted, I should have realized that. Angry not scared. Then you found Jack Price at his agency, knew Santos was dead before the police called you officially. You had to have been out there, seen Linero. You were sure he'd killed Santos. When they came to the house, Vicario Silva pulled a knife on you, you were scared and shot him."

"You don't think Paz killed Santos?"

"Linero sounds and acts like a man who wants to find out something. As if he doesn't know who killed Santos or why and that worries him."

She thought about that. "He'd want to know."

"Would want to talk to you about it. And anyone else Santos maybe worked with." I watched her. "Like the Genius."

She shrugged. "I never met Mr. St. George."

"But you were looking for him too."

"Santos liked him, helped him when he could."

"Helped him do what?"

"With money, food, other things. For the street people who live in the house with Mr. St. George. The people who fight the corporations, the polluters, the military. Who work for the poor who have nothing while the generals and landowners have so much."

"That doesn't sound like a man who wants to be a rich Anglo in a big house with a swimming pool and two cars."

In the hammock, Inez Ortega rocked, her eyes closed but not asleep. Out in the *barrio* lights came on in the windows as the janitors and sweepers and dishwashers and cook's helpers got up to go to work even on a Saturday. The lucky ones who had work.

"He wanted what all Americans want, Mr. Fortune. But he didn't forget who he was."

"Who was he?" I said.

"A man from a million miles away in Mexico I met a thousand years ago and married."

Chapter Twenty-Seven

Francesca Ortega from Santa Barbara, meets Santos Torena, who says he is from Los Angeles, at a dance in Oxnard where she had gone with a cousin. She is eighteen. In the *barrio* that is old not to be married or living with a man. Francesca's mother is herself American born, her Mexican-born father has worked hard to adjust to the ways of his new country, and Francesca does not like most of the boys in the *barrio*.

Too many of them are loud and violent, or sullen and silent. Macho and in trouble, or lazy and mean. Poor and excluded, they sink into apathy or go to war, sometimes both. The apathy of an underclass with no way out, or a

war of rage and violence to have a share. Slow
death or quick death.

Francesca doesn't want either, and while
there are boys who manage to follow the
normal path to an almost Anglo life, they are
few and hard to find. So she goes to dances
with cousins, hopes to meet the right boy,
knows at once that Santos Torena is not from
Los Angeles. His English isn't good enough,
his Spanish is different. He is too polite, too
courtly. And too pompous and macho, without
being aggressive, at the same time. He is too
openly eager, not cool and laid back. He thinks
Oxnard is a wonderful city.

"In Santa Barbara we think Oxnard is dull,
a bus stop."

"Then Santa Barbara must be heaven," he
says.

They are speaking Spanish. Francesca has
switched quickly to put him at greater ease.
He would have struggled in English as long as
she spoke in English. She likes this, senses that
he is a kind man as well as proud. Because she
wants to put him even more at ease, give him
a chance to tell her he is really from Mexico,
probably an illegal, she tells him about her
father.

"My mother and grandmother were born in
the States, but my father came up from Sinaloa.
His father and the *patrone* wanted him to work
on the ranchero, but he knew that if he stayed
he'd never do more than work on the ranchero

his whole life, and he wanted to do more. So he saved his money and came up here. It was easier in those days, the big growers here wanted workers and *La Migra* let almost anyone come over."

"It is not so easy now," Santos Torena says. "Sometimes *La Migra* is not the worst."

"You would have to want to come to *El Norte* very much to take such a risk," she offers.

"That must be so," he says, evading, unsure of her.

She backs off. "My father was lucky. Because he was a single man, didn't have to send money to Mexico, he could save and leave the fields to find work as a gardener. Eventually he came to Santa Barbara and opened his own gardening service. He did well, but then he became afraid. Something happened with money they had hoped to make, he wasn't really happy in the Anglo world where they laughed at his English and had no respect. My father is an important man in the *barrio*, but outside in the world of the Anglo he holds his hat in his hand."

"For that," Torena says, "he could have stayed in Mexico and worked for the *patrone* like his father."

She sees in him what the sullen boys have given up and the violent boys will never get—the simple ambition to have what Anglos have. He is gentle, neither weak nor arrogant. A man without being a bully or a tyrant. She sees, too, that he likes her. But he is shy, is in Oxnard to pick lemons which he does not want her to know so can't tell her where he lives, has no car and no telephone. She solves the problem by returning twice to the dance, giving him her address. When he writes to ask her to meet him outside the dance, they both know they are serious, and he finally tells her who he is.

He tries to tell her in English. "I live in Lost Angeles three year. I am cook. I from Morelos. Zapata is from Morelos. My father teach me to be cook. I want to have res . . . rest . . ." He gives up, switches to Spanish and they both laugh.

His father had worked in good restaurants in Mexico City. His father married and had many children and returned to Morelos to open a small restaurant for locals and an occasional tourist bus that wandered into the town. His father talked of the great city of Mexico and its fine food the locals did not appreciate, and of the time he almost went north to the even great-er city of Los Angeles with his chief chef who had been invited there. His father never went to the city of Los Angeles, but Santos listened and learned all his father could teach, started north to open a fine restaurant. He spent two years in Mexico City, learned more and saved money, and moved on. To the border.

"They are animals, thieves, and vultures, and we are all the chickens. The *coyotes*, the *mules*, the bosses, the fixers and arrangers, the police and soldiers. They take our money, pluck our feathers, send us north in our skin. Everyone knows this, and hides his money where the animals do not know. But there are the bandits. The bandits know."

"They are Americans? These bandits?"

"No, they are our own people. In the deep canyons between Tijuana and your San Diego. It is eight miles of canyons inside the city of San Diego where more of our people try to cross than anywhere else. Sometimes thousands a night, and the bandits wait for them. There are the people who will sell you food, clothing, tequila and whisky, marijuana and more. And there are the bandits. They all work together. If you buy they know you have money and they lie in wait after dark inside the States and rob you, attack you, murder you. I was lucky, I was only attacked, my arm broken. They did not get my money, I was not murdered."

"I'm glad," Francesca says, holds his hand.

The rest of his story ends with a different kind of bandit and he is not so lucky. Once safely in the States with his small amount of money, he soon learns how small the amount is by the standards of the north. All it buys him is a share in an even smaller *barrio* restaurant where he goes to work as night cook on a salary that barely pays rent for a single room in the back of the principal owner's shack. Still, he has a restaurant, he is a chef, and he is in *El Norte*. He is on his way to success his father never had, the success he could never have had in Mexico.

"I cooked for two years. The hours were long at night, and not much fun. Nobody wanted me to cook the dishes my father had taught me, I was paid the same the whole two years. But my share got always bigger. The owner I lived with showed me how much money we made each month, put it all safe in the bank. A month ago I went to work and there was a lock on our door. A paper on the door says we owe much money. I go home, the owner is gone. His wife cries, but she does not know where he is. He has taken his car, his clothes, his rosary. But it is the restaurant that owes the money, and when everyone is paid there is nothing left. All my money is gone. They sell the stoves, the fixtures to pay the bills. There is not even a restaurant. So I am here to pick lemons, save more money."

"Couldn't you get a lawyer?"

"I talk to a lawyer, he tells me what they are doing is the law. The money must go to our creditors. All I can do is find the owner and sue him for my money. The lawyer tells me to have good luck. He does not think the owner has money, and if he has no money I cannot get money. Besides, I am an illegal, I can be deported if the owner tells."

That night they find a motel where Francesca can comfort him. She is happy because she knows he is not beaten. The hope he brought with him from Mexico has not died nor turned into rage. He will work in the fields, find another restaurant, be smarter next time. Shyly, she speaks of her getting a better job, saving her money, and later that week, after she has talked to her father and other older men of the *barrio* in Santa Barbara, they meet again.

"My father made a telephone call. The man owned the cafe and the land it is on. His wife says come back and operate it and share the profits with her instead of rent."

"It is a restaurant with walls and floors and nothing else."

"My father says I can get a loan from a fund for minority businesses."

For the first time she sees him grow tight.

"Why can I not get such a loan?"

She squeezes his rough dark hand. "You are illegal, Santos. One day you won't be, but . . ."

She can feel the muscles all the way to his back, but he nods, smiles if not happily. "One day."

They are married, get the loan, return to Los Angeles and the restaurant in the *barrio* where Santos is now the boss. The deserted wife gets them a house near the restaurant. Francesca's mother finds them furniture from friends in Santa Barbara. It is, he tells her, a miracle, and it is she who has made the miracle happen. He is the most fortunate man in the world. Francesca is happy. She has a man who has hope and ambition, does not take drugs and carry a gun, drink and stare at the TV after a day of mindless work, or drink and take drugs and stare at the TV all day because he has no job.

A miracle, perhaps, but even the miracles of *El Norte* need some help. Their savings are gone quickly on rent and food and new clothes and being young and in love. The restaurant does not make enough yet to support them. There are expenses, overhead beyond the loan, and money must be plowed back into the business.

"I'll get a better job," Francesca says.

She feels him tense again beside her in the tiny bedroom. The muscles that reach all the way back to the town in Morelos. New ways are not easy, but he is trying. This time his smile in the dark when she turns to him is better, more real.

"In this country we are together, Santos."

She gets the better job, and one better than that. The restaurant prospers. They do not have children. This is hardest for Santos. In Mexico a man is still measured by the number and frequency of his babies. But Santos is learning the mind of his new country.

"For most Mexican men, there is not much more to show."

Francesca does well in her work for a large corporation, returns to night college to study as a paralegal. Her boss, a vice president, likes her. Santos does well at the restaurant, hires another chef and two waitresses.

Customers come from beyond the *barrio*.

Santos expands the restaurant, meets Latino businessmen and community leaders. He even meets Anglo businessmen. They are talking about a child, when the opportunity comes.

Call it another miracle.

One of the Anglo businessmen loves Mexican food, operates a string of topless bars with food service. The food end is losing money, and, besides, he doesn't like the food his managers serve. Why not Mexican food? How would Santos like to take over all his kitchens as a concession? Break into the Anglo world? All he has to do is find the cash to operate ten restaurants completely on his own—food, staff, the works. Selling the restaurant, borrowing, using their savings, they still would not have enough to stock, hire, and start up the ten concession restaurants. Santos sits and adds and figures and schemes, but he always comes up short. There is no one left to borrow from, he must have another ten thousand dollars, at least.

Miracle, perhaps, but in the United States God helps those who help themselves, and Santos is at a dead end, his hope is dying.

"I'll get a loan from my company," Francesca declares.

"You can do this? So much money?"

He has now been in the United States many years, has learned much. He has particularly learned that money is a serious matter.

"They have special funds to help employees. For a big company it isn't all that much."

She is not eighteen anymore. The money is there, yes, and it is a small sum to a large corporation, yes, but she knows that no one gives a loan of any size that freely. She will need help, influence, an angle. Her boss, the vice-president, likes her very much. For over a year he has taken her to lunch once or twice a month. For the last four months he has asked her out for a drink after work. He has made no secret of what he wants. They are both adults, both married. He likes her, and if she likes him even a little?

"We need a loan, my husband and me," she tells him in the cocktail lounge on Wilshire. "Ten thousand dollars. A business opportunity."

"Why not?" he says.

They get the loan from the corporation, sell the restaurant in the *barrio*, operate the Mexican food service in the Anglo's topless bars, and Santos is on his way at last.

When Santos finds out how Francesca got the loan from her company, they have the crisis of their marriage.

"You . . . ?"

"Yes."

They are in the small kitchen of the tiny house in the *barrio*. "How long . . . ?"

"I needed the job. The loan took time."

Chasing Eights

In parts of Mexico, when a barnyard animal such as a pig becomes a pet allowed into the house, it is called *Sancho*. When a Mexican man goes north to work, he leaves his wife at home. The man can be gone a long time, even years. The woman is alone. A male "friend" moves in, is kept by her, becomes a pet. *Sancho*. Or Senor Gonzalez. It is a serious matter. Women have killed their children by a *sancho* so the husband will not find out when he comes home. But husbands find out, and many wives and *sanchos* have been murdered by returning husbands.

"Now?"

"I don't need the job."

The food service is a success, they move into a real house in the *barrio*, have their first child. Santos puts on weight, has prestige in the Mexican community, but wants more. They are about to buy a house outside the *barrio*, open a better restaurant outside the community, when the Anglo who owns the topless bars is murdered by rival gangsters and the new owners no longer want Santos to have the food concession.

Santos has learned. He has money in the bank, his agreement is in writing for a fixed period with an option for a new period, and he had made friends inside and outside the *barrio* who help convince the owners to pay him a fair price for cancelling. He comes out well, he and Francesca decide to move to Santa Barbara where her mother lives alone, and where Santos feels he can do better in the long run. He opens his new restaurant, branches out into construction, real estate, and any business where there is a good dollar to be made.

Francesca doesn't always like what he does to make the good dollar, but she has learned to accept his need, as he learned to understand her need to help him any way she could. She senses that as her need to help grew from his ambition, his need to succeed has grown greater from her action.

Chapter Twenty-Eight

Jack Price walks through the unit in the bungalow court on lower Salsipuedes Street. A kitch-
en with an ancient refrigerator. A bedroom with
a single narrow bed. Two canvas chairs in the
living room behind a dirty window that faces
the narrow courtyard between the two rows of
semi-detached units dark in the night. Paintings on every wall, unfinished canvases on the
floors.

"Where the hell are we? What is this place?"

"My studio," Max Mellecker says. "My hide-
out. My cave."

Jack looks around again. "What for?"

"For painting. For hanging out. For hiding.
For me. How do I know? Want another beer?"

The only light is in the kitchen and outside over the door. Jack sits in one of the canvas chairs. A red sling, butterfly, whatever they call the damn things now. He forgets almost at once what he was talking about, his interest in where he is. "Why not? Might as well get loaded all the way. Right?"

Jack looks out the dark window at the silence and the low stucco buildings joined in identical pairs like Siamese twins. Max Mellecker comes back with the beer. It is Anchor Steam. Mellecker sits in the other canvas chair and laughs as he looks at his bottle. "Jesus. Always the expensive beer. No matter how hard you want to run away from it."

"Who's running away?" Jack says. "I don't run away."

"I do," Mellecker says. "At least I'm trying to. Or I think I'm trying to run away."

"Run away? From who?"

"From me, I suppose."

Jack drinks. "You can't run away from yourself."

"One good cliche deserves another. I'll drink to that. Don't let the bastards wear you down." Mellecker drinks. "Not from myself, Jack, from the other me. The me who never was. The me someone else painted over the real me."

"You're as crazy as that Genius."

"You think the Genius is really crazy?"

"Crazy or stupid, and you know he isn't stupid."

Mellecker drinks. "No, he isn't stupid."

He joins Jack in staring out the single window of the dark living room. They sit, each drinks from his bottle, continues to look at the nothing in the one small light beyond the window. Jack is detached from the room and the silence outside. The dark seems to fascinate both of them, mesmerize them, as if they are waiting for something. If they are, all they see is the empty night, all they hear is the hum of a car on the freeway bridge, a cough in the shabby court.

It is Mellecker who talks. "The Genius thinks we're insane, our whole world. You ever think he might be right? The Genius and his crazy friends with their underground newspaper, memorials to street people, stashed guns, rockets in the backyard? The ones with dreams for the future."

Jack has slid down in the sling chair, butterfly chair, or whatever they call it now, still stares out the dark window, sucks on his Anchor Steam. His eyes are alert but unfocused, as if seeing everything in front of him and nothing at all.

Mellecker talks. "Most of us never think about what we do as a country, where we're going. The Genius may be crazy, but he thinks about real things. We're sane, but we act as if TV card-turners, gossip columnists, fashion models, and jet-setters are important. Our president named a nuclear missile *peacekeeper*, obviously not having read George Orwell. We actually believe a certain kind of automobile will make us strong and masculine. We believe we have what we want."

In the sling chair, butterfly, Jack has his eyes closed. He opens them every few seconds to look out the dark window at the deserted courtyard in the feeble light of the single bulb over the door of Mellecker's unit. He looks at his bottle and finds it empty, goes into the kitchen, comes out with two more bottles. He has forgotten the opener, returns to the kitchen for it, sits back down with his opened beer.

"The Genius is right?" Jack says.

"Sometimes I wonder."

"Murdering the President?"

"Getting their attention."

Jack's eyes turn sharply. He has seen movement out in the shadows of the bungalow court. Rigid, he leans forward, eyes straining to peer through the night and shadows. But there is nothing. Maybe a cat. A racoon. Jack slides back down in the sling chair. He continues to watch the empty courtyard, but his eyes are no longer alert as he tilts the beer bottle, drinks.

Mellecker talks. "What are we doing here? Now, tonight? Why are you here? Why did someone kill Torena? Is it all so sane? Normal? Rational? The right way to live?"

This time it is a cat that darts from the shadows across the courtyard outside. Jack wipes his mouth, the sweat from his brow, watches the shadow of the bush where the cat has vanished.

Mellecker talks. "A Saturday a year ago I woke up, couldn't make myself move. I felt shut tight, chained. I realized I'd been chained my whole life. From the moment I decided I wasn't going to be a feed store owner like my father. Then I heard my voice say, 'What's wrong with running a feed store? At least you could have really painted.' That's when I rented this place to start painting the way I'd wanted to paint back in high school. Abstracts. Like Pollock, De Kooning. That's old hat now, but I've got a lot of years to catch up on before I can move on to something new, something real."

A light has gone on in one of the other units across the burned-out grass. Shadows cross the drawn blinds of the single window. This is the lower east where people go to work early even on a Saturday. Jack, who has been half-dozing, his beer empty again in his hand, jerks upright. Another light goes on in another unit. It is still pitch black, the dark before the dawn, but the night is ending. Jack stares at the lighted rectangles across the courtyard. Mellecker talks.

"If I go on living how I'm living, doing what I'm doing, I'll never even know I've lived. Thoreau said it, didn't he, but he was crazy too, right?'"

A door slams somewhere up the court to the left. Too far left for either of them to see. The girl comes along the narrow concrete path directly outside the window of the darkened living room with its walls of abstract paintings. She walks slowly, her head down and her face lost in a cascade of long black hair. Her body is slim. Small high breasts loose under a man's shirt. Narrow hips in a tight blue skirt, and long legs that wobble at the ankles in her high heels. Adolescent. As she passes the window she stops and removes the high heels and they see her face. It is the brown face of an adolescent not much more than a child. Blank and unsmiling. She holds the high heels in her hand with a bra and blouse and panty hose. Barefoot, she walks on, head down and face hidden again in the long black hair.

"What?" Mellecker asks into the silent room. "Her first sex? Did she really want to, or was it the thing to do to be a grown-up? Sent home right after, kicked out carrying her underwear? An older married man who couldn't take her home? Some macho stud who fell asleep? A young boy who had to go to work, poor and going nowhere? A rich boy about to leave town who had to be home when momma called? A rite of passage like a million before her. Where does it take her? Home to cry it out? Suicide? A hatred of all men? Cynicism?"

Jack still looks out at where the girl had stopped to remove her wobbly high heels, put them with the rest of the clothes she carried in the pre-dawn hours. He put his beer bottle on the floor, stood up. "Nothing's ever worked out. I don't know why. If this deal goes down the tubes I lose all my money. I lose the best chance I've ever had. I lose the car agency. I go home a failure, and if I fail again it's all gone. My whole life down the drain. I can't blow it this time, Max, no matter what Brower is doing. I don't care what he's doing."

He stands with his back to Mellecker, still stares out at the spot where the young girl had stood with her head down, her clothes in her hand. Mellecker stands behind him.

"Jack, someone killed Santos Torena. Maybe it was those *coyotes* or because of them. But other people are out there shooting. It could be the Genius and his street people, only it could be Brower's deal too. Torena wanted to talk to you, and he's dead. Go home, call the police."

The silence rests heavy on the small room.

"All right." Jack turns, smiles. "We'll both go home."

Chapter Twenty-Nine

The narrow night street at the foot of the Riviera was as silent as an exhibit in a museum.

Francesca Torena had left me on the porch in the *barrio* with her mother asleep in the gaudy hammock. She didn't tell me where she was going or why, suggested I stay there for at least ten minutes. She did say, when I asked her what Torena did for the Genius, who the Genius was and where he lived, "Santos never forgot that Emiliano Zapata came from Morelos."

I walked along the wall around the Genius's house, wondered about a man who exploited his own people and still remembered he came from the same roots as the greatest Mexican revolutionary. It was a high wall, but the sturdy branches of at least four trees hung low over it. There was a smaller door in the heavy wooden gate. It was open, swung in easily and silently.

Inside, a chair stood against the wall. There was no light in the big house across a wide courtyard of cement over old cobblestones. My eyes accustomed to the dark, I saw a newly planted sapling at the edge of the cemented courtyard, three figures close to it under blankets or in sleeping bags. I became aware of shapes on the ground all through the trees and brush, the sound of many people asleep in the night, like the slow pulsation of some unknown machine.

I looked at the empty chair against the wall. A ceramic mug on the ground still held coffee. Warm coffee.

When I found him he was still warm.

In the small beam of my penlight his face was mottled, his thick throat bruised red and purple across the windpipe, but that wasn't what had killed him. The blood, the two holes like burned red mouths in the head, showed what had done that. Two bullets from a small pistol fired into his brain. No more than 7.65-mm, maybe smaller, that had not even awakened the sleeping yard. An automatic, silenced and probably muffled.

I stood over him in the night, a solitary mourner.

A big, bearded man, long hair held off a weathered face by a red band, he looked able to take care of himself. Only none of us are strong enough to take care of ourselves against men with guns who want us dead for reasons we don't even know.

My old cannon out, I stepped over and around sleepers like moving through a mine-field. Through the windows of two outbuildings there were only the darker shadows where more people lay asleep. Along the sides and rear of the old house windows were open to the night air. The canvas-covered objects were in the rear yards. I lifted a cover.

Who has rocket launchers in his backyard? Why?

The rear of the wide garage had horizontal casement windows open under the overhang of the roof.

"Price was here, we know that. Where'd he go?"

"Hey, you point us to old Jack, okay?"

The voices were faint but clear through the hard-edged echo of an empty room. Thin light moved inside, but the windows were too high to see inside. A sound like a butcher hitting meat with the flat of his cleaver. Another sound, muffled.

"Price and the other guy, they drove some-where."

"You're gonna tell us, friend."

I could hear the bone break, the blood spurt, the choked sound that was a scream that couldn't scream.

A broad red eucalyptus grew close behind the

old carriagehouse. I pocketed my cannon. To climb a tree isn't easy for a one-armed man, but I climbed. I had no way of knowing who or what was inside the garage, how many and how strong, what they would do to who they had if they knew I was around. Or to me. The eucalyptus had low branches. I found a thick limb, then a thinner one where I could see inside the high horizontal windows.

The two who had chased me in Isla Vista stood on either side of a man slumped in a chair. His feet were tied to the chair, but not his hands. A yellow pad rested on his knees, a pencil lay on the floor under one of his dangling hands. His head hung, only his red hair visible in the weak light of a camp lantern on a table. Blood all over his camouflage fatigues and the floor. There was an old Ford, stacks of crates, scattered parts of a computer, some open crates that held AK-47 rifles and their large, curved ammo clips.

The two men had no interest in the rifles or the scattered computer. Only in the man slumped in the chair.

"What're the guns for? Those rockets?"

He was the broader man in the suit. A brown suit with a brown tie, white shirt, drab brown shoes. Late forties, a square face. Both face and eyes without expression. He picked up the pencil, put it into the bleeding man's hand.

"Who're the greasers? What're you and Price doin'?"

Chasing Eights

The eyes of the man in the chair were swollen shut, the nose broken, his cheeks, chin, brows a mass of bloody flesh. His mouth was taped, gagged. He couldn't scream aloud, but he also couldn't speak. The man in the brown suit guided his hand to the yellow pad on his knees. His bloody head shook once. The man in the brown suit looked at the younger one. Brass knuckles on a massive fist slammed the bloody face. The pencil fell to the floor, the scream came out a muffled gurgle.

"Hey, you're a genius. Be smart before I bust my hand."

The taller second man had laid his blue blazer neatly over an empty crate. In his early thirties, he breathed almost as hard from the hitting as he had from chasing me.

"Who hired the private dick? Where the hell does he fit?"

In the tree I let go of the branch I was holding, gripped the branch I sat on with my knees and leaned back against the trunk. Cursed the limitations of a one-armed man and got my cannon out of my pocket. Tried to steady and aim through the high windows down at where the older one talked and the younger smashed his brass knuckles into the bloody face of the man in the chair.

"Price went somewhere, goddamnit."

"What does the fucking private want?"

I couldn't hit two men with one shot, and if I missed both of them? Fell? I wouldn't help

275

the man in the chair, would be a sitting duck in the tree. Miss, and I would get the man in the chair killed. I had no illusions about that. One, maybe two, shots, that was all I would have. From a tree. One hand to hold steady a big pistol, and if . . .

"Shit, Messick, he's out for the fucking count."

"Get your fucking coat."

The older one put the small silenced automatic to the bound man's head. I barely heard the sound. Saw not heard. The thick hand, the pistol, the white knuckles, the sharp jerk of the bloody head as two bullets hit in the brain. The younger one carried his blue blazer over his shoulder as they went out.

I slid down the tree, almost fell, stumbled around the carriagehouse garage. They were already at the gate and through. Life comes before death. Inside, the blood dripped to the floor. I cradled his bloody head, pulled off the tape and the gag but didn't move him. The phone was in a corner. I called 911, the paramedics, the police, sat on a packing crate.

Excuses? Or honest judgment and bad luck? Everyone fears, but judgment is all we have.

"Genius?"

They stood in the doorway. Two men not that different from the two who had gone. Both with rifles aimed at me.

"He's dead," I said. "I called the paramedics,

the police. Dan Fortune, a private investigator. There were two of them. They were looking for Jack Price. I'm looking for Jack Price too. You know where he is?"

"Dead?" He was an older man in a worn navy blue suit. He lowered his AK-47.

"We heard someone at the gate, found Walt Frank." A much younger man in the same camouflage fatigues as the silent body in the chair. Worn camouflages, faded where the rank and unit had been. A soldier. He didn't lower his weapon. "You got a gun?"

I showed them my old cannon, told them the whole story of my actions inside the gate. "Either of you recognize those two?"

"No," the soldier said. "How do we know you're not lying?"

"You saw my gun, it didn't shoot your friend."

"You could be with them," the soldier said.

The older man said, "Why?"

"Why," I said, "is what I'm trying to find out. Why and who and what. Santos Torena, a *mule*, now your friend. The Genius. Was that his name?"

"Stan," the older man said. "Stan St. George. I'm Harry Klossner, he's Nolan. I mean, why Stan?"

An edge of hysteria had come into his voice. Whatever he and the Genius and the soldier named Nolan were doing was flowing away from Harry Klossner and leaving him with nothing but the reality of the death of a friend.

Nolan heard it too. Klossner would crack, fall apart.

"Tell the others, Harry. Warn them the cops are coming."

Alone, the soldier and I looked at the dead man in the chair. No sirens whined in the distance toward us. At 4:00 A.M. even the paramedics and police move slowly.

"You think the same guys killed Torena?"

"Torena worked with you. Doing what?"

"He was good at getting stuff we needed."

"Assault rifles? Ammo? The Stinger rockets out back?"

"Genius built the launchers all himself from scratch." Nolan had a kind of wonder in his voice. "His own design, you know? The rockets too. Torena got some of the parts."

"What for? The rockets? What were you going to do with them?"

"Shoot down old Reagan. We took too long. Genius said we'd use 'em on the next clone-clown. He liked that, *clone-clown*. Made him laugh." Nolan stared at the dead man as if waiting to hear that laugh. "He'd never of used 'em, not when it come right down to it. He just liked to think about it. About really doing something, making a difference."

"With the guns too?"

Nolan nodded. "A revolutionary army, you know? You like to think you can do something and make it all happen. Not just talk, yell, drop out." He stared at the dead body. "He said most people'd never go along with tryin' to change it, not in this country. We got too good a job of thinking control. So we'd stockpile the guns for the future, for when it all got to collapse."

"The rockets weren't for stockpiling," I said. "Who knew about them and the guns, could want to stop you?"

"No one I know."

"What does Jack Price have to do with you?"

"Nothing."

"He was here tonight. Why?"

"I don't know. Seems like he knew Genius. They talked a lot. Just talking."

"Torena did more than talk. He was a hard-nosed businessman who pulled any deal to make a buck. What was his angle here?"

"Santos believed with us."

"A man who cheated his own people? Smuggled illegal aliens? Wanted to be a wheeler-dealer? The big man in the *barrio*?"

Voices moved outside the garage. The sounds of many feet, of anger and confusion. Sirens had begun in the distance. Up deserted Garden or Santa Barbara Street, coming across from Cottage Hospital. Nolan listened to the sirens.

"Santos used to say he was like me. I had to be a goddamn soldier, he had to win in the Anglo world. But he knew what it did to him, all those he hurt, all the slick tricks and angles to make a bigger buck. He said Zapata was right, the wise one he called him. He said they had to kill Zapata because the people might listen to him and ruin the system. He said he worked with us for Zapata. A payment, he said."

The sirens had turned from their race up the north-south streets into the cross streets. The paramedics were in the lead. The voices and movement outside had stopped. Nolan got up, walked to the door. I went out with him. The courtyard was deserted, the house silent, the thick brush empty under the trees. They had all faded away into the night, scattered to a hundred safer havens. Nolan nodded once, disappeared around the house as the sirens turned into the small street.

The first ones through the gate were the paramedics. I pointed to the garage door, they trotted past me. The uniformed police were next, stood me against the garage wall until the same sergeant from outside Mellecker's house recognized me.

"You get around, Fortune. Any new wounds?"

"Unscathed this time."

Chavalas came in last. He watched the patrolmen tape off the murder scene, listened to my report, went into the garage. He came out within seconds.

"Dead," he said, lit a cigarette and coughed for two solid minutes. "4:00 A.M., I got to smoke. Okay, tell me."

I gave him a full report of the two killers from Isla Vista to here, of Claire Broberg, Inez Ortega and Francesca Torena. The two paramedics came out of the garage closing their cases.

"You've been busy."

"With nothing to show."

"You got two killers with faces and descriptions, that's more than we have. All I've come up with so far is that Brower looks to have a cash problem all around. Anything else on his deals has to wait until morning."

"How about this gang here? You have anything on them?"

"The protesters and dropouts, sure. The dead guy, nothing. Guns and rockets and shooting presidents is all new. More fun that keeps until morning. Not that we'll find anything or anyone now. One crank with nutty notions, and he's dead."

"Jack Price?"

"We're still looking. He seems to have friends."

"What do you do next?"

He dropped the cigarette, watched the coroner's crew arrive and go into the garage. "Put out the word on your two killers, then go home and go to bed. You better do the same." He went into the garage.

I went out to my Tempo, drove along Foothill Road that was as abandoned in the pre-dawn hours as a road in some war zone, to Cathedral Oaks Road and Turnpike. There was no light at the Price house, no cars in the drive or carport, no sign of anyone inside through the dark windows.

There was nothing more to do but go home.

Chapter Thirty

Jack Price sits in his Jaguar in front of the small house on Camino Corto and looks at his watch. It is 4:00 A.M., but there is a light in the house behind the low fence. Jack likes the house, there is something warm about it. Your wife and kids waiting for you when you come home with the new car and they all come running out, excited, almost awed.

He looks at his watch again. It is still 4:00 A.M. on the digital he can't quite get used to. 4:00 A.M. and fifty or so seconds, but the seconds don't register like the hands of an analog watch. Anyway, it is very late, or very early, and . . .

"Jack? Is that you? For God's sake come in."

Claire stands in her open door in a white robe with the living room dark behind her. "How long have you been sitting there?"

Jack gets out of the Jaguar, walks to the door. "Just drove up. You must have heard me."

Claire doesn't question, steps back and closes the door as he passes her into the living room. "I've been watching TV in my bedroom. God you look cold. I'll get coffee. Sharon's asleep. Go on into the bedroom."

Her bedroom is half a sitting room with an armchair, red loveseat, coffee table and color TV. Jack sits in the armchair, hopes he has heard the invitation in her voice he thinks he has. He needs something to tell him he is the same man he has always been, that the world is still his world, that he will go to work tomorrow and have lunch and talk about women and the Dodgers and that fishing trip to Baja for marlin he has never taken because he never had the money and Angie wouldn't go anyway. A charter out on the deep blue ocean after the big ones and then back to the penthouse suite in the best hotel.

"Cream and sugar?"

"Both."

She smiles, goes for the coffee. He leans back in the soft chair, rests his head, almost closes his eyes. The way he is sitting reminds him of his father. His father after a hard day in court or a long meeting of the town council where someone had crossed him. Maybe it's the small house where he feels secure, comfortable, the way he had back in Minnesota.

"Sugar *and* cream. You're sinful."

"I never did have any willpower."

She sits on the loveseat. Not in the center but at one end with room left for Jack if he wants to move. Jack drinks the hot coffee, realizes how cold he is in the late night, looks at the empty space on the loveseat. He glances at the TV as if he has just noticed it was on. A late movie on a cable channel.

"How come you're watching TV so late?"

"It's Saturday. I don't always sleep well." She smiles straight at Jack. "Living alone isn't much fun."

"I know what you mean," Jack says. "Sometimes I feel like I live alone all the time."

"I can believe that," Claire says.

It is a mistake, shifts Jacks' mind from her to himself. He frowns over the coffee. "Sometimes I wonder what it is with her. Angie, I mean. She used to be fine, you know? Back in college. When we got married." He drinks the coffee, shrugs. "She changed when we came out here. She liked the newspaper in Tulsa, but we had to take that Spear offer. It was a big step for us, careerwise. You have to go as far as you can, build for the future, the family. It wasn't my fault Spear didn't work out, that old bastard was crazy."

His face is almost inside the steaming coffee cup, as if he needs the warmth like a man crouched over a campfire. Claire doesn't really want to talk about Angie, or his past, she wants to talk about herself, them, and shifts on the loveseat to get his attention again. Tucks her legs up under the robe, flashes thigh to show she is naked under the robe, her eyes warm. Jack doesn't seem to notice.

"It's like she never wanted me to be someone. She hated all the jobs she's ever had, but never wanted to stay home either. I'd get home and she'd never even make me a drink. Probably not even have dinner started. Reading and writing that stuff of hers never made us a dime. Hell, it's more fun having a drink before I go home." He shakes his head. "I figured when we had kids she'd straighten out. She doesn't bitch about money, yell when I quit some job that's going nowhere, push me all the time like Maggie does Max, like the She-Wolf did when I was a kid. She makes me feel like nothing, you know? No one."

Claire sees that he's going to talk it out, and maybe that's best for her in the long run. She remembers how her father had talked his problems out with her mother, knows her role is to listen, encourage. "It doesn't sound like any homelife, Jack."

He laughs. "You can say that again. It's like a museum most of the time. I don't do a god-damn thing right. She doesn't bitch, but I can feel it. She hated our camping with the kids, hates my workshop, the Jag I bought to give me a sharper image. Always putting me down. It's like she thinks she can do it all better, wants to be the man." He nods, angry. "That's it. She wants to wear the pants in the family. Her and her writing. All those classes, that conference every year. Leaving me with the kids. Off on her own. Even in bed. Always talking about sex, coming after me. That can turn a guy off."

He broods over the almost empty cup. Claire knows that too from her memories of her father. His mind is still on himself, on Angie, and that is not where she wants it. She needs to lead him out of himself and back to where he is, to her, to them.

She shakes her head. "You wonder why so many people have to go it alone, build-up their own weak egos instead of working together. Both my ex-husbands were weak, you know? Rudi wasn't much better than Matt. He was a commercial fisherman with his own boat, didn't gamble but had no more ambition. He drank too much, took long cruises alone when he was needed at home."

"A long cruise on my own boat sounds pretty nice to me sometimes," Jack says. "Like right now."

"You wouldn't go unless you'd done your job, and you'd take Angie and the kids with you. You're a responsible man like my father. You want to hear how Matt really died? A forty-year-old man with a job other people depended on and a young daughter?"

*Matt Ramovsky left his Newport Beach con-
dominium that fatal morning with his blonde
live-in, Cindy, beside him in his 1989 Porsche.
They drove to brunch at his friend Ivar's house
to celebrate Ivar's divorce. A triple celebration—
Ivar had gone to Vegas for the divorce, won big
at the crap table, and met Ingrid who had just
moved in with him.*

"All the Ivars I met while I was married to
Matt. Every one with an Ingrid he'd met at the
track or the casino."

*Matt held the same job as manager of a large
motel in Laguna for four years. On the day he
died, he was making good money and expecting
to buy into the business. Ivar was a mechan-
ic who specialized in Porsches, kidded Matt
that morning about joining the establishment,
according to Ivar's brother who, with his wife,
were the only other guests at the party. They had
eggs Benedict and lobster crepes cooked by Ingrid,
a chocolate mousse cake brought by Matt and
Cindy, and plenty of champagne.*

"Angie used to like to give parties," Jack says.
"I don't know what happened. She never seems
to have any fun now, doesn't talk to our friends.
She's angry all the time."

*The celebration brunch at Ivar's led to a cel-
ebration flight that afternoon. The men decided
it would be a kick, and Ingrid fell right in with
the idea. Only Cindy wasn't as enthusiastic. She
told Ivar's brother and his wife, who didn't go
on the fatal impulse, that flying with Matt in his*

Piper had shown her all the things that can go wrong, that it wasn't all that safe. She tried to talk Matt out of it, especially since he had had a lot of champagne, and that was against FAA regulations.

"Childish impulse. Rudi too. Rules, regulations, common sense, neither of them gave one damn about any of it. Whatever candy they saw in front of them."

Ivar wanted to show Ingrid his friend's private plane, and Matt was eager to cap the celebration. Flying was important to him, his sense of being alone on the edge even in a crowd. Not that he flew that often, with his job and his need to gamble and play the stock market. Mostly he just went up for the thrill of it, sometimes took a vacation trip. He had never qualified for more than the basic private pilot's certificate, never seemed to have the time or interest to learn more, and his flying record showed minor citations and one major citation for not following proper procedure.

Claire shakes her head over fresh coffee. "Matt never learned to do anything really right."

The four squeezed into Matt's Porsche, drove to the airport where Matt kept his Piper. After checking and fueling, Matt taxied to the takeoff spot on the runway. He reported over the hand microphone that the Piper was ready to takeoff. The tower cleared him, he increased the power, the Piper began to roll. Matt laughed with exhilaration. He reached takeoff speed, lifted the plane

*free of the earth and into the air, and the engine
misfired, sputtered. The Piper gained thirty-five,
forty, fifty feet. The runway lay straight ahead. A
hundred feet. The Piper began a turn . . .*

"No," Jack says. "No."

Jack sees himself behind the controls of the
Piper as it goes on coughing and sputtering and
the plane begins to lose altitude. He steadies
the Piper on a straight course. There is over a
thousand feet of runway still ahead. Even with
the wheels down, that is enough room for the
Piper to land safely. Fighting the dying engine,
Jack brings the plane down slowly, slowly.

"I didn't know you knew how to fly, Jack,"
Claire says.

"Everyone knows you never turn a plane
that's losing power, for Christ sake."

*. . . the Piper turned until its wings were
almost vertical to the ground, apparently seeking
the safety of where it had come from. The safety
of home. The reflex that was wrong and should
have been educated, trained, out of any pilot. The
error of a careless man. The engine stopped, and
the plane, on its side and the wings pointed at the
ground,, dropped like a stone and crashed into
the concrete. All four dead on impact. Ingrid
from Vegas, Ivar the newly free man, Cindy the
tootsie, and Matt Ramovsky who left a motel and
a daughter without support.*

"I'd like to have my own plane, a boat, a
condo in Newport Beach."

"You can have those things and be reliable,"

Claire says. "My father did, your father did."

She moves once more on the loveseat. Jack sees she is naked under the robe, is sure now he has seen the signals he thinks he has seen. But he has seen something else too: Claire is looking for a man like her father. They have talked about their fathers before. They agreed in those talk sessions after work that their fathers were what men should be, what Jack himself is, or will be once he gets a break.

"Maybe you need a new wife, Jack. A wife and a break."

The men Claire married never acted the way her father did. They were always doing what she could not understand or control. She sees in Jack the husband and stepfather she can live with without having to change much of how she lives now alone, which she really likes except she has no man and she needs a man. The way he needs a woman.

"She's all wrong for you, Jack, like Matt and Rudi were all wrong for me. You need someone to help you, not tear you down."

She sees him as a better version of her father. That's how he sees himself, but not how Angie sees him. Angie doesn't want him anymore, not for a long time. Claire wants him. Her other husbands wanted what they wanted not what she wanted. What does he want? What he wanted when he got out of college, what he was supposed to get by doing what he was supposed to do.

"We'll be a team working together for the family. Just what you want, Jack. You deserve to take it easier, not have to fight so hard all the time, fight the world and her."

Jack has never seen any of this before, has never thought like this before. He is scared, feels a great knotted lump in his gut where the coffee has gone cold. He panics.

"Let's talk about it. Tomorrow, okay? I better get home."

He almost runs from the bedroom and out the front door to his Jaguar silent on the residential block where the faintest light touches the eastern sky.

DAWN

"Tell 'em where you got it,
and how easy it was."

—ANONYMOUS

Chapter Thirty-One

Kay watched me in the dark.

"How long have you been awake?"

"Since you came in."

"Sorry."

"Why? I want you in bed with me. I want you home. I like to know you're home and in bed with me."

Our bed faced the open windows. Unseen, the sea broke on the beach a few hundred yards away as the crow flies, across the freeway and the Southern Pacific tracks. I had undressed thinking she was asleep, had slipped in beside her and seen her eyes.

"How do you feel?" she said.

"Like a deserter."

"You don't have to be a hero, Dan."

"He's still out there somewhere."

"And it's your job to save him? Even from himself?"

"Yes." The steady pound of the surf was clear in the pre-dawn hours. There is a little fog in the winter.

"What happened, Dan? Tonight."

I told her about the *coyotes*, about the attack on them, Jack Price and me. She switched on the light, sat up.

"Let me see that side."

She examined the bandage.

"It's sore and stiff. I'm all right. Other people aren't." I left out the chase in Isla Vista, told her of the death of the Genius and his gateman. "He ran his house like a rescue mission for the homeless and dropouts, had a kind of revolutionary gang who look crazy but could be deadly if they acted on their plans. Someone might not have wanted to take the risk."

"The government?"

"Always, but not this time."

"Then who, Dan?"

"Someone worried about Price, the *coyotes*, me and the Genius."

"Why you?"

"Probably because I'm asking questions."

She said nothing, turned off the light, settled back on the pillows. I felt a stirring, but my brain wasn't in it.

"There are only two kinds of winners at

poker, and a hundred different kinds of losers. Except that all the losers have one thing in common—they live on hope, on what might be, on the bright future that will be theirs someday. They don't have the skill, the drive, or the boldness to do what is necessary to make them winners."

Trucks had begun to pass on the freeway. Fresh produce for Los Angeles.

"Only the house and the professional win. The one who runs the game, and the one who plays all the angles. Winners never depend on hope, and they don't think of what might be. They deal with the real, look for the advantage. They don't play a hand unless it will win. They know that bold always wins more than timid. They don't wait for fortune to smile. They don't hope for a winning hand, they *have* a winning hand. If they don't, they don't play. Over the long run chance evens out, and they win. That's how the game is set up."

High in a Monterey pine outside our windows an early season mockingbird sang a mild display of its abilities. The real pyrotechnics would come at the end of spring in the same old tree. A Monterey pine is a popular tree in Santa Barbara. It is tall and full, pleasing to the eye, grows fast but doesn't live long. An imposing shadow without much substance.

"I read a report about the American Dream. It seems it's alive and well all over the country. Ninety percent of those surveyed think they have the same opportunities as most other Americans. The median income for all these happy pursuers of opportunity was twenty-three thousand a year."

"Give an Irishman a horse," Kay said, "and he'll vote Tory."

There was a vague lightening in the sky beyond our bedroom when the telephone rang. I felt Kay tense, knew she didn't want me to answer. Let the machine answer, she would say if I asked. I picked up the receiver.

"I think he just called me, Dan."

"Think?"

Kay turned on the light, held a pen and notepad toward me. I shook my head. Angela Price's voice was agitated.

"I let the phone ring six times before I answered. Nothing. I said hello, hello, Over and over. I even said his name. But there was only silence. I'm sure it was him, Dan. I told him to come home, I didn't care about the deal. He never answered, just hung up."

"How long have you been home?"

"Half an hour. He hasn't been here. No one has."

"Where's Brower?"

"He went out somewhere."

"When?"

"About an hour ago. That's when I came home."

"Where did Brower go?"

"He didn't tell me, Dan."

I told her what I had learned since we'd talked in Ed Brower's office.

"A poker player? Dead? I don't understand."

"A friend of Santos Torena and Jack," I said. "Is there anything you haven't told me, Angie? Anything about Jack and Torena and the Genius?"

"No."

"Anywhere else he might hide you haven't told me?"

"No."

I could hear her breathing, but she said nothing more. I wondered if she was alone.

"There's still one place I can try to pick up on him. Stay there, I'll call. If he shows, call here."

Chapter Thirty-Two

Over Max Mellecker's rustic street the shadows of the mountains had begun to emerge in the sky. Jack Price's Jaguar was gone.

Light and movement in the kitchen of Mellecker's half-hidden hillside house told me someone had recently come home, or that one Mellecker got up early on a Saturday morning. Whoever it was let me ring four times before flinging it open.

"This is a fine hour to . . . Oh, I thought you were Max."

Maggie Mellecker stood with one hand on the doorknob. The anger that had been prepared for Mellecker couldn't shift to deal with me. In worn gardening clothes—loose white coveralls dirty at the knees, hiking boots, a floppy straw hat—she stood there, regrouped the attitude triggered when she thought she had heard the closing of the car door she had been waiting for.

"You're that detective."

"He's not home?"

"Even a bad detective should have guessed that."

"He hasn't come home at all?"

She folded her arms across her chest under the coveralls. "You don't ignore what I say, Mr. whatever your name is."

"You don't take your anger out on me, Mrs. Mellecker. I'm trying to help Jack Price and maybe your husband. And the name's Fortune, Dan Fortune."

"I couldn't care less about Jack Price, Mr. Fortune, and I'm not all that sure about my husband."

"That's clear, anyway."

"Good."

We stood facing each other off, getting about as little out of that as usual. She blocked the doorway, didn't invite me in, but didn't close the door in my face either. She wanted to talk out her anger, didn't much care who the listener was, and I still needed information.

"Price's car is gone."

"What is that supposed to mean?"

"It was parked across the street. When did he come back and get it?"

"How should I know?"

"Your husband would probably have driven him back."

"If he did, he didn't come and tell me, and he didn't stay. I'm not sure I care if he stays when he does come back."

When people need to talk about what is eating them inside they will eventually let it out. The pressure will inexorably turn the talk to what they can't tell even themselves but must tell.

"Where would your husband be at this hour?"

"Anywhere. Communing with his muse, touching his soul. Painting the dawn like Constable. Searching for what the world denied him with its crass demands. How do I know where he is or what he's doing? He doesn't care what I know or want. God, does he think I'm some kind of fool? I don't know he wants to turn his back on everything we've accomplished, what we've struggled to get? Well not me. I've earned my comfort, my rewards, a nice life without anything I have to do. He can chase his ridiculous muse if he wants, but he'll chase it without me and what's mine."

"You think he's out painting? At this hour?"

"Painting or just sleeping pure and alone in his attic, his secret hideaway." She laughed in the chill dawn, wrapped her arms tighter across her chest, cold now as well as defensive. "Another thing he thinks I don't know. After all these years does he really think he can fool me so easily? Rent a hideaway I won't find out about?"

"What hideaway? Where?"

"Some scummy bungalow court down on the lower east with the bearded soul-searchers and transient scrawny blondes out of the sixties he's suddenly decided he should have been with."

"You have an address?"

"No."

"Jack Price could be there. I think he's in danger. That means Max could be in danger."

She was bitter, but she'd been with Mellecker over twenty-five years. "It's on Salsipuedes near Cota. The Aurora Court."

"Thanks."

"Tell him to be home by five if he wants any dinner."

The first thin light of dawn is a leveller.

Deserted streets, dark gray and silent. The passing of a solitary car. A thin cat and a derelict dog. The same among the stately mansions and trimmed hedges of the upper east, and the bare shacks and lumber yard and weed-grown lots of the lower east. The cover of night fading as the shadows emerge.

Aurora Court was a quarter of a block up Salsipuedes from Cota. I got out and walked into the court where the dirty, uncurtained windows looked at me like the eyes of caged animals in the pound. The tarnished brass slots on most doors were empty, but the third in from the street had a cut business card: *Max Mellecker*. Middle-class habits die hard.

I rang three times, heard no ring inside, and knocked.

"Yes? Who is it?"

The voice was distant from the door.

"Dan Fortune. The detective looking for Jack Price."

"The door's unlocked."

A tiny living room had two canvas chairs and walls of paintings sharply different from the seascapes at Mellecker's house. Abstract, post-expressionist, groping. Mellecker lay on a narrow bed in the smaller bedroom. He studied a canvas on an easel, a table of brushes and squeezed tubes beside it. A faint head in a jungle of thick, grotesque color.

"He went home."

"When?"

"An hour or so ago."

"He's not there now."

Mellecker turned his head to look at me. "I drove him up to his car, he went home."

"He didn't make it. Not yet, anyway."

He went on looking at me, then turned back to his painting on the easel. "How'd you find me here?"

"Your wife."

He lay silent for a time. I looked at all the paintings. He'd been busy. They were all the same combination of hidden figures behind

305

thick, bold, jagged blocks of powerful color.

"She'll divorce me." He watched me study his paintings, followed my eyes around the dawn room. "If I drop out now, try to find out what I really wanted to do. I've got enough money to make it, but not the way she thinks we should live, not in that house, probably not in Santa Barbara. I'd have to leave, and she won't come with me. Why should she? It's the house, the town, the friends, the lunches, the money in the bank that count for her. The outer life. You know Herbert Marcuse? His work?"

"Some of it."

" 'Individuals identify themselves with the existence imposed upon them, are indoctrinated by the conditions under which they live and think and which they do not transcend.' Something like that. The way things are, is the way things should be. What you see is what you want. Maggie and Jack." He looked at his work in the room. "I took him to the Jag, he said he was going home."

"Where else would he go?"

"Anywhere. Something's wrong with Brower's deal. I know it and Jack knows it, but he won't quit on it. He's got to win this time, make it work out for him, bring home the prize. Are you a poker player, Fortune?"

"Off and on."

"We both play in Morgan's game. High-low poker: seven-card stud or hold 'em. Jack always stays in a hand with a possible eight low. Chasing a possible anything is bad poker, but chasing an eight is hopeless. Real players chase a six at worst. They have an eight made, might win with it, but they never chase it and often fold it. Jack chases an eight when it's the best hand he can get. Most of the time he won't even get the eight, and if he gets it he loses." He looked away out the single bedroom window at the gray dawn over the bungalow court. "He's out there chasing an eight right now."

"In what game?" I said.

"That's the question, isn't it? I'm sure it's Brower's game, but I could be wrong. It could be Santos Torena's game, with or without Brower, or even the Genius's mini-revolution."

I told him about the Genius. About the two killers.

"My God." Even his voice was pale. "Who are they? What kind of men could do . . ."

"Ordinary men. Just like you and me."

Through the single narrow window he watched the first light of another morning. "Not like me, and I don't think like you. Feed and fuck, work and sleep. They serve who pays them, and they don't chase eights. I laugh at Jack, but I've begun to realize my whole life has been chasing eights, and someone wants it that way." He shook his head to himself this time. "I'm going to find out what I wanted to do. I'm going to try. I think I'm going to try. It might not even be too late."

"It could be too late for Jack Price."

"What do you want me to do, Fortune?"

"Think of somewhere he could have gone."

"Home, Brower's office, Claire Broberg's, how do I know? He believes, you understand? He believes the whole thing."

Chapter Thirty-Three

They are behind Jack Price when he drives away from the phone booth on Hollister Avenue. The Cadillac has more power but it harder to handle and less responsive then his Jag. He has the better car and he knows what to do with it. They'll eat his dust, be left standing with egg on their faces, see a blue streak waving *sayonara*.

He is almost happy as he cruises through the dawn toward the freeway. He feels powerful with the wheel in his hands, the surge of the six cylinders under his feet, in his total control. The chase through the new morning light. He is doing what he has seen in the movies a hundred times, concentrates on his driving skill, his mechanical superiority.

He has recognized the skinny *coyote*, Paz
Linero, and the heavyset *mule* in the Cadillac
that is chasing him, and he is happy about that
too. Glad it is the *coyotes* who must have been
waiting outside Claire's house, not the "experts"
Brower brought in. It has all been a mistake.
Those two, Messick and Gretzer, have never
been chasing him. Brower isn't doing anything
illegal, isn't worried that Jack will spoil whatever it is Brower is doing to close the deal.

So he feels almost exhilarated as he drives
along Storke Road and over the freeway and
straight on toward the mountains where the
road becomes Glen Annie Road named for the
ranch of old man Hollister who owned this
whole area once. Hollister named the ranch
after the wife he brought to rule over his
domain carved from the Spanish Land Grants
when the Americans came in to take over a
sleepy land and make California great. Now
the wife and the ranch have a road named
after them to show where they were and how
important Hollister had been.

Jack makes a left turn into Cathedral Oaks
Road, speeds up past Dos Pueblos High School.
The Caddy lurches onto Cathedral Oaks far
behind him. Jack ducks into the first left, Ala-
meda Avenue, floors the pedal in the residential
tract, twists through the small streets with their
lawns and cul-de-sacs and dead ends, and parks
in a hidden turnaround. He hears a heavy car go
by, catches a glimpse of the Caddy two streets

over and moving south toward Calle Real. He laughs aloud, makes his way to Glen Annie again, turns left to Cathedral Oaks, then heads east. It is time to go home.

He drives the smooth Jaguar easily, lightly on the almost empty four-lane boulevard. He starts to sing the fight song of The Golden Gophers ... *Minnesota hats off to thee ...* when he sees the blonde in white climbing into a red Mercedes 450 SL convertible, her long, lean body arched and tight and smooth in the gray dawn as she and the unseen man in the car prepare to drive somewhere for a glorious weekend, and even more glorious weekend nights, golf clubs jutting from two bags in the back seat and ...

It is his first summer home from the university. His father takes him to the country club. The timbered Minnesota hills enclose the neat white buildings and the small figures that walk on the rolling green of the fairways. In the pool behind the clubhouse there is the shouting and high laughter of children. On the shaded terrace next to the pool and overlooking the first tee half-hidden people drink cool drinks.

His father is on the board of the club, has been for as long as Jack can remember, is greeted many times as they walk across the gravel parking lot. Jack stands apart. Now that he has been six months a man of his own he won't be Joe's boy, in the shadow. Instead he watches a tall woman in a green dress, her long red hair that shines in the sun, the dress that swings as she walks into the clubhouse.

The odor of the locker room is hot and sweet, thick with steam and the smell of talcum powder. Older men, solid and substantial, sit naked on the benches. Jack knows many of them, the friends, associates, and enemies of his father, but naked they seem even larger than he remembers. They don't ignore him, but after a smile, a nod, it is his father they talk to.

Jack slips into the shower. He stands under the hot water a long time. He is at that age when he is acutely aware of his body parts, the warm liquid flowing over them and him. The heat stimulates, but also soothes and tranquillizes, and that is no way to prepare for golf with important men. A warrior doesn't go into battle soothed and tranquillized.

The shock of cold water. Icy, whipping. Jack thinks of those naked Vikings who stand in hot steam and pour ice water over their bodies. Sit in waves of searing heat from fired rocks, then plunge into Finnish lakes ringed with the snows of winter. Whip their naked bodies with birch branches in ritual preparation for battle. Cleanse body and soul and mind for the purity of battle.

He has no birch branches, but stays under the numbing cold water until he can't stand it anymore.

As he dresses in the golf clothes his father has bought him, a fat, tired, gray-faced man sits down beside his father. The man smiles a stiff, almost grotesque smile.

"Sorry to hear you're all so snowed under over at B. of E."

"We're all busy, Tom."

"Guess that's why the contract renewal hasn't come through."

"I don't handle that directly, you know that. You'll have to talk to Walt Beaver."

"But you're my man, right, Joe? We've been together a long time."

"A long time, Tom."

"That counts, right?"

His father smiles, bends to tie his golf shoes. The fat man looks at his father's bent head and Jack sees something die in his eyes. The man stands, pulls on his zipper that doesn't quite close his fly all the way over his paunch.

"Well, come over to the house sometime, Joe."

"I'll do that, Tom."

After the man, Tom, has gone, and Jack and his father are on their way to the first tee, his father talks about Tom.

"Tom Berti, I've known him thirty years. He thinks it gives him privileges with the Board of Education, and within reason it does. He's a solid businessman, and a friend, and that counts, remember that, Jack. But only to a point. He's let his family, his house, his hobbies distract him, hasn't kept up with the competition. We've got two new firms we know are cheaper and better. Business is business."

A tall old oak shades the first tee. The two men they are to play with are waiting, smile at Jack, talk to his father. A judge and a prosecutor, both on the Republican Committee. They discuss handicaps, find that Jack has no handicap, decide to give the boy a twenty. Jack's father says with a handicap that big he'll play with Jack. Everyone laughs. Jack will tee off first.

He has played with his father since he was sixteen, but he is conscious of the people on the terrace, the lawyer and the judge. He hurries his drive, tops it, sends it bouncing less than a hundred yards down the fairway. The others laugh, but not meanly, make remarks about their own bad shots. Jack stands back under the tree out of the way where he doesn't have to look at the terrace.

As it happens, while his father and the prosecutor make good, straight drives for distance, the judge shanks his and ends in the rough near Jack, and Jack has a decent two iron second shot. He only boggies the hole, is congratulated somewhat tightly by the judge who has double-bogeyed and cost his side the hole. Jack makes a fair drive at the second tee, settles down to the safe, plodding game his father taught him.

As his father, the judge and the prosecutor talk business, politics, and cases they are handling, Jack feels a thick silence like deep water settle over the green of the grass and the blue and sun of the Minnesota sky. Voices, close and distant, become faint and detached from him. Voices

*without direction. A kind of tunnel vision. He
sees the trees, the sky, the grass and the flight of
his ball. He watches his ball in the sky, watches
it hit and bound and roll, but is detached from
the ball too.*

*The soft grass of the fairway springs under his
feet. The thicker rough catches his shoes and
pants, he pushes through like an explorer in the
jungle. Sun filters through the leaves of the trees
where he walks alone. He walks with his father,
the judge and the prosecutor, but he walks alone.
Only the grass, the trees, the flags fluttering on
the greens. Isolated. Around him they talk but
he doesn't hear. He answers, but he doesn't hear,
not even himself. Words seem to float in a haze
miles away.*

*Then they are on the eighteenth green, Jack
and his father have won. The judge and the prosecutor congratulate him, his father accepts the
money with a laugh, and they go into the clubhouse. In the locker room Jack showers again,
changes into his bathing suit. His father and
the judge will meet on the terrace to discuss
an important case. Jack will join them later.
The prosecutor has some other business. Jack
goes out to the pool.*

*In the shallow end children scream in a mass
of arms and legs and splashing water. It has
not been that long since Jack was there in the
shallow end, even less since he was out in the
middle with the teenagers playing tag, dunking
the girls and each other, smirking at the adults*

who sit in deck chairs under hats and read books or talk and drink their drinks. He climbs the diving board, tries a swan dive, hits hard, hears the teenagers laugh. He swims, knows they are all watching him on the terrace and in the pool, and soon gets out to sit on a deck chair before he joins his father and the judge.

Jack sees the girl in white. She is tall, but not as tall as he is. Slimmer than he is. Young, but older, a woman not a girl. She is blonde. Not much older, a year, two years, yet he knows she is much older than he is. A white dress with a high-necked halter top that shows her slim bare arms and her bare back down to where the swell of her buttocks begins. A lean, smooth, taut, silken bare back. The long curve of her spine that swells into the curve of her hips and breasts and no bra. He stares in wonder at the bare back with no brassiere strap, wonders if under the dress there is some female secret he doesn't know.

She crosses the pool area, walks up onto the terrace, sits alone at a table. The waiter brings her a drink. She sips and looks out over the rolling green golf course and the Minnesota hills. Jack sees himself there at the table with her. He has a drink, is leaning back in the white terrace chair, one ankle crossed on his knee. She is smiling at him, reaches to take his hand and look into his eyes. He touches her hand, smiles back.

Then the prosecutor is at the table, bends to kiss the woman in white, sits down, waves for the waiter who hurries to him.

Chasing Eights

Jack goes into the locker room to dress, joins his father and the judge, hopes they have finished so he can go home.

On Cathedral Oaks, Jack drives faster in the cold dawn.

The afternoon of the woman-in-white. The day of the judge and the prosecutor. The judge died years ago after a bribery scandal, the prosecutor went on to become state attorney general. His father died, Jack went on to play a lot more golf. Where is the woman-in-white?

Jack stops for the light at Patterson Avenue, the Cadillac is not behind him.

If he'd had the woman-in-white he would have gone far. Played a better game of golf, a three handicap. Any woman except Angie. Waiters to run when he waved. A different man.

The light turns, Jack guns up the sweeping curve toward Turnpike and his turn. The Cadillac is nowhere in sight.

He drives on past Turnpike.

He isn't a different man. He is Jack Price. He never played golf well, he never really liked to play golf. Angie is the woman-in-white.

He turns into Highway 154 and drives fast up the steep curves into San Marcos Pass.

Chapter Thirty-Four

Dawn rested pale on the Price house and the cul-de-sac of the older upper-middle-class tract. Still hours before the sun rose above the mountains, only a loud dog alone on a neighboring lawn was up to greet me. There was no yellow Jaguar, but the old Chevy station wagon sat in the carport.

No one answered my rings.

I walked around the house through the side gate to the back.

She was in the hot tub.

"Jack?"

Head back, eyes closed, hair up and tied in a twist, her body under the steaming water, Angela Price opened her eyes.

"He still hasn't come home?"

"No."

"Called again?"

"No, Dan."

The hot tub was on a raised platform, our heads on a level where I stood below.

"Join me."

"I'd fall asleep."

She looked away toward the dawn and the mountains. "I can't sleep. I ache in every bone. I'm a little scared. In here it's hot, almost peaceful, even rational."

"Brower tell you anything more? About Jack? The deal?"

She closed her eyes, leaned her head back against the side of the tub again. "Not in so many words, but I could feel it. I wasn't being cute when I told him he gets an extra thrill out of fucking both of us. I know he's using Jack, but at the same time I think he's concerned about Jack, worried about something."

I described the two men who had chased me, shot the Genius and his gateman. "Ever seen them around Brower?"

Her eyes opened. "This morning. At least, I think so. When he left I looked out, saw him talking to two men in the parking lot. It sounds like them. There was something frightening about them. The way they stood, the way they looked at him. The older one especially."

"Yeh," I said. "What did they do?"

"Nothing. Got into their car, drove away."

"With Brower?"

"No. He was alone in the lot for some time after they'd gone. I thought he was waiting for someone else, but then he got into the Rolls and drove away too. I dressed, came home." She floated under the steaming water in the dawn. "Is Jack in real trouble, Dan? Danger? Or is he part of whatever Ed's doing?"

"I think he's in danger whichever way it is."

"You mean if he's part of it or Ed's pawn?"

"I think Brower has some scheme to raise money he needs for an even bigger project in Nevada, and so do the police. Chavalas is digging into it now, or he will be in a few hours. If it turns out something's illegal in the condo deal, Jack is president of El Bosque Homes. Brower is clean, Jack takes the fall."

"Santos Torena was vice-president," she said. "He wanted to talk to Jack, he got killed."

"Yeh," I said.

I climbed the steps to the hot tub, sat on the railing. The steam rose into the cold morning air. Her body was diffused under the surface, but long and lean and female. It was a shame to waste such a body, and mind, on Ed Brower. When I raised my head to look at her face, she was looking at me. She knew what I was thinking.

"He wouldn't kill anyone, Dan."

"If you go to bed with tigers, you risk getting eaten. When you call up demons, you can't always control them."

"Those two men?"

"And Brower."

Closed in by the mountains, sound carries a long way in a clear winter Santa Barbara dawn. A jet thundered into takeoff at the distant airport. Angie Price listened to it until it had faded away to a faint echo pulsing in the pale sky. "What they strive for is so finite, so small. Nothing is more transitory than power, not even money. You ever realize that nothing gained by force has ever lasted? It must be a terrible thing to know that all you've done, all you are, will last such a short time."

She let her long body float slowly up to the surface of the tub as if to make me look, but she really wanted to look at and within herself. She shook her head as if unable to understand.

"What did you get out of going to Brower tonight?"

She went on looking at herself where she floated in the rising steam. "Me, I think. I think that's why I hired you. When I sent you to look for Jack, I was looking for me. Until now I couldn't have hired you. I'd have waited at home until it was all over, lived with the result. I couldn't have sent you to find Jack. I couldn't have decided to go to Brower." She laughed in the hot tub, let her body sink slowly to the bottom again. "Brower needs to be a winner. Tonight he wasn't the winner, I was. The one who needs the other least always wins. To need anything too much is always to lose. Tonight

Brower needed me more than I needed him."

"What does Jack need?"

"Certainly not me." She looked again toward the mountains around the lush city as if waiting for the sun to come up so she could fly away. "I thought I had to be what Jack wanted me to be to have any life. Now I know I never wanted that life. He doesn't want me or the life we have either, but he doesn't know it." A morning hawk soared in the dawn. A red-shoulder. Her eyes followed it across the sky. "Jack liked our old Mesa house. It was a blue-collar neighborhood, he was the only one with executive position on the block. Out here he's just another professional among the crowd. It was after we moved that he started to sleep late, take days off, nap on the weekends. After a time it seemed all he wanted to do was sleep, hide in bed. That was when I started fucking around." She watched the hawk in its slow circles looking for prey. "I think if someone offered to support him and the house and the family for the rest of his life, he'd go to bed and sleep all day every day."

A car drove slowly into the cul-de-sac beyond the house. I listened. It was a big car. Too big for a Jaguar, too rough sounding for a Rolls-Royce. I didn't know what kind of car the two killers drove, put my hand on my old cannon in my pocket. Angela Price didn't notice.

"He should have been a carpenter, he likes working with his hands. Instead he's a mediocre businessman with the wrong wife. He blames me, and maybe he's right. Or he was until tonight." She came down from the hawk to me. "I think I'm free now, Dan. I hope he'll be too."

"Just like that?" I said.

She looked down through the water at her long, slim body once more. "Until a few years ago I was as heavy as Jack. Flabby, out-of-shape, dull. As soon as I started to fuck around I took up running. I go early in the morning while the house is still quiet. I slip out through the patio and just start running. At first I could only do a mile, but by the time I'd gone to bed with the fifth man I was up to almost ten miles. The morning air is so clean on my face. I become aware of my muscles, the rhythm of breathing. I'm alone out there, and I run until it hurts so much I have to stop. Then I feed the kids, send them off to school, sit with a cup of coffee and listen to the birds. I'm aware of my whole body, yet out of it, as if I've run right out of myself. Out of myself to find myself.

The big car that had driven into the cul-de-sac had not driven out. I listened to her and for any sounds that didn't belong to the quiet neighborhood. There was nothing. Only the morning birds, the rustle of some small animal in the underbrush outside the back fence.

"And lost Jack?"

"I don't think I ever really found Jack. Only a husband, a home, and children. Exactly like my parents and his."

Chasing Eights

The car with the big engine still hadn't started up again. Probably a neighbor coming home from an early morning errand. I hoped it was a neighbor.

"You don't sound exactly like your parents," I said.

"How do you think I ended up in this hot tub? Behind my house in a good middle-class tract, waiting for my husband to get home? Why do you think I married Jack, *wanted* to marry Jack when he was probably the worst man for me?"

"You parents wanted you to marry him?"

"It's not that simple. It's who they are, what they expect of themselves and you. Did you ever read a mail-order catalog for tall girls?"

"Not that I remember."

"I have. I was almost six feet tall at fifteen. I lived inside a tall girl's catalog."

Chapter Thirty-Five

Angela's father is only an inch over six feet, and while at five feet nine inches her mother is taller than most women, she is not excessively so, especially in Minnesota. So they are surprised when, at fifteen, Angela suddenly spurts from a nice, average, well-rounded five-feet-six to a long, sleek five-eleven.

At first Angela is delighted. It is a time of healthy food, exercise and slim-is-beautiful even in Minnesota, and she has been dieting to lose weight and girth for as long as she can remember. Too soon she finds that growing abnormally tall is not an accepted method of slimming for a female. She towers over most of the boys her age, isn't much shorter than the tallest of her school's athletes even on the basketball team.

If she were athletic, it might not be so bad, but she isn't, and doesn't want to be, and most of the girls as well as the boys consider girl athletes freaks. Angela doesn't want to be a freak. She wants to be liked, popular, average, exactly the same as everyone else. Her mother is worried and her father is a little annoyed, he doesn't like girl freaks either.

Angela wants the same clothes as the other girls, but it is hard to find them in her size. Nothing really fits. It is a small town, her choices are few. Her mother tries. She takes Angela to Minneapolis. Even then, most of what high school girls are wearing that year or any year is not made in sizes so long. The fads and tastes of high school girls are mercurial, have a brief shelf life, are made in average sizes. Minneapolis isn't Paris, or even New York, they can't afford the time or money to go to Minneapolis often anyway.

Mail order helps, and her mother tries to make Angela's clothes. That works for size and fit, not for style. The truth is that Angela does not look good in what smaller girls wear no matter what size it is. So most of the time Angela must wear clothes too big in the waist, too short in the sleeve, never long enough, and that don't really suit her in the first place.

She is a relatively happy girl, does not cry much, but has few boyfriends. She tries to be the same as the other girls, wears the same clothes no matter how small on her or how poor she looks in the styles of smaller girls, but she does not get boys. Tall boys don't want a girl who can look them in the eye, short boys have to bully her. It goes on this way into her sixteenth and then seventeenth year.

It is a week after her seventeenth birthday when she finds the tall-girl catalog. An aunt who has moved to New York sends her the first real pair of tight, faded jeans that fit, and with them she notices this catalog from a special shop in New York—Tall & Tasty. Not all the clothes the smaller girls wear at her school are in it, but more than she has ever seen. She is ecstatic, plans everything she will buy, including shoes that don't make her look like the world's worst frump.

That is when she really cries for the first time.

Without realizing it, Angela has been changing. She has not become a rebel, but she has begun to accept that she is not the same as all other high school girls, has her own personality, and will, she has decided, eventually find a boy who will want her as she is. The catalog is a wonderful moment, but as she looks for the perfect pair of high heels for the spring dance that is only a week away, she begins to notice something odd. At first she is only puzzled, and then, as she slowly turns each page of the shoe section, she bursts into long, hard tears.

No shoe in the catalog has a heel over two inches. Dancing slippers, party pumps, business shoes, pointed toes, rounded toes, spectators, slings, suede, leather or the flashiest patent. Nothing has a heel more than two inches high, most have less. All other clothes are in every style. Not the shoes.

All tall girls want to be shorter. All tall girls know they have to be shorter than their man. All tall girls know they must be shorter to get a man.

At school that week she is silent, says little, watches the boys and the other girls. She watches herself. She sees how she bends forward and rounds her shoulders when she walks, stands with one hip thrust to the side, shoulders down. How she always eats lunch half lying on her elbow on the grass so the boys do not look shorter when they eat with her. The way she slumps in her seat in the classroom, looks no taller than any other girl from the front or back. How often she stands hunched, her arms crossed on her breasts.

Two days before the spring dance she goes out to the most daring women's store in town and buys a pair of four-inch black patent pumps even though they are a size small. She buys a slim black dress with a bare back and a high turtleneck that is her size but only in regular. Black net pantyhose, a new underwired black brassiere, and on the day of the dance has her hair done in an upsweep.

When she is dressed, she comes down to wait for her date, a quiet boy in her class she is only friends with. It is a group date, but the boy has been hinting that maybe they should be more than friends the last year of school. When they're seniors and all. Her parents stare at her.

"Oh, honey," her mother says. "You . . . look nice."

Her father says, "What do you call that outfit?"

"I'm going to a dance," Angela says. "I'm wearing what all the other girls wear."

She has little makeup, only small silver earrings, and the slim black dress is not at all gaudy. But with the four-inch heels and upswept hair she is now taller than her father, and the sleek line and high turtleneck of the dress, the high thrust of her breasts in the new bra as she stands up straight, accentuate her height even more.

"You look . . . older, dear," her mother says.

"You look like a streetwalker," her father says. "That woman on *Batman*, what's her name, Catwoman? You look like a—"

"Now, Tom—"

"Why?" she says to her father. "Because I'm wearing high heels, a tight dress, standing tall? I'm not wearing any makeup, flashy jewelry, loud colors. I'm just tall."

Before her father can say anything more, her date arrives. She now stands a full six inches over him. Her breasts, not all that big, seem to thrust out at him. He stares, isn't happy. In front of Angela's parents, of course, he is polite but everyone is awkward. He and Angela leave as soon as she gets a light coat. In the car he is not polite.

"Christ, what're you doing, Angela? I mean, that outfit, the hair and all. Jesus, what're you trying to do to me?"

"I'm wearing what all the other girls wear, George."

"Well, shit, it makes me look stupid, for Christ sake. You don't think I'm going into any dance with you like that?"

"Because I'm too tall for a girl, George?"

"Because I'm not gonna get laughed at." He drives her to where they are to meet the others, and he drives off and leaves her alone with her two girlfriends and their dates and one extra boy who couldn't get any date at all. Everyone is inches shorter than Angela in her new clothes, and as they go into the dance everyone outside and inside turns to stare.

The night is a disaster.

The girls giggle, the boys stay away. The two chaperones aren't pleased. No one dances with her. The boys don't laugh, some even seem to understand her flaunting of her height at them and don't hide their anger. At one point the boys try to push the tallest boy, a skinny center on the basketball team, and then the shortest boy in school, out to dance with her.

Chasing Eights

They laugh when they do that, but their eyes don't laugh. She goes home early, driven by one of the chaperones who doesn't speak to her.

The second chaperone has called her parents. When her father starts to lecture her, she runs upstairs, cries alone in her room more than she ever has in her life. She never wears the dress or the bra or the four-inch heels again, has no boyfriend the last year in high school, goes off to college in a height minimizing shirt-waist dress and flat shoes, her hair medium length, and wearing a simple brassiere with no underwires.

Chapter Thirty-Six

As Jack Price drives up the curves and sheer drops of San Marcos Pass, he knows that Angie will leave him.

He drives fast, knows she's gone this time if he goes home without the deal. The woman-in-white won't wait forever. Buy into the car dealership, a partner, or he's out of her life. He realizes as he hugs the curves and feels the wind in his face that he's known for a long time she'd leave him if he didn't make his move soon, wonders why he didn't know all along that Angie was the woman-in-white, how he'd missed it all these years?

The woman-in-white doesn't hang around if a man doesn't deliver. Time is money. If you're not the man to drive the fast car, then stand aside and let him pass. A man makes his own destiny, sink or swim. The woman-in-white knows what she wants.

She will walk out, take the kids, probably the house. The wife always gets the house, you can't make the kids leave their home. The house and the furniture, the cats and the hot tub. For him the Jaguar and the open road. No more house, no more golf, no more business. Like Max said, find the real Jack under all the paint. A condo in Newport Beach, his own plane.

At the top of the pass, Jack pulls off into Camino Cielo and parks among the trees. He looks out at the brush and old oaks, listens to the dawn. He sits there in the silent car among the morning birds and green old trees washed clean by winter rain.

He can go to Vegas. In Vegas there is always a game to sit in on and take money from strangers. He is a good poker player. Not as good as the Genius, but who is? He can hold his own.

Go back to Minnesota.

Then knows that at his age it is too late, and Jack Price doesn't run away.

The deal can go through. The men looking for him are those *coyotes*. They've made a mistake, he knows nothing about Torena. All he has to do is tell them. If they know enough about him to find him at both Max's house and Claire's, they know where he lives, are probably waiting there for him right now.

Jack drives back down the pass.

Abruptly pulls off before he reaches the bottom.

He gets out this time, stands at the edge of a sheer drop and the early dawn panorama of the coast and the far out islands.

Ed Brower is doing something that could get them all in deep trouble, is worried about Jack. It isn't only the *coyotes* out there. Messick and Gretzer have been told to watch him. He still can't go home. Not until the deal is nailed down, or Brower calls off his dogs. He has to talk to Brower, tell him that he, Jack, isn't going to crack, but that he has to know what Brower is really doing so he can decide if it's all right.

Before he gets back into the Jaguar, he takes his Sharper Image binoculars from the glove compartment. The sweeping view on a clear dawn is too good to miss. He focuses on the distant islands so clear he can see actual hills and valleys. On the thin traffic of the freeway on a Saturday morning. On the harbor where some boats are already putting out to sea. On his house to the right along Cathedral Oaks.

His house is out of sight, but he continues to look. He sees the neat, orderly lines and angles and rolling green curves of the community golf course. The sun is not yet up, but tiny figures already move across the grass that seems almost painted on the earth. They swing invisible clubs at invisible balls. From this height they are like robots that swing and move without clubs or arms or even legs. Only the rigid motion of a slow dance across the green lines and squares and curves.

There is no light in the elegant old house that is Ed Brower's office. No cars in the parking lot, and the door is locked. Jack stands alone in the morning in front of the locked office door. He looks up at the dark second floor windows. He looks around at the empty parking lot and the streets on both sides where no one walks and only a few cars drive past.

He could wait, but he doesn't want to wait.

He gets into the Jaguar, drives north on Garden Street, then east to the board and care home where Angie's mother lives. They get up early, the old people at the board and care. The staff is small and there is a lot to do to get ready for the day. Most of the rooms are dark, but there is light in the kitchen, bathrooms and dining room. In the living room where all through the day the old folks sit and stare out the windows or at nothing, the stained and dusty furniture waits empty. Last night's magazines are still on the tables and chairs.

The cook, who is also foreman of the staff, looks out of the kitchen. "Oh, it's you Mr. Price. Don't think your mother's up yet, but you can go look. She's been kind of tired last few days, but she's eating pretty good."

"Thanks, Mrs. Gallardo."

Chasing Eights

Narrow halls lead off the living room to clusters of small rooms. Angie's mother has the corner room on the right. They all think she is his mother, and he has never corrected them. He and Angie almost never visit the old lady together, so Angie hasn't heard what they think, and the old lady doesn't care. She doesn't seem to know exactly what a son or daughter is, or the difference between a son and a son-in-law.

"You awake, Mother?"

Her eyes snap open as if she has been faking, lying in wait to attack him. "Who are you?"

"It's Jack."

"I want to go to the bathroom."

Jack helps her to the bathroom across the hall, helps her settle on the seat. He leaves the door open an inch, goes back into her room to sit on the single armchair. She has been in this room for four years, everything Jack and Angie have bought her is all around: the TV set, the radio for her baseball games, the recliner that takes up too much space in the tiny room but gives her both pleasure when she watches TV and pride when any of the other old people see it. The stereo and cabinet of CDs so she has her music. The bureau. All given to her since she came here. Nothing of her own, except the bed. The double bed she brought from Minnesota, the bed she and Angie's father slept in for fifty-two years.

"Where are you?"

He helps her out of the bathroom and back to her bed. When he tries to help her into the bed, she pushes him away.

"Turn on the TV."

He turns on the small color set that is all the room will accommodate, switches channels until she decides which early morning show she wants. It is an exercise program, she watches it as if she were doing every movement herself.

"I want to get dressed."

He gets one of the attendants to help her dress, goes out to wait alone in the living room. He will have breakfast with the old lady. He likes to visit her. She needs help and he can give it. The staff have to dress her, but the rest is something he can do: cut her food, open the cereal boxes and wrapped crackers, change channels and stations, read TV Guide, walk her around the block, put her Books-On-Tape cassettes on the stereo and give her her earphones.

In the empty living room with the debris of last night's games and reading Jack decides he will come to see the old lady more than the once a week he does most weeks now. She needs him, is probably the only one who does. She's like a dying planet, a dying sun, and needs him. The She-Wolf never needed him, he never could please her. She never wanted him, only his father. Angie's mother likes him, is grateful even if she is bossy as hell, and he will visit her more often. He still wonders why Angie wouldn't let the old lady live with them, but at least he can visit her more, maybe every day.

"Here we are, Mr. Price. Aren't we beautiful this morning?"

The attendant sits the old lady facing Jack, leaves to help another resident. The old lady glares after her.

"She's so stupid. They're all so stupid here."

"She's just being nice, Mother."

"I want to watch TV."

Jack helps her back to her room, settles her in the recliner. He plugs her earphones into the set, turns it on, reads TV Guide. She always lets him read the programs for every station, always decides on the same one—cartoons. He sits with her a few minutes as she stares at the cartoon mayhem without a single laugh or even a smile.

Breakfast won't be for half an hour.

Ed Brower could be in his office by now. Or out at the Hope Ranch house.

"Have a good day, Mother," he says as he leaves. "I'm going to try to visit you more often."

The old lady says nothing, stares at the cartoons.

Brower's office is still dark and locked.

Jack drives to the freeway, gets off at Las Positas Road, takes the back way into Hope Ranch and Brower's mansion at the edge of the sea. The gate is locked, the house is dark.

The garage is open through the fence, the Rolls-Royce is not there. Jack doesn't want to ring at this hour if Brower isn't home.

He sits for a time, the islands like floating shadows far out above a still dark sea.

Angie will leave him.

He thinks of Claire Broberg.

Chapter Thirty-Seven

Angela Price stepped out of the hot tub tall, slim and naked, her body steaming in the cold dawn.

"You know how long it's taken me to be able to do this? How many years to unlearn all that was put on me?"

"How long do you think it's taken me to learn to just sit here?"

She reached for a bath towel on the redwood deck. "Another time, another place."

"Two different people."

She shrugged at that, dried herself, put on a blue terry robe. "I had an aunt in Minnesota. She was dirt poor, anorexic, had four sullen kids and a gaudy alcoholic husband who bat-

343

tered her and beat her down and strutted around chasing other women. But she sent the most expensive Christmas cards we ever got. She sent Christmas cards to everyone even when she couldn't really afford the stamps much less the cards." She sat on the redwood railing in the robe and stretched her neck back and forth as if it were as stiff as the rail. "Where *is* he, Dan? Where? What?"

"Take it easy," I said.

She took a cigarette out of a package in the robe pocket, lit it. "What is he doing? What's happened to him?"

I didn't know what had happened to Jack Price or where he was, but I had a good idea what he was doing. "He's staying away until the deal is sealed and he can come home successful, the winner. I think he knows something he doesn't want to know, doesn't want to tell you or anyone."

On the railing above the hot tub, her cigarette smoke mixed with the steam rising from the tub in the cold morning air. "You mean he's hiding. Running in a circle." She slid down to the deck, sat against the railing, knees up and wrapped in the robe. "I said he was a standard male chauvinist, Dan, but he's not. He only thinks he's supposed to be, should be. It's all a role. It always has been."

The cigarette moved like the smoking wand of a magician, the incense of a sorcerer. "He's been playing a role all his life. The way some actors play the same character until they come to think it's really them. An old actor named Ned Sparks played a character who spoke in a deadpan monotone in a hundred movies. Humphrey Bogart got into fights in night-clubs, always lost. The police said Bogart's problem was he thought he was Humphrey Bogart. Jack is what he thinks he's supposed to be. He's never known what he wants, only what he was supposed to want. Jack Price—successful businessman, breadwinner, fast-lane male whose wife stays home and has babies."

On the deck she was bent all the way forward, rigid as a statue, the cigarette forgotten, a long ash about to fall.

"All these years he's been playing his role, and the echo role I thought I had to play almost destroyed me. His whole life is false, and now he's out there in a real world he doesn't know anything about." She spoke almost straight down to the redwood deck. "I have this terrible need to go out there, find him and comfort him. Hold his head, tell him it's all right, it'll all be fine, everything will be good again soon. But I can't. I won't be destroyed again."

"He's got to come home sometime."

She looked up at me. "You're a rational man, aren't you, Dan? Logical and clear eyed."

"I try to be."

"It's not something we're particularly taught." She looked away. "Jack would reject any comfort from me anyway. The real man who's going

345

to hit it big with all the other movers and shakers doesn't need any help or comfort."

I said, "He should come home soon. Morning does something to us, you know? Makes everything better, a new day. He should want to talk to someone, have breakfast, take a shower. Where would he go to get breakfast? A bath, a bed?"

"Max Mellecker's house. Maybe Brower."

"I don't think so."

"The agency? He has a key."

"Claire Broberg?"

She dropped her burning cigarette over the rail to the wet morning ground. "She's a lot the way I was when I married Jack. When I thought I was supposed to marry what Jack was supposed to be. If he can't come home to me, he might need a mother."

"If he comes home before I get back to you, call the police. Tell Sergeant Chavalas."

I left her still seated on the wet redwood deck, hunched inside the thick robe, the tub steaming behind her. A brighter white tinged the sky behind the peaks of the mountains around the city. Voices broke the dawn as I walked around through the side gate and cut across the lawn to my Tempo.

The skinny Latino, Paz Linero, stepped from behind a palm in the next yard. He wore the same windbreaker and greasy western hat, had the same heavyset *mule* in white behind him with the same gun aimed straight at me.

"Hey, man, we talk, okay?"

The Cadillac stood in front of the next house. There was no one to see except the now quiet and well-behaved dog in the next yard. The *mule* waved the pistol from me to the car. Linero walked behind me. In the Caddy, the *mule* sat in the back with the gun. I got the passenger seat up front. Paz Linero drove.

"You workin' for the Price guy?"

"The wife."

"Yeh." His pale eyes watched the road. He turned into Cathedral Oaks going west out of town. "You find Price?"

"I don't know where he is any more than you do."

He drove slowly and carefully. He didn't want to be stopped for some driving mistake.

"How you know I don' know where Price is at?"

"You weren't waiting at his house for me."

He thought that over. "Okay, why I wait for Price?"

"You want to know who shot Santos Torena and why."

The *mule* in the back gave one of his grunts. Linero kept his eyes on his driving, even though the Saturday morning road was all but deserted this early.

"You don' think we kill Santos?"

"I know you didn't."

Now he looked at me, the pale eyes hard

and sharp and no longer behind the mask of *chicano* distance.

"At least two men killed him, maybe three. They held him on his knees by his wrists. A big gun with a silencer. Up close, execution style. You were alone when I saw you, didn't attack me. You're asking questions, looking all over town. You want to know who killed him and why. If you'd killed him, you'd have been long gone, not hanging around, even going to his house."

Linero thought it over. "That ain't knowin'."

"I wasn't the only one you saw there last night. You saw two other men: a big, flashy guy in a blue blazer, and a shorter, heavier guy in a brown suit. One of the questions you want answered is who they are."

He glanced at me again, pulled at his drooping mustache. "So who? *La Migra*? Anglo gang muscle?"

I told him who they were.

"That rich guy runs the real estate stuff with Santos? Why the hell he want to kill Santos?"

"They were in a big real estate deal together. Price too. Something's wrong with the deal, something illegal, and Torena knew it. I think he was going to blow the whistle, at least to Price, maybe screw up the whole deal."

We had reached Glen Annie Road. Linero made a right, did a U-turn from a left turn lane, got back to Cathedral Oaks, turned left and drove back the way we had come.

"We come up for a meet with Santos, you know? He don' show. We goes to the house. Francesca she say she don' know where the hell he is, 'cept he got this poker game, you know, an' he was gonna talk to some guy at the game. We goes out there, Santos's wheels ain't parked at the game, so we looks around an' Vicario spots the wheels on that road runs by the freeway."

"Via Real or Oak Avenue."

"We waits, you know? It gets dark, Santos he don' come back. I tell Vicario an' Nacio stay with the car, I go look. I'm back up that road goes to the mountains, you know, I hear like shooting. I heads to the shooting, sees them two guys come out of the bush. Just like you tells they looks, you know? They gets in this wagon an' drives. It's maybe five minutes 'fore I finds Santos. I spots you when you sees me. So I take off fast, figure I got to find out who kills Santos like you says. We been checkin' all night, you know? Find nothin', ever'body clean, got alibis. So I figures you right, it's those two an' their boss, ain't nothin' with our business." Linero grinned, called back to the *mule*, "Hey, Nacio, we outta here. *Vamanos!*"

I said, "What time was it you talked to Francesca Torena? When she sent you out to Toro Canyon?"

"Aroun' 4:30, 5:00."

"She was home then?"

"Her an' the old lady."

We were back to Patterson Avenue by now. He looked at me as if expecting another question.

"You saw her out in Montecito too?"

He nodded. "Yeh. After I find Santos, see you an' split back to the heap, we sees her up by Santos's wheels. She runs off, we lose her. How long she out there, you know? Maybe she tell us, goes out herself, you know? She know how to go faster 'n we does. Maybe those two guys kill Santos, on'y Francesca she out there too, hey?"

"That's why you went back to the house to find her, why you've been looking for her."

Linero turned off Cathedral Oaks toward Jack Price's house.

"She killed your other man, didn't she?"

"We go to talk, the old lady says she ain't home. We waits. Francesca shows up, we go talk to her. The old lady tells us to get lost, you know. Vicario he shows his blade, okay? He tell her we're gonna talk or cut her fucking head off. Francesca she come out o' the house, she got this goddamn big gun was Santos's gun. Vicario he says she puts the gun down or she gets hurt. She got the gun both hands, blasts Vicario off them steps. Me an' Nacio beat it."

"She thought you'd killed Santos," I said. "It was only later, after she talked to me and the police, she realized she could have been wrong."

He parked in front of Price's house. Jack

Price's Jaguar still wasn't there, and the old Chevy wagon was gone.

"The *chingada* kill Vicario, but what the hell. My business you takes chances, right? Vicario shouda watch out better, hey? Maybe I come back sometime, get her, maybe not. She ain't no problem to me no more, right? Business is business."

I got out. "Thanks for the information."

"Hey, *de nada*, right?"

He flashed me a grin, put the Caddy in gear. The *mule* got into the front, the Caddy drove out of the cul-de-sac.

The house was silent, no one answered my rings. At the front door, the side door and the hot tub, there was no message from Angela Price.

Chapter Thirty-Eight

There was no Jaguar outside the small house on Camino Corto, only the Chevys, Dodge and Ford wagons, Toyota pickups, but there was light in Claire Broberg's living room. I rang three times before she opened the door.

"Mr. Fortune." She sounded stiff and distant. A tight, formal voice. "Come in."

The big younger one closed the door behind me. The older one in the brown suit sat on a blue upholstered couch in the living room. The younger leaned against the door and grinned. His face was flushed, his eyes watery as if he could barely keep awake. The blue blazer was wrinkled, the gray slacks had lost their crease. The pale gray striped shirt was open at the

353

collar and dirty with sweat, his tie hung loose and crooked, and the pistol in his hand was a big automatic with a silencer.

"Hey, Messick, look. One arm. The private asshole. I bet he knows where the hell old Jack is."

Messick's gun was the small caliber silenced automatic he'd used to kill the Genius and his gateman. His off-the-rack brown worsted looked pretty good for all night, his white shirt only a little dirty around the collar, the brown loafers still shined.

"You talk too fucking much when you're drunk, Gretzer."

Claire Broberg sat in an old-fashioned high-back wing chair. As if she'd been sitting there before I rang, had gone straight back to the wing chair where she sat stiff and silent and scared.

"Stick your nose up your ass," Gretzer said. "We oughta be gone outta here, for Christ sake."

"Everybody worries," Messick said.

"Fuck you, asshole."

Gretzer wasn't smiling, and it looked like Messick never smiled. Claire Broberg had forgotten how to smile. I didn't have anything to smile about. Messick turned his blue eyes toward me. There was something inexorable about all his actions.

"Who you working for?"

"Price's wife."

"He playin' around on her?"

Gretzer did a grind at the window. "Way to go, Jackie boy."

"She thinks something's wrong with Ed Brower's deal."

Gretzer came away from the window. "What the hell she—"

"Get the fuck back there and watch," Messick said.

Gretzer slammed his massive fist on a lamp table. The lamp crashed to the floor. "Shit, shit, shit!" Both hands on the big automatic, he held it out at Messick. "Off my back, you hear? You screw the boss lady, you think that makes you big man?"

Messick looked at Gretzer. "You couldn't find your way home alone."

Gretzer's face flushed redder. Messick was impassive, but his small gun was aimed almost unseen at Gretzer's belly.

"Go watch for Price," Messick said. "Half an hour. Show or no show, we're gone."

Gretzer went back to the window. His watery eyes came alert again, looked out as if nothing had happened.

Arguing, violent, busy with each other, neither of them took my old cannon.

"How's the wife figure something's wrong?" Messick said.

Up all night, drinking, over some timetable, they were as on edge as the nerves of a death row guard. Maybe they didn't care if I had a

355

gun. I'd never get to use it. Strongarm men aren't the smartest men around.

"The way Price was acting. The extra money he had to put into the deal."

Two men like us, I'd told Max Mellecker, like me and like him. Ordinary, normal, reasonably intelligent. Probably some college for Gretzer at least. The difference was inside. Like poker players, they lived in a world without reason or purpose. Life is a game, no one wins except for the moment. Today's winner is tomorrow's loser, the money goes around the table. You live high when you win, don't cry when you lose. Spend it, you know you can't keep it.

"What's the wife want you to do about Price and the deal?"

"Find him, talk to him."

"Pull him out? Blow the whistle?"

Only a jerk plays by the rules. Only suckers work nine to five, drive the kids to school, take a two-week vacation and work their ass off all year to pay for it.

"Never got that far."

"No?" Messick said.

He scratched at his beard stubble with the silenced pistol, looked around the room. At Gretzer, at Claire Broberg. At the closed door. Aimless and restless. Something missing inside.

"You know where Price is hidin' out?"

"No."

In the end, no more than walking appetites,

monsters who serve the barons of our freebooter world. Where there is a market, something or someone will always appear to satisfy it.

"Who're those goddamn greasers you an' Price was talking to up at that house?"

"When you shot us all up?"

Claire Broberg made a sound from the wing chair, small and trembling. Fear was all her body and mind had room for now. Anger mixed with uneasiness in Gretzer's voice from the window.

"Who the fuck's talkin' all over now, Messick?"

"Don't try to figure it out," Messick said.

"It half an hour yet, boss man?"

"I'll tell you when. Who the fuck are they, Fortune?"

"*Coyotes* Torena worked with bringing up illegals. They wanted to know who shot him and why."

"Wanted?"

I sensed the mistake, but I couldn't evade. "They're gone."

Gretzer looked at me from the window. Messick leaned in his chair.

Gretzer said, "Gone where?"

"How do I know?"

Messick said, "You told them."

I edged slightly around to my right, to hide my good arm.

"Told them what?" I said.

"Told who what, for Christ sake?" Gretzer said.

Messick had his little automatic half off his lap where he leaned. "He told them we snuffed Torena. He told them, an' they said thanks a lot, we're clean, we don't need to hang around here no more, and they went on home."

"How the hell'd he know?"

"He's a smart peeper." Messick's lightless eyes were still fixed on my face. "He found out Mr. Santos Torena was going to clue in our Jack Price, blow Brower's whole deal. He found out we got hired by Brower. He put two and two together."

I edged farther around. My empty sleeve faced Messick as well as Gretzer. My hand inched into my right pocket.

"He maybe even told that cop," Messick said.

Gretzer moved suddenly away from the window to stand and breathe down on me. So close I could smell the night's boozing on his breath, the big automatic under my nose. "I'll blow his fucking head off right now."

"Later," Messick said. "Get the fuck back to the goddamn window. That cop could even—"

Gretzer held the .45 under my nose, pushed the barrel into my nostril. "Why the shit we hanging around, for Christ sake. We're all done, ain't we? It's set up. Who cares if that asshole Price busts now, cries to the cops?"

"We care you stupid dumbhead. He blows

they come looking for us after, for Christ sake."

"Then we blast 'em all now."

"I said later, goddamn it!" Messick raged. "We'll waste both of them later, now get your stupid ass back—"

Claire Broberg half-screamed, covered her mouth, the fear like a tent over her.

Gretzer whirled on Messick, "Stop tellin' me what the fuck to do all the—"

Messick turned on Claire Broberg, "Shut your—"

I didn't wait. My lone arm gave me an instant of edge. They both saw only my empty sleeve, subconsciously forgot the arm out of sight. I jumped back, shot Gretzer twice through my coat pocket. Hurled myself at the couch.

Gretzer's automatic fired into the chandelier and the ceiling as he went down. Messick got off one shot. I took the small slug through my pinned-up sleeve, hit the couch, went over it on my face.

Chapter Thirty-Nine

Behind the couch, I listened.

A weak crawling. Then silence.

"Fortune."

Messick's voice was across the room. On my belly, I peered around the end of the couch.

He stood behind the high-backed wing chair. Claire sat in the chair, her fear become terror. On the floor Gretzer had stopped moving. There was a lot of blood. We are animals, we protect ourselves, but I've never really learned how to live with it except to not think about it the same as everyone else. That never really works. I remember every one, live with that.

"I've got the lady, Fortune. Toss out the gun."

He had his little automatic to her head, still

with the silencer on it. His eyes searched around the couch for a sign to tell him exactly where I was.

"Shoot her you lose your cover. I've got the position."

He thought that over.

"Okay, she's my cover to the door and out."

"You so sure I won't shoot?"

"The good guys don't take chances with innocent bystanders."

"Maybe getting you is worth the risk."

He knew I wouldn't shoot Claire Broberg, or even take the risk of shooting her. But he wasn't *sure*. He would shoot her to get to me, we all tend to judge everyone else by ourselves.

"Bullshit. You're squeaky clean all the way. I can spot a sucker ten miles off. You got principles."

"Make your break then."

Sure but not sure. He didn't move, went on searching all around the couch for a glimpse of me, something to tell him where to watch, where he could maybe try a shot through the couch even with the small gun.

"When I'm fucking ready. You ain't going nowhere."

His face above Claire Broberg was as impassive as ever, unchanged by the death of Gretzer or his own danger. Without fear. Imagination wouldn't be his long suit. As long as he stood with a gun in his hand and plans for escape he wouldn't be afraid of anything. The fear would come only when hands held him, the cell door slammed shut. Or not even then. Not until they came to take him to the chair, the noose, the gas chamber. No fear, only calculation. Would I risk Claire Broberg's life? Would I kill her to get to him? He knew he would, but everything in his experience told him I wouldn't. It was there on his square, blank face with the pale blue eyes.

I said, "It doesn't matter if I'd shoot her or not, Messick. You can't walk out of here and leave me alive."

"Shit. Outta here ain't no one got a gun on me, and the lady's a hostage. My ticket out of town. You gonna have to decide you want to waste her or not."

"Out of town, out of the country, where do you hide? If they don't gun you down, you end in the gas chamber or in the joint the rest of your life."

"They got to catch me first, that ain't gonna be so easy."

He didn't care about how he looked, how handsome he was, or even how rich. He had only one vanity: how tough he was. Hard and cool and independent. That, and maybe his sexual prowess.

"Sooner or later, Messick, sooner or later."

"For everyone, buddy, and ain't nothin' matters except you live good here and right now. I live high on the hog, buddy, how do you live? Now, you gonna let me walk, or we gonna shoot it out through the scared lady here?"

Hard and cool and independent, that was how he saw himself. A powerful man in all ways, and that was his weakness.

"You don't live good, Messick. All you get is what they throw you. The bones, the short change. You're the biggest sucker of all. A hired hand, a laborer, a goddamn servant of the big boys who pay you. You do what they want you to do, buddy, and not a fucking thing more. You think you're real independent, but you can't walk out of here without wasting me first or you won't get out of the state."

A red flush spread up his face. "You trying to get yourself killed, asshole? You're as dumb as fucking Gretzer. You—"

Concentrating on each other, watching for an opening, neither Messick nor I heard anything until the outside door opened and Jack Price stood inside. He stared at Messick and Claire Broberg in the wing chair.

Messick, still thinking about what to do and when, about time and if I would or wouldn't shoot at the risk of killing Claire Broberg, saw the man he'd been looking for all night and took an automatic step out from behind the wing chair. A reflex, his gun turned on Price.

I came up from behind the couch shooting. Four shots. All I had left.

Three hit, spun Messick around, his little gun firing and shattering a window four feet to Price's right, slammed him into the wing chair splattering blood all over the chair and Claire Broberg, and flung him flat down on his back.

The fourth shot missed.

Claire Broberg slid unconscious to the floor.

Messick stared up at nothing.

Jack Price leaned against the wall inside the door, looked at Messick's blood on his wrinkled, stained suit.

I sat on the back of the couch.

I'd hit Messick three times in the chest. From less than ten feet. On the floor he hadn't crawled or moved, a bloody rag doll in a cheap brown suit, one loafer still on, the other five feet away. Jack Price stopped looking at the blood on him, saw for the first time Gretzer on the floor with Messick.

"They're both dead."

It wasn't a question.

"You killed them."

That wasn't a question either. But I answered this one.

"They killed themselves. That's what you tell yourself. Help Ms. Broberg. I'll call the police. You ready to talk?"

"Talk?"

He made no move to go to Claire Broberg.

"About Brower. Who these two were, what they were doing."

"I don't know what they were doing."

He looked away. At Claire Broberg on the floor. At the walls. I went to kneel over Claire

Michael Collins

Broberg. Her eyes were fluttering, her head moving, but she made no sound yet, still afraid someone would hurt her.

"For starters," I said, "they were chasing you."

Claire Broberg's pulse was good, her breathing less shallow as she came around, opened her eyes to stare up at me.

"They killed Torena, your friend the Genius and his gateman, wanted to kill you and me."

I got Claire Broberg up and back into the wing chair. Her eyes stared at me, asked questions she didn't want answered.

"Those *coyotes* killed Torena," Price said. "He was mixed up with them, smuggling aliens. He—" My words broke through the wall of denial inside his mind. "The Genius? No one killed him. I was with him a couple of hours ago. Me and Max. We were at his place for hours. He—"

Claire Broberg touched blood wet on the wing chair, began to shiver. I helped her across the room to another chair that faced away from the two dead thugs on the floor.

"They were looking for you. They shot him."

He looked down at Messick and Gretzer, then away. "Experts he called them. Brower. They came to help him on the deal."

He was strung out, not all the way sober, running on pure adrenaline. In a state of confusion, exhaustion, fear, denial, need and hope that made him think and speak in disjointed

366

blocks. Half hyper, half in a fog.

"They're dead." He even smiled at me. "You stopped them. It's all over."

"Brower's not dead," I said.

"Brower?"

I walked close to him. "Whatever Brower planned could still go down, probably will go down. Gretzer said they were finished, nothing more to do. The whole thing'll still happen, whatever it is, and Brower gets his deal."

"It can still go through?"

"It can still go wrong," I said, "and that means you can still take the fall with it."

"I've lost deals before." He shrugged. "Angie'll walk out this time. I don't know, maybe it's best. A new start."

I studied his eyes. "You really don't see it, do you? You don't want to see it, know what's happening."

Almost petulant. "Brower never told me what he was doing."

I half leaned, half sat, on the back of the couch. "He made you president of El Bosque Homes, Santos Torena vice-president. On paper all that shows is that Brower Management invested in a company run by you and Torena. But he'll have fixed it so if the deal goes through he gets the cash, and if it goes wrong you're the fall guy, Price, the dummy front. Whatever Brower brought those two in for isn't something safe and legal. Torena figured it out, that's what he wanted to talk to you about. He must have made the mistake of letting Brower know what he was going to do and those two killed him."

He listened to me now, almost following my lips as I talked.

"What is it? Some swindle? A con game? A big insurance scam? Double books to hide assets? Muscle someone into buying that white elephant mansion? Steal some land? Chavalas'll find out. You have to tell the police everything, hope they can get you off the hook."

Across the room Claire Broberg had begun to rock in the chair as if we weren't there. Price looked toward her.

"He said he wanted me to be president because he was too busy to do it right, I was the the best man for the job. I'd need the experience for running the agency when he sold me a share, maybe all of it. He was giving me a big chance."

"A real opportunity," I said.

He laughed. It was a fake laugh, empty. Not a laugh at all, a nervous reaction when he didn't know what to say or do.

"That's why Angie hired you. She thinks I'm a damn fool."

"With Torena and those two dead there's no one to connect Brower except you."

"Me?"

"You can tell the police enough so they can get to him."

He watched my face as if he could see his salvation there, an escape from being a fall guy and a fool. Claire Broberg had stopped rocking, suddenly stood up.

"Coffee. We all need coffee."

She walked around the two bodies, stepped over the blood, and went into the kitchen. I could hear her running the water, opening a coffee cannister. I went to the living room phone.

"Think of everything you can tell the police," I said to Price, dialed 911. When I reached the police I told them all that had happened and where. I asked to talk to Chavalas if he was in. He wasn't, but they would call him, stay right where I was. "They'll be here—"

Jack Price was at the door. He held Gretzer's big .45.

"Put it down, Price."

He laughed that fake laugh. "I know what he's going to do, I can stop him, fix it all."

"Don't be any more of a damn fool—"

It was a mistake, the wrong word. Price waved the big pistol straight at me. Claire Broberg came in carrying sugar and cream on a tray. Almost dropped them. I didn't think he could hit much, not with a .45, but it wasn't a chance I could take.

"Tell the police I'll call them. I know what I'm doing. You got those two so Ed's alone, I can handle him."

The grin was almost manic on his soft face, the big gun now steady in his pudgy hands.

"Price, listen—"

He backed out the door. I got to the window, my old cannon ready, aimed at the Jaguar's tires. The gun clicked on empty. I swore inside. He was already in the car headed in the opposite direction from my Tempo. By the time I reached it, backed in a U-turn, he'd be out of sight. He knew the streets better than I did, and I didn't know what he was going to do or where he was going. There was nothing I could do but watch him screech away like every hero in all the Hollywood movies.

I walked back to the telephone, called Chavalas. He hadn't come into his office. They thought he was on his way. Claire Broberg still stood in the door, the two gunmen still lay dead on the floor.

"We might as well have some coffee," I said.

She put the tray on the coffee table, got the coffee pot and cups from the kitchen, poured.

Chapter Forty

Sergeant Chavalas had arrived after the sheriff's department patrol deputy and sergeant, before the major crimes detectives, the crime scene investigation detectives, the coroner's detail, and a pair of UCSB officers. While the deputies strung their yellow crime scene tape and swarmed over Claire Broberg's house, Chavalas got my story. Then he took the patrol sergeant aside and explained about me.

The coroner's team worked over the bodies, were ready to slide them into their bags and carry them out. The sheriff's sergeant wasn't being easily convinced of my value to Chavalas and the case. They had examined my credentials and gun, taken my statement and Claire

Broberg's statement as an eye witness. I would appear whenever they needed me for the hearing.

Claire Broberg drank her coffee as if she were alone in her living room, looked at no one.

The bodies went, the UCSB cops wandered out. The morning was still a thin white on the front yard outside. Chavalas finally shook hands with the sheriff's sergeant.

"Let's go, Fortune." Outside he stopped between his car and mine. "Brian F. Messick and Duane Gretzer. California driver's licenses, addresses in Palm Springs, some credit cards, a lot of cash. That's all they had on them. Not a damn thing to say what they were doing here, who they worked for. Sheriff's on the pipe to the Springs now. You have anything more you haven't told me?"

"No," I said. "You found nothing to connect them to Brower? To Jack Price or Torena?"

"Not a damn thing. We better hope the sheriff's people come up with something from the Springs, or we may never know what they were doing. You shoot too all-fired straight, Fortune."

I followed his car to the freeway, and east into the morning light and the city. With Messick, Gretzer and Torena dead, it could turn out that there was no way to connect Ed Brower and the condo deal to them. Except Jack Price. At Brower's office, his Rolls-Royce was parked in the lot. So was Angela Price's old Chevy station wagon. But no Jaguar. Chavalas rang. Brower's voice from somewhere inside was terse, annoyed.

"We open at ten."

"Police, Mr. Brower."

We waited. Chavalas held his identification ready. His other hand pushed his suit coat back away from his pistol.

"The door's not locked."

Brower was behind his desk. Angela Price sat in the Eames chair across the big room. She was in slim khaki jeans now, a striped man's shirt of thick bed ticking, low western boots, her hair tied back in a blue ribbon at the nape of her long neck. Brower was in a gray business suit. White shirt and tie, ready for a day with bankers. Chavalas showed his credentials.

"You're working early, Sergeant."

He watched me not Chavalas.

"You're up early, Mr. Brower."

"I'm due in Los Angeles by 10:00, should be on the road now but Angie here wanted to talk."

I said, "About what?"

"You'll have to ask her, Fortune." He stood up. "I really have to be on the road."

Chavalas said, "It won't take three hours to make L.A. Or is there some reason you want to be on the road this morning?"

"I like a leisurely drive, Sergeant, usually take Highway One, stop to look at the sea. However, if it's important—"

He sat down again, smiled at us and at Angela Price in the Eames chair. Chavalas nodded to her.

"What did you come to talk about, Mrs. Price?"

"My husband. I suppose you know he's been away from home all night. I hired Dan to find him, talk to him about Ed's deal. After Dan left this morning, I got restless, came to ask Ed if he knew anything about where Jack was, if he'd seen him."

"I haven't," Brower said. "Not since early last night."

"How early?" I asked.

He was making no attempt to like me now. "I really don't know, Fortune. 8:00 or so." He looked from me to Chavalas. "Has something happened to Jack?"

"You think something could have happened to him?" Chavalas said.

"Obviously he never went home last night. That isn't usual for Jack or any other normal person, now is it? Anything could have happened to him. An accident. Car crash. Drunk and passed out. Attacked, robbed. The streets aren't exactly safe these days even in Santa Barbara."

I said, "Your nice world has gone all to pot."

"Very funny, Fortune. Tell me, has anyone thought to check the hospitals? Or are you all too busy building theories about Jack?"

"He's not in a hospital," I said. "I talked to

him less than half an hour ago."

Angela Price said, "Where, Dan? Is he all right?"

"At Claire Broberg's. He was okay physically."

Chavalas said, "I understand you went out very early this morning, Mr. Brower. Can you tell me where you went?"

Brower glared toward Angela Price. "No, I can't. It was business, and it was my business." He stood up again. "What the hell is all this, Sergeant? I have to leave for Los Angeles, if you have something specific on your mind say so."

"It's about this condo deal you have with Price and Santos Torena and some others," Chavalas said. "About the two men Mrs. Price says you met in the parking lot when you went out on your business early this morning. We'd like to know who they were, what they do for you."

"Two men? I don't know anything about two men. Angie must have imagined it, or she's lying for some reason. Who are these two men? I mean, what's your problem with them?"

"Why would Mrs. Price lie about it, Mr. Brower?"

"What do I know about women? We had a big bed night, she's mad as hell at me about something. Who knows, maybe women have to hate any man who fucks them."

"A real gent," Angela Price said.

"You want a gentleman, act like a lady."

"Just how does a lady act, Ed?"

"Shit," Brower swore. "So who are these two? They have names, Chavalas?"

"Messick and Gretzer. Brian F. Messick and Duane Gretzer, both apparently from Palm Springs."

"Never heard of them. I haven't been in Palm Springs in over a year. Now if that's all, I really have to leave."

He said it, but he didn't do it. He stood as if about to walk from behind the desk, looked at both of us. Waited for us to do something. Give up and stand aside, or make some move to stop him. He wanted to leave, but he wanted to know how serious we were in questioning him, what we really knew. Chavalas nodded to me.

"Tell him everything you told me, Fortune. From the start. All of it."

I watched Brower as I talked. "The condo deal took a lot of cash, stretched everyone to the limit including yourself, then something went wrong. I don't know what, Chavalas will find that out sooner or later. You came up with a scheme to save the day that required importing a pair of what Jack Price says you called 'experts.' Enter Messick and Gretzer. You'd already set Price and Torena up to take the fall if it went wrong. But Torena found out what you were doing, realized the position he and Price were in. He must have made the mistake of letting you know he was going to warn Price, so Messick and Gretzer killed him before he reached Price."

Brower said nothing.

"I don't know if you told them to kill Torena, but when you call up men like them you can't always control them. They kill to protect their own skins. If Angie hadn't hired me they might have come and gone without any more trouble. Once I was in the picture, they got worried about Jack Price, me, anyone who could bring the police down on them before their job was finished, or put two and two together after they did what they'd been hired to do. That worried you too, so you let them go on trying to find Jack Price and me. They'd have killed us to cover themselves, the only code they know is kill before you're killed."

There was a faint twitch at the corner of Brower's mouth, a nervous tic, the smooth tan a shade sallow.

"You better not ever repeat that story, Fortune, or you'll be talking to my lawyers." His voice rose hard. "Not ever, you understand?"

Chavalas said, "We've found out you have a big note due on the condo deal, have a lot of cash tied up in a Nevada deal, Mr. Brower. We heard you're getting a shaky, high-interest loan. Messick and Gretzer wouldn't be connected to whoever you're getting money from would they?"

"I think, Chavalas, you better remember my lawyers too," Brower said. "Where did you get such a crazy story, Fortune?"

"From a lot of people," I said. "But mostly from your two goons and Jack Price."

The office became silent in the warming morning as a thin yellow glow slanted down the cross street outside. Traffic was moving now, the city almost awake, people beginning to walk. Brower's voice had become quiet. The nervous tic had stopped.

"If those two men, whoever they are, even say they know me, they are lying. Any more conversation will be with my lawyers, and I suggest you produce those two men in a court before you ask me another word. Now I'm leaving, and so are you."

He walked from behind the desk, aimed his considerable weight directly toward me. I stepped aside. Chavalas didn't.

"Fortune tells me those men had set up what they came to do. It was all finished, they could go. You figure that has anything to do with you being on the road and out of town this morning?"

Brower's calm deserted him. "I'm going to sue you and the city for everything you have, Chavalas, you hear me? Where are these liars? Show them to me. Before you accuse me of any more crimes you better read my rights, let me call my lawyers, and arrest me!"

Chavalas said nothing. Brower stalked back behind his desk, picked up his telephone, glared at us. Angela Price watched us all, puzzled. Chavalas watched Brower.

"It could go easier on you, Mr. Brower, if you tell us what those two set up for you."

Brower dialed. "Tell him it's Ed Brower, urgent. I'll hold on." He shook his head angrily. "I'm warning you, Chavalas, any more accusations and . . ." He stopped, held the phone away from him, the receiver pointed at Chavalas like a magic wand. "You're saying that those two men told you they worked for me, that they killed people, but they didn't tell you what they came to do?"

The silence was deeper this time. Not even the traffic out in the morning seemed to penetrate the office.

"By Jesus," Brower said. "You don't have them. You can't produce them. You can't prove that crazy story."

"We'll get the proof, Mr. Brower," Chavalas said.

"Something's happened to them! You're not arresting me because you know you can't. You don't have those two men to stand up in a court. What are they, dead? Shot up resisting arrest? Wild animals, right? By God, you don't have them to tell their lies."

"It probably doesn't matter, Brower," I said. "Jack Price should be all Chavalas needs."

Chapter Forty-One

Jack Price sits once more in the Jaguar. He holds Gretzer's big automatic on his lap.

He is parked far in from the Montecito side road in a grove of oaks and pepper trees beside the long driveway of El Parador, the great estate El Bosque Homes had to add to the condominium package at the insistence of the buyer. He is watching for Ed Brower, or anyone Brower might send now that his "experts" have been killed by that one-armed private detective, Fortune. Two of them by one man with only one arm. Jack holds the pistol in both hands and raises it to point out the window at the mansion, feels the blood pump in his chest.

Michael Collins

Where he is beside the abandoned driveway with its potholes and invading grass, Jack can see the only entrance into the estate, and both the back and front of the mansion. The empty condos are closer to the road through the forest of trees. The bulldozers, backhoes and trucks have been at work, but sit idle and silent this dawn of a Saturday morning. The monumental Italianate mansion itself looms across its overgrown lawns and gardens. Silent, rundown, and deserted. Leaves blow across its stone terraces on a cool wind.

Jack is on edge and a little sick. Sick because he has never seen dead men before except in an open coffin rouged and powdered and lying in white satin with hands crossed on the breast of a blue suit. He has never seen death lying crumpled and twisted in a pool of blood and bone on a living room floor. Gaping mouths open in a silent scream you can almost hear, empty eyes that stare up with no light left in them. Eyes that had seen moments before, mouths that had been talking even as he entered the room.

He knows what Brower is going to do. He thinks he knows, and he can still stop it. The detective is right, he sees that now. He is the fall guy, but he can still stop Brower, make it right. So Jack sits in the Jaguar that always makes him feel better when he's in it. He touches the smooth burlwood of the dash, the soft leather of the seats. He had been afraid he would be too late, but when he drove up everything was quiet.

He remembers when Brower told him he would be president of El Bosque, when they bought the great estate because the buyer demanded the extra land, and when, later, Brower bought the insurance policy for him to sign. A big insurance policy on the mansion and all the condos.

"Routine," Brower told him. "That damn mansion's worth five million alone. The buyer wants all the land, but we'll have to resell the mansion, we need it well-protected."

It sounded logical, good business, routine. No sweat. Sign here, Jack, you're president. I'm just lending the company the money, buying the stock. You and Santos do the paper work while I handle raising the money.

"How does it feel to be president of a company, Jack? Good, right? Gives you that feeling, that charge."

Jack Price, the president who did nothing. The figurehead, the front, the paper boss, the fall guy. Him and Santos Torena, and that was what Torena had wanted to talk to him about. What they had stopped him from talking about. Messick and Gretzer. Because they were afraid if Torena got to Jack he would blow the whistle, ruin Brower's plan and end the whole deal.

Sure.

He sits in the Jaguar, looks at the silent mansion, and wants to drive on down East Valley

Road to the poker game. Walk in to the shouts
and laughs, the smile of Morgan the owner,
the deadpan of the Genius, a pat on the back
from Benny. Take off his coat, slide into his
regular seat to watch the cards go around the
green under the familiar light. Look at his hold
cards, make his bet, sit back and study the
intense faces of the other players as each card
falls, reach out with both hands to rake in the
mound of chips.

But the game doesn't start for twelve hours,
there are no shouts and laughs in the old Victorian house at dawn.

He wants to go home, hide in Angie as he had
hidden once in the She-Wolf, but there is no
way he can do that, admit to her or to anyone
that he even wants to hide. A man doesn't admit
such things, and never to Angie. All wrong for
him, but there was nothing he could do. Not
after the kids came along. No way he could
let her raise them alone. A boy needs a father.
Angie never wanted to be part of the family.
Now she'd walk out, take the kids. Not the boy.
No way he lets her have the boy.

Cars pass far off through the trees on their
way to the golf courses.

Brower belongs to The Valley Club. Takes
Jack there once or twice a year. Not Messick
and Gretzer. They wouldn't have fit in at The
Valley Club. The mansion stands Venetian and
silent across its overgrown gardens, and he
wonders if maybe it could still work? The

insurance to bail out the deal, bring him the money to buy into the car agency. Experts, Messick and Gretzer, no one would know. Only they were dead, they had killed Torena and the Genius, the police would come, and if Brower went through with it they would know, and he, Jack, would be arrested, sent to prison. The fall guy.

Jack regrips the big automatic, stares down at it. He'd missed the army, Vietnam. In the Jaguar, Jack wonders if he hasn't missed more than Vietnam. Nothing ever works out the way he expects, his luck is always bad. But there is still time. He can still make it right. Stop Brower cold and go home to Angie with his head up. Fix everything. Save the day.

Nothing moves through the trees or around the vast mansion with its crumbled balustrades and choked terraces. He gets out, walks across the overgrown grounds and up the broad terraces to the carved stone of the front door. The door is unlocked, Jack walks into the towering entry hall and cavernous living room that echoes to his footsteps in the morning light through the tall windows with their Venetian stained glass. A folding chair, and a cardboard box set upside down for a table, are near a fireplace so big Jack can walk into it and look up the vast, blackened flue. There is an empty beer can on the box, an empty bag of taco chips on the floor. Jack sits on the folding chair, rests the big automatic on his knee.

The high ceiling is painted like the Sistine Chapel Jack saw once in a movie. The great fireplace reminds him of a book he read as a boy. *The White Company* by Sir Arthur Conan Doyle, the same guy who wrote all the Sherlock Holmes stories. The great castles with their enormous fireplaces. The English knights fighting the French and Spanish for The Black Prince who was so great he didn't even need a throne, sat on a little stool with the kings of Spain and Navarre on thrones behind him but everyone knew who had the real power, who was the real boss. Jack hadn't wanted to be The Black Prince, dreamed of being the greatest knight of them all—Sir John Chandos, a captain with one eye who'd come up from nothing to be The Black Prince's best general and closest adviser. The *red pile of Chandos*, a red V-wedge on a background of silver. He remembered drawing that shield, putting it up over his dresser in the old house back in Minnesota.

All he'd wanted back when he was a kid was to be great, a knight, a famous captain. A kid's dream, and you have to grow up, but every kid has dreams he takes with him and it's a crummy world where a kid's dream can't come true. Maybe not the details, there sure weren't any knights and castles anymore, but something like them. Something wrong with a fucking world where a kid's dreams don't come true.

Jack gets up and walks on through the rooms of the mansion. There have to be twenty rooms on the first floor alone. They are all empty. Beer cans and food wrappers where Brower's workmen have been, but no one and nothing else. In the kitchen Jack looks around with a kind of wonder. The kitchen is as large as his whole house. He tries to think about, imagine, the kind of people who built this place, had the money and the power. Oil barons, railroad tycoons, industrialists. The real men of the country. We didn't really have those kinds of men anymore, everything held back by rules and regulations, the goddamn Federal bureaucracy in Washington.

At the kitchen windows he looks out at the grounds behind the massive mansion that seem to roll on forever beyond the garages that had once been stables. If it isn't the rules it's something else that always stops a guy. Times change and the dream you had as a kid can't happen anymore. If never works out. Not for most guys, not for him. With his rotten luck he wonders if he was really cut out for California. Glitzville, Tinseltown, La-La Land north, Lotusland. Too fast and too *mañana* at the same goddamn time. Bad for a real family man like him. Out here the family didn't count, the backbone of the nation lost in all the glitz and drive to make a big fast buck. Angie's kind of world, California. Driving and striving, always looking for something outside the family.

In the kitchen that echoes to his footsteps, Jack thinks about his Dad. Lawyer, school board, politics, influence all over the state. Maybe he should have stayed back there. The smaller time, the slower pace. Solid values. The heartland. Even Angie might have been different if they'd stayed, not so driving, so hard to get along with. Maybe she'd have backed him more. They had roots back there, something to grow on, the old values all around them, his father's footsteps to follow.

Sure.

Joe Price's boy. Running errands for the She-Wolf. Small-town and small-time. He'd never have gotten out from under his father. Joe Price's kid. He had to find his own way. Bigger and better. Not yet, maybe, but it would work out. He'd had a lot of bad breaks, like Randy Castro losing that election. Half the jobs he took turned out to be small-time and dead-end. He'd done okay, nothing to be ashamed of, but he could do better. After he got this all straightened out, stopped Brower's scheme, saved the day, got his money back and . . .

He hears a noise. Behind a door to the left. A sound he can't identify. He grips Gretzer's big automatic, crosses the echoing kitchen to the door.

Chapter Forty-Two

Brower held the telephone receiver. "Jack doesn't know anything that could possibly hurt me, Fortune."

"He knows Messick and Gretzer were working for you. He knows you have some scheme to raise money for the condo deal."

"He doesn't know those two men were working for me, because they weren't. Find anything you can on paper. If Jack says he saw them with me, he's lying. His word against mine."

"Everyone can't be lying, Mr. Brower," Chavalas said.

"Why not? Especially a husband and wife with a reason to get me into trouble." He sat forward, nodded into the telephone. "Paul?

Ed Brower. I'm having this problem with the police. No, no arrest, and I don't think there will be, but be ready with writs and bail. And Paul, see what you can find out about two men who may have been in a fight with the police or a private detective named Fortune early this morning. Probably fugitives or dead. Messick and Gretzer, I believe. Check hospitals, the morgue, the sheriff." He hung up, swivelled to us. "That will do it. Now, perhaps we should all leave so I can get to Los Angeles sometime today?"

I said, "Claire Broberg and Max Mellecker know about Messick and Gretzer."

"No, they don't know anything. Hearsay and lies, Fortune. Disgruntled employees."

Chavalas said, "We'll get the details of your deals today, maybe tomorrow."

"Talk to me when you do."

He sat behind his desk still making no move to leave as if he were waiting for more questions. I think he was enjoying it, sure he was safe. The knock on the door startled us all. Brower looked at his watch, swore, called out.

"Closed. We don't open until ten."

An outside voice, "Sergeant Chavalas?"

Chavalas went to the door.

"Neither of you know where Jack is?" I asked Brower and Angela Price.

"No," she said. "At least Ed says he doesn't."

"I don't, damn it, and I don't care. He's a clown, and he's acting like a clown."

"You made him president of the company," she said. "You don't do anything unless there's an advantage for you."

"That's called life," Brower said.

Chavalas came back into the office. "The mansion El Bosque Homes bought out in Montecito next to the condos is on fire. Out of control, and the fire department tells us they think a man's inside." He looked at Angela Price. "There's a yellow Jaguar parked in the trees near the mansion."

"Jack!"

Angela Price ran out of the office. Reflex, as if she were going to run all the way to Montecito.

Chavalas said to Brower, "I guess we know why you wanted to be on your way to L.A. The land is all your buyer needed in the condo deal, the mansion was a five million dollar white elephant. You could probably sell it, but that would take time. You didn't have time on your Nevada deal, and you saw the chance to unload the mansion, ease the condo deal, and make a bundle to put into Nevada in one shot. Three for one, no waiting. If your experts screw it up, Jack Price takes the fall. Only they got out of hand, and now we've got you. We better go and get your statement on paper."

Brower shrugged. "Speculation, Chavalas. I'll call my lawyer to meet us."

He called, we went out into the parking lot. Angela Price paced next to Chavalas's car, watched us emerge. Brower suddenly stopped in the middle of the lot.

"By Christ, Chavalas, if that's Jack inside El Parador there isn't a damn thing you can charge me with! He's president of El Bosque, he set the fire, I don't know a thing about it." He laughed in the clear morning.

Chavalas said nothing, only motioned for Brower to go to the car. Francesca Torena stepped around the corner of the building. She still wore the tight jeans, man's shirt and multicolored wool poncho. She didn't have the big handbag, and her hands were out of sight under the poncho. She walked toward where Brower stood and laughed at Chavalas.

"Chavalas!" I shouted.

Francesca Torena held the big .357 Magnum out in both hands. The two shots echoed like a cannon in the clear dawn air. Brower flung over backwards, his blood spraying the air and the lot. Chavalas had his gun out. Angela Price didn't move. Francesca Torena circled around us to have another clear shot at Brower. I walked straight at her.

"No," she said.

The big pistol in her small hands was aimed at me. I took the gun. Her eyes reproached me, but she didn't shoot.

Chavalas and the second detective holstered their guns, crouched down over Brower. Angela Price walked toward her Chevy wagon. Cars on the streets slowed to stare. The second detective went to his car, bent in to talk into the radio as Chavalas continued to work on Brower.

"You all right?" I said to Francesca Torena.

She looked past me at Chavalas and Brower.

More police had arrived. Patrolmen took charge of the parking lot, waved the curious on. The siren of the paramedics' van approached. Angela Price had taken her station wagon to drive to Montecito and Jack.

Francesca Torena said, "He wanted to beat the gringo world. I loved him, but he became less the man I had married every year. He became like Brower, then Brower killed him. I heard Brower laugh. The courts will do nothing."

The paramedics had taken over with Brower, Chavalas had gone back to his car to talk on the radio. The other detective and two patrolmen walked toward where I stood with Francesca Torena. She watched them.

"You remember that loan we got from the vice-president in my office? Santos found he had crabs. Only I could have given them to him. He came home from the doctor, found the lice on me, used the doctor's medicine to treat me. He treated me until they were gone, the lice given to me by another man. He never spoke of it again. I loved him, and that man killed him. For money."

The detective and patrolmen were there. I gave them the gun, they took Francesca Torena to a squad car. The paramedics had Brower on a stretcher, covered him with a blanket. Chavalas beckoned me over.

"I'm going out to that mansion, you want to follow me?"

"Brower?"

"He took one through the lungs, the other in the shoulder. They says it's not that bad, he'll make it."

"What about Mrs. Torena?"

"She shot him."

"He had her husband murdered."

"That's up to a jury."

Flames still spurted from the great mansion of El Parador, but more of it was already smoking stone walls jagged against the dawn. The red Montecito fire trucks were there, and two yellow county trucks. They don't take chances with fires in Southern California. The thick brush and trees had caught, but the firemen had that out. The empty condos beyond the scorched trees were intact. Chavalas talked with the firemen and the deputies. Angela Price stood beside the yellow Jaguar.

"It's his car," she said. "They told me he's still inside, if it's him. In the kitchen. He has a gun. If it is him."

"Jack had Gretzer's gun," I said.

She was tall and slim in the jeans and high-heeled cowboy boots, her face tired but calm under the stress lines she would never lose. Not cold or indifferent, not even resigned. Only aware of the end of the night, of a part of her life. Chavalas came toward us across the overgrown lawn. He had a damaged digital watch.

"They reached him. They'll need medical records to make a real identification, but they found this."

He held out the watch. Angela Price didn't take it.

"It's his. He had that Jaguar watchband made for him."

Chavalas put it into a small plastic bag he took from his pocket, put the bag back into the pocket.

"Fire captain says it was a gas explosion. Can't say what set it off yet, but the pipes are old, pilot lights all over. There's a dead cat in there too. They checked and found the gas was turned on only about a week ago on an order signed by Santos Torena for El Bosque Homes. There's no evidence of arson so far, but someone inside makes them suspicious. Captain says if its arson it's a real pro job and going to be damned hard to prove." He looked at the smoking ruins. "Torena's dead. Fortune killed Messick and Gretzer. Price bought the insurance, headed the company. If they prove arson, there's no one to tie in Brower."

"The gun is Gretzer's gun," I said. "It's odds on it killed Torena."

"So Brower's lawyers pin that on Price too. We won't even indict Brower. The only good part is if it's arson the insurance company won't pay off. There isn't any loan to pay off the due loan, he was lying to Price and the others. He couldn't get a new loan, that's why he hired Messick and Gretzer. Now he won't be able to meet that note on Monday, both deals go down the drain, he takes a financial bath."

"His lawyers'll fight," I said. "The insurance people need more proof of arson than Jack Price inside, and I don't think they'll get it. Messick and Gretzer were pros. With a probable big insurance settlement he'll get an extension on that due note, come out fine."

"Maybe we can still find a paper trail from Brower to those two gunmen."

"Don't bet your house on it, Sergeant."

"We better find something, or Brower smells like a rose. Home free, on to bigger and better deals."

"Tell 'em where you got it and how easy it was," I said.

Chavalas walked away to talk again to the fire captain who stood in a knot of fire officers. They all shook their heads as they looked at the mansion that had stopped burning now. Angela Price had been silent all the time Chavalas and I talked, her eyes toward the smoking mansion as if she could see Jack Price through the jagged walls.

"I expected you to find him," she said. "Tell him the truth, drag him home. Or I expected he'd drag himself home, beaten but still full of every answer and reason, still pompous, still playing the patriarch, the successful executive. I never thought he'd be so scared of himself he'd try to be the hero."

"What will you do?"

"Try to explain it to the kids. You can't hide if you want a real world."

"Then?"

"Go back to work, do my writing at night until I start to sell if I ever do. It's what I want to do, we'll get by."

I said, "If the insurance company doesn't pay Brower he'll lose the condo deal, Angie. You could lose the house."

She nodded.

"Jack had life insurance?"

"Of course."

"They'll pay on that," I said. "I don't think they'll prove arson anyway, Brower's deal will go through, you'll get enough money to save the house."

She looked for some time at the smouldering ruin. "I can sell the Jaguar. It won't be easy to tell the children. I won't miss him, Dan, I'm not sure the children will. In a way he never really existed. An empty space." She looked once more at the smoking ruins. "You'll send me a bill."

"No," I said.

"She smiled. "Thanks. I'll have to get used to being poor. Maybe I can give up smoking."

She took her old Chevy wagon, would send someone for the Jaguar. She had put in her

time, Angela Price. Knew who and what she
was, and maybe even what she wanted. I
watched her drive down the long estate driveway and turn toward the city.

The sun was finally coming up over the
mountains behind the charred mansion. Like
so much we wait for, even when it came it
wasn't what it was supposed to be. No more
than a hazy orange ball through the smoke. A
two-bit sun, a four-card straight. Through the
blackened stone I could see Jack Price being
brave, saving the day, making it all come out
right, playing his role to the end. Had he realized in those last moments, the flames around
him, that the house cut the pot and the pros
always had a six? That he was the one who
built the pots for Ed Brower to rake in?

I knew better.

They used to meet the immigrants at the
boat, the factory owners and tycoons, tell them
it was all milk and honey two hundred miles
west, but they met Jack Price in the cradle. It's
a great game, son, everyone a winner. Play the
game, make a name. Catch an eight, make a
straight. They get you to chase an eight all
your life, the owners and the big boys, draw
to sixes themselves, and when you get a flush
they've got a boat. It's their game, Jack, they
know only a few can win, so step right up and
chase that eight. Don't look too close, they don't
like that. You could change the game to one
that was good for you and not for them. It's

the only game for a real man, if you're not in you can't win.

Behind the smoldering ruin they loaded what was left of Jack Price into the morgue wagon.